ATTENTION DEFICIT

NIGEL PICKARD

Weathervane Press

Weathervane Press

Published in 2010 by Weathervane Press
22a Hilton Crescent, West Bridgford, Nottingham NG2 6HT
www.weathervanepress.co.uk

ISBN 978 09562193 5 0

Cover image © Costa 007 www.dreamstime.com
Font for title www.vtks.com.br

Designed and printed in Nottingham
by Parker and Collinson Limited.

This is for H.

"The facts are closing in."
('The World Of Facts' - Martin Stannard)

1. Lewis

the fist thing you shud no abowt me is my dad. my dad woz in a bike accident a motorbike, his legs doant work no more, he doant like to go out, you see it messd up his head aswell as his legs, peepel used to do what he wantd now that doant happen no more, so thats a reson why he doant bother, most days his in bed, he dusnt get up

my mum trys to make him and she carnt, he doant like to do bogall, wen shes mardy with him i go and see him, that happens quiet a lot, i make him his tea his faverite is fish fingers and beans, i make them krispy cos that is how he likes them krispy and crunchy, the beans i do in the micrawave, my freind bath head once nickd a micrawave, then cos it dint work he tuck it back to the house heed nickd it from, his culled bath head cos his head is full of water ha ha

i like to talk to my dad becos he tells me things i shud do, like he sez i have a new start, they doant no you there, they doant no abowt you, so that is why im doing this for you now becos it is my way off tellin you abowt me.

2. Harry

"Okay, everybody, let's get this down. Remember to use a ruler to underline the title and the date, unlike me. Not a good example, eh, Sharon? Everyone's got a pen now, yes? Even you, Brett, good." I glanced out of the classroom windows which were smoky with dirt, meaning that most days I couldn't really judge the brightness beyond them. Outside, the police helicopter was continuing to hover around, more over the school than the estate at present. It was a sound I was generally inured against and it took me a while to work out what was missing when it wasn't there, the security of its cough, its recurrent chuckle. I focused back on the class of eleven and twelve-year olds, a group who could barely read or write. My six-year old daughter, Eve, was more literate than all of them. Even after a decade of teaching I still couldn't properly comprehend how this stalling might occur, though I wasn't going to give up trying to do something about it. "Right, ready to roll."

After introducing my topic and jotting some useful words on the whiteboard, I sauntered over to the back of the class and talked to Connor, a pale, straggly little kid whose unwashed white shirt was now so unwashed it was more of a brown-grey colour. Connor smelt brown-grey too, a stolid mixture of sweat and dirt which meant I wasn't keen to get too close to him. He was leaning back in his chair so that it balanced on two legs against the wall, chewing the half-sized broken biro that he'd borrowed from one of the girls in the class at the beginning of the lesson, and staring into space; still not having written anything beyond what he'd copied badly from the board: 'cage' had become 'caj', 'animal' 'anmal' and so on.

"Right, Connor," I said with a kind of ironic enthusiasm I'd perfected over my career, always verging on a subversion of what I said while at the same time being seemingly committed to it, "have you ever had a pet?"

After a long pause, as though he'd had to dredge more than forty years of memory, Connor reckoned he might've had.

"What pet was it?"

"Er, hamsters."

I crouched down next to him, now irredeemably deeper into his fug, while continuing to keep an eye on the rest of the class, who were apparently getting on with the work. Or, at least, it was quiet and most of them were staring in the general direction of their exercise books, some a little hypnotised by the effort of this, by the empty lines, the white space, white *matter*, as my colleague Jon had called it; like dark matter, only more alarming. "Hamsters?"

"Yeah."

"Still got them?"

"Nope." Connor took a small piece of plastic biro casing out of his mouth and examined it like it was a precious stone; examined it first one way, then the other, as if he was trying to catch the light to make the plastic sparkle. It was dull plastic however, and it remained dull plastic, and chewed dull plastic at that: the light was sludgily trapped inside it. Not that this restricted Connor's temporary enchantment with what he was doing.

"Hamsters, eh?"

"Yeah."

"What were their names?"

"Wha'?"

"Their names, Connor. What were they called? Your hamsters."

"Oh. Them."

"Well?" I said.

"Wha'?"

"Wha'? Wha'?" I said merrily. "Their names, Connor." I sounded, I thought, like a policeman with a suspect. "Their names." Again: "What were their names, Connor?"

"Twit and Twat," Connor said, flicking another piece of

3

casing from his fingers onto the desk in front of him, then lining up a shot to land across the floor.

"Right," I replied, not missing a beat, now beginning to remember as I did most days what it was I liked about this place. Much better than some dreary establishment where the kids drove more expensive cars than the staff. Kids with hamsters called Pereguine and Xanadu. Kids with fountain pens. Kids with pens, full stop.

Connor was off: "Y'see, the thing wor, sir, Twit were bigger'n Twat. He wor a bloody monster. Huge beggar. He kep' tryin to eat Twat. You should've seen him, great big teeth like a vampire. Chasin Twat round the cage. It wor a right laugh."

"Probably not for the hamster."

"Twat?"

"Yeah."

"Twit loved it though. It made 'is day. Every day. He wor after Twat every day. But Twat wor right fast. He kept runnin and runnin."

"You never had hamsters, you, Connor - you're a liar!" This was Yusuf, sitting on the opposite side of the room. He was an overweight boy with a convict's haircut and thumb-sized brown eyes.

"Did," Connor threw a bit of the casing in Yusuf's direction, but missed woefully.

"Never."

"Alright, Yusuf, thanks," I said, getting up off my haunches and stretching up to my full height to make the point. I felt a stiffness in my knees as I did so, alongside a pull in the backs of my calves. I felt increasingly creaky. I pictured a cartoon can of oil to rid myself of my rust. I pictured my robotic self, the lubricant running in the crevices. I caught my reflection in one of the windows: my short, sandy-coloured hair, my darker ever-present stubble. I stood in the centre of the desks - well, tables, more than desks in the old-fashioned ink-blotter sense. I'd arranged them in any number of patterns over the years, but I was currently on a traditional run: all of them facing the front.

4

"He's a bloody liar, sir," Yusuf continued. "He never had no hamsters, I've been to his house, sir. They've got loadsa mice an' rats running about there, but not bloody hamsters."

"Yusuf, shut it. And watch the language will you?"

"Sorry, sir. He gets me mad. He's always lyin. I can't help meself."

"Yer mum," Connor said, under his breath, but loud enough.

"What you say?" Yusuf pushed his chair back and stood up, the swag of his stomach swaying. There was no doubt he'd be able to demolish little Connor in a matter of seconds.

"Alright, Yusuf, sit down. You've made your point. Badly. But you've made your point. What animal are you writing about anyway?"

"My pet beaver," Yusuf answered, returning to his chair, a manic-looking grin on his face, a wart of spittle at one corner of his mouth. "Beaver, d'you gettit?"

"Very good, Yusuf. Get on then." I nodded to Jane, the teaching assistant, and she moved away from Louise, a quiet girl she was helping, over to the demanding lad.

"No, no - my *beaver*, sir," Yusuf's mouth looked like it might annex his face, swallow the rest of it or most of the air around it, at the very least. His head was a bowl and his smile was a giant fish swimming across the bottom of it.

"Yeah, very good, Yusuf, that'll be different," I replied, resisting the trap. That was best. Pretend not to understand. Play innocent or dumb. At heart, teaching was a manipulation, a con-trick. The best teachers were simply propagandists for their subjects, for themselves. And quite right: anything to get that work done, that knowledge in. "Write about that then."

"Oh, *sir*!" Yusuf shook his head as Jane sat down next to him. "Miss," Yusuf said, "d'you get it? *Beaver*."

"Yusuf," I said, the two syllables weighted with a greater sense of threat. Then to Jane, "Miss, see if you can get any sense out of him. It might be difficult. I think he's been eating Skittles for breakfast again. Skittles and coke. Anyhow," turning back to Connor, "what are you going to write about your hamsters?"

"Dunno."

"Well, describe how you looked after them. What you did. Each day. Like cleaning them or feeding them."

"I din't," Connor said.

"No?"

"No, me mum did. That was her job."

"Your poor mum."

"She wor good at it. She liked doin it."

"Did she?"

"Yeah." Connor replied, after further consideration. "Two things she wor good at - drinkin and lookin after me hamsters."

"Okay, describe how she looked after them."

"I'll tell you what I liked doin with 'em." Connor leant back on his chair again and sucked at his rapidly disintegrating biro: the stem of the ink cartridge grew from the bombed-out wreckage of its casing.

"What was that? What did you like doing?"

"Throwin matches at 'em."

"Connor."

"I did."

I rolled my eyes back and shook my head. "Write about that then." I knew there were other children I needed to get round to seeing before the lesson was out; but at the same time I didn't want to lose Connor's laconic enthusiasm.

"Once, I threw this match and the straw set on fire, the whole cage were goin up, so I got me dad's beer and poured it over it, to put it out. Me dad gave me a right slap when he fount out. Nickin 'is ale. Twit's fur wor black. All over. Grew out alright in the end though. Weren't bothered. Good as new."

"Loads, you see. Tell me about all that."

"I just did."

"Yeah, well, write it down, it's a funny story, I'll enjoy reading it."

6

"Do I have to?" More than a hint of a whine.

"Yeah, Connor, you do."

"I don't want to 'ave to write it. I mean I've told you, you know it now. What's the point?" Connor said. "You'll be bored 'avin to read it."

"Nothing you write ever bores me, Connor." There was a knock at the door. A tall Year 9 girl sauntered in with a note.

"Hiyah, blondie!" Yusuf called over to her, his smile erupting once more. The girl raised her middle finger at him and scowled.

"Yusuf, you're on thin ice now," I said. "One more thing and you're outside."

"Yeah," Connor agreed. "You're on thin ice now, Yusuf." He threw another piece of casing at his enemy. It missed again.

"Shut up, Connor, for God's sake, or I'll have to send you out too. Get on writing."

"Sir," the girl tried, "it's from Mrs Hibbert, she's says it's urgent and you must reply. Right now, sir."

"Yeah, yeah. Thank you." I took the note, opened it and read what Alice had written - using our own euphemisms, of course. I scribbled *Yes* back and then returned the note to the girl, but that was it for the rest of the lesson: thinking about Alice again; my head full of her, her touch, her voice, how she felt when I held her; not pets or whatever it was I was supposed to be doing. I paced up and down, helping those who had their hands up, keeping Connor and Yusuf apart and watching the helicopter swoop over the school again, its rotor blades now sounding like a slowed-up Maxim gun: one, perhaps, to quell the restless natives.

3. Lewis

startin somewhere new is wierd isnt it. your new you sed so you no what im talking abowt, also i have to cum on a bus im not from here no thanks, so i doant no nowon, a cupple of peepel but nowon propa.

this school is diffrent to my last one, there if you coffd rong you got in trubble, it was rank, i was always in trubble, i dint meen to be, not always, but i always wos, it wos reel stric they dint like me there, there wos one teacher who thort i wos safe but the other teachers dint like her so that was probly why?

i play it kinda quite here, just now i am keepin an eye on peepel, i am keepin an eye on you, your my best teacher ever, i no thats becos your young and all that but your a gud teacher to, you let us have a laff but then we do sum work, sum peepel do im sorry if i doant. i am workin now though arnt i, you carnt say im not, luck

i am writting this, im useing an exersise book from your desk, you werent lookin and my mums pen, she dunt no ive got it, shell strop if she finds out, thats enuff

4. Harry

Alice's husband, Simon, had left her two years previously. She was forty-three years old, nine years older than me, and she'd been flattered by my interest in her; or that, at least, was how I'd perceived it. I'd promised Alice I would find her a new man, but had ended up finding only myself. Naturally there was a risk that we might wreck the good relationship we'd enjoyed for three or four years, but Alice said we ought to try and see, and that "It would be for the best, and after you've slept with me you can tell me to piss off, and I can hate you till one of us leaves. Which, actually, Harry, will be you."

The fact that I told her I'd never done this before was also something which Alice liked. I knew this, and I knew that she'd chosen to accept I was telling her the truth, and though she did allow herself to mention Sarah, my wife, and Eve occasionally, we'd agreed that whatever happened wouldn't get out of hand, that it would remain superficial and lightweight, a sort of bodily banter; that it was, more than anything, an easy way of cheering each other up.

I'd endured my own rough times recently - I'd plenty of worries about money, while other things could be a strain at home. This was to be our secret, and all the more fun for that. "A secret life," Alice said, "I've always wanted one of those. I've never had a life which no-one else has known about. Everything about my life has been played out more or less for everyone to see. It's all been so *obvious*." She'd barely told anyone of the affair, only her oldest friend, Jackie, whom she rarely saw but needed some news for, and she might have given a subtle hint to Donna at aerobics, but Donna might not have picked up on it, because they were also laughing about my 'stalker', which was something of a joke for most of the staff-room at that time too. It had

9

started as a joke to me as well, but had begun to become moderately more irritating the longer it went on, especially now that everyone else had forgotten about it. Kimberly, the girl, was pretty screwed-up as it was - as if she wouldn't be, having a fixation on *me*, huh! - but the whole scenario seemed to be compressing my other concerns so that they too were uglier and even more out of joint. It wasn't as though Kimberly actually did anything wrong or compromising: it had merely reached the point where she'd learnt my timetable by heart, the days I did duties, the fact I managed to pub it on a Friday lunchtime without anyone knowing; and, as a consequence of this dedication and feat of memory, she was invariably in my vicinity. Okay, so she was only in the habit of finding me and talking to me. That was partly the problem - if she'd written me a note it would have been more straightforward: I could have passed it on to her Head of Year. As it was, the situation was merely a tad wearing. Kimberly would try and talk to me with what she trusted to be an easy-going adult intimacy. Instead, unsurprisingly, given her age, she was more often than not a weird mixture of the earnest and the coy.

I was also convinced that Kimberly had got hold of my home telephone number, which I found difficult to understand, seeing that, like most teachers, I was ex-directory. Calls kept coming through that when answered were met with silence and static and the hint of a giggle in the distance. It didn't bother me unduly because I was fairly certain I knew who the instigator was, but I still resented the small waste of time their receipt was intermittently becoming. And, I also wondered, if Kimberly had my telephone number, did that mean she also knew where I lived? Which would be great: her turning up on the doorstep one day. I could imagine the way that might play. I saw tabloid exclusives and overuse of the words 'sex-crazed'.

So here Kimberly was at lunch-break while I was on duty in the yard. She was a skinny girl of medium height with a washed-out pallor and dyed off-blonde hair, the colour of butter thinly spread on toast. "Hello, Mr Monk," she said.

"Oh, hi, Kim," I replied, as though her appearing was a shock. "How are you today?"

"Terrible."

"Why's that?"

"I've got the coursework, and it's doing me head in. I've got History and French, then there's Science that Wilding says I've got to do again, but I'm not going to, Wilding's gay."

"Kim -" I said with mock indignation.

"He is. And I've got to go to work tonight and tomorrow." I knew that she worked at a pub or restaurant, but I didn't know where. "And so I really don't know when I'm going to do it all, I really don't. And I had my bike nicked from round the back of our house last night, which is well annoying. My mum says she's going to start rolling up the grass and putting away the flowers every night to stop them disappearing too."

"Right." I tried my best to sound interested: actually that was rubbish about Kim's bike.

"How's your brother?" Shane had left school four years previously.

"He doesn't live with us anymore."

"Oh, okay."

"What's he up to? Still working at Jessops?"

"Think so."

Some boys were playing basketball. I watched them for a while. There were clumps of kids across the yard, an expanse of newly laid tarmac surrounded on all sides by school buildings, mostly squat sixties constructions. It was like the architect hadn't really believed in what he was doing and then the builders had run out of energy too. It was a bright March day, the scarce cloud high in the sky, the helicopter cutting across from left to right, an alien insect, a few seagulls wheeling about at roof-level. I watched one flit around then dart down to pick up a crisp from the tarmac, before swiftly returning to the safety of the air. It was dangerous territory down here compared with up

11

there. Kimberly smiled at me. I thought I'd better walk over to the smokers, show my face, make the right noises, but instead noticed something in the far corner of the yard: two Year 11 boys, Aaron and Steven, were squaring up to each other while a third, Matthew, looked on. The three of them were talking, it seemed quite rationally, but then, without warning, Steven had Aaron in a headlock. I started to walk towards them, though I wasn't sure if what was happening was serious or not, seeing as none of the other kids had noticed it going on, which was unusual in this situation. Typically, the first I knew about a fight was when a chant went up and a hundred pairs of legs stampeded over to get a ringside view.

Matthew was still becalmed, impassively watching Steven and Aaron. I shouted to him as I approached the boys, "Matthew, Matt, are you messing? Is it for real?" Matthew ignored me. A seagull swooped low over the boys, brightly white, sun-struck. Steven hit Aaron in the chest, and Aaron staggered backwards. It wasn't playing, that much was now apparent, but I wasn't close enough to do anything about it, so I shouted again, "Oi, Matthew, break it up will you?" Matthew again showed no interest in what I'd said so I started to run. A crowd began quickly forming around the three boys, iron filings to a magnet. Aaron had freed himself from Steven's arm and landed a punch close to his ear. I pushed through the melee, saying "Out of the way!" as I did so - this was always the time when my heart started racing, the physical effort, the claustrophobic sense of reaching the core of the crowd; it invariably took me longer than I expected, kids not wanting me to make it there - and I grabbed hold of Aaron while shouting "Break it up, both of you, break it up!"

Aaron was the same height as me, six feet tall, while Steven was smaller, but stockier, and I knew I was in trouble as the boys weren't stopping, were wrestling now, while about the four of us, including Matthew, the crowd was shouting, pushing and jostling. It was similar to being up to your neck in the sea, its current threatening to take you first one way then the other. I steadied myself and remembered the security cameras, hoping that someone might be watching so another adult could be alerted. I glanced over to the entrance of the main block, but nobody emerged. Seagulls strafed the sky. The crowd went forwards then backwards. I tried once more to get hold of Aaron and this time succeeded in hanging on to his arms. "Matthew, will you hold Steven?" My voice came out hurriedly and with shallow breath, and still Matthew paid no attention.

The problem was that the more successfully I held onto Aaron, the more I was giving licence to Steven to hit his opponent wherever he liked: the stomach, the chest, the face. My hand was grazed and I felt my tie get pulled as I attempted to force my way between the two of them. "Matt!" I said, hoping yet again that Matthew might intervene with Steven; but rather than this occur, Matthew swung his fist with slow, lazily careful calculation straight into Aaron's nose. Blood spurted over Aaron's face, onto my shirt. Great. The crowd cheered and laughed and shoved some more. It was like being surrounded on a bouncy castle. "Jesus," I said, loosening my grip slightly on a further incensed Aaron, "Matthew, what did you do that for? What for? Steven, will you stop now? Come on. Enough's enough."

Then, thankfully, the cavalry. Three other Year 11 boys came running over and helped me part Aaron and Steven. One of them, Jaware, was turning to the crowd around us and saying, "Right, it's finished. It's *finished*. Now will you all piss off. Fuckin *piss* off, will you? Haven't you got a *lesson* to go to? The bastard bell's gone, for fuck's sake. *Dicks*." Most of the crowd recognised that the fight was over, and that Jaware's intervention was only hastening the post-bout dissolution. Kids began to drift away, laughing and joking, re-enacting the key incidents of what they'd just seen.

"Thanks, Jaware." I was getting my breath back while loosening the noose of my tie.

Jaware laughed at me, "Sir, you're gettin old, man! Can't break up fights no more. You old."

"I think you're right. Get Steven out of the way over there, will you? Aaron, you better come with me, get you cleaned up. Matthew, wait outside the staff room."

"Me? Why?" Matthew asked, pulling a face as though his brain had revolved 360 degrees inside his skull.

"Do it, Matthew."

"I never did nuffin."

"That's right, Matthew, that's absolutely spot on, son, you didn't."

"I didn't," Matthew said. "How can you say I did? That's shit, that is."

"Do as you're told."

"No."

"Right then, don't do as you're told and make it worse for yourself." Matthew shrugged and shook his head, muttered something about it being unfair, before walking off slowly in the direction I'd suggested, just as Ray Chiltern, the Head of Humanities - a heavily-lined, ruddy-faced man with white bushy hair, a full moustache and a Bob Dylan fixation - appeared. "Good timing, Ray," I said, "as usual."

"Perfect," Ray replied. "I'm sorry, I should have been with you quicker, but I only just found out, but good job you did there. Are you okay?" He was, in fact, properly bothered. "There's blood on your shirt by the way. Just there and there, look. On the bright side, I expect it's all on video. Ought to make the term's highlights. Are you okay? No, seriously - are you okay?"

I nodded. Ray always made me feel calmer and better than I was. It was as if I assimilated some of his decency, kind-heartedness and blessed sense of conviction. Ray had been a teenager in the sixties, while for me it had been the eighties: that seemed superficially to sum up the differences between us. What we'd lived through at our most impressionable. He'd come out one way, and I turned out another. Sixties Man. Eighties Man. There were times when

14

I thought I might want to be Ray. Without, of course, the moustache.

Blood was continuing to drip from Aaron's nose as we reached the main building. Kimberly was next to me, saying, "Are you alright, Mr Monk? Are you okay? I really thought you were going to get hurt." It was she who had alerted Ray about the fight.

"Yes, I'm fine, thanks, Kimberly," I said. "Fine. Thanks for getting Mr Chiltern, I appreciate that."

"That's alright, sir. I thought I better had. Are you sure you're alright? Is there anything I can do?"

"No, thank you. But thanks for asking."

As a result of the note Alice had sent me, we met an hour after the end of school at a pub that was fifteen minutes drive away. The pub had uncovered floorboards, trestle tables and whitewashed walls which narrowed at one end down towards the kitchen, and this was always the area where Alice and I sat. Less chance, we both thought, of being caught unawares by anybody: facing the doors, the bar, the Mafioso of - whatever. "How are you?" I asked as she arrived. I'd already bought her usual drink, a double-vodka and diet coke.

"I'm fine." Her voice had a convent school assurance about it. I liked that about her, she didn't try and hide where she'd come from. "And how are you, after your punch-up?"

"Absolutely brilliant," I said to her. "But you already know that." Then, "Joke, obviously." I smiled and kissed the front of my index finger before placing it on her cheek. I put my right arm round her shoulder and pulled her closer to me, then whispered something pornographic into her ear.

"Promises, promises."

"I always keep them," I said seriously. "I'm very predictable like that." Alice thought this funny. I didn't know why, but kept my surprise to myself. When people reacted in a way which I construed as being critical of me, I was at first more deeply hurt than I should have been; but, conversely the hurt soon evaporated - within seconds on occasion - and I quickly recovered my composure. Like now. "The trouble with you," I said to her, "is that you're too bloody gorgeous. I want you every second I'm with you and I can't stop thinking about you when I'm not." I did think about Alice far too much. I still couldn't quite picture her naked and still found it surprising when she undressed in front of me. She had a fuller figure than Sarah, she was taller and everything about her was bigger - her shoulders, her breasts, her waist, her thighs - there was more flesh there, more skin. More of her. I liked her substance. Sarah was, in comparison, frail. She was slight and bony. Though I'd initially been attracted to that daintiness, how I could encompass her easily: which must have meant something to me at some point.

"The trouble with you," Alice replied, "is that I don't believe a damn word you say. But the truly wonderful thing is - I don't need to."

"Me? I always tell the truth."

"Harry," Alice said.

"I always tell the truth," I told her, downing my pint as if this was proof of my statement. "That's one of the great things about me. I'm the most truthful person I know. No, don't laugh, I am. I've plenty of faults, Alice, I know that, but I'm not a liar. I can't see the point. No, really. Really. Don't believe me then. Is anyone at home?"

"Yes."

"Don't they have rugby to go to? Or is it indoor cricket now?" Alice shook her head. "Chess club?"

"No."

"Isn't it the school play? It must be the school play. Nick must be in line for a starring role by now."

"It's the bloody spring term, Harry."

"I thought they had productions once a term at that place you send them." Alice's sons went to the city's major private school, which was always a joke between us. "Anyway we need to fix something up."

"We do," Alice agreed.

"Isn't there a conference coming up? A weekend one? Behaviour management?"

"You know I think there might be. Maybe next month. Friday through to Sunday."

"At a nice hotel, somewhere in the middle of nowhere." I looked down and could see the slope of Alice's breasts in the opening of her blouse. "A very nice hotel, in the very middle of nowhere."

"If you think you're up to it."

"I'm not totally knackered yet," I yawned theatrically. "Not totally." Alice held my hand then bent her head and lightly kissed it. In public this was as far as we chose to go. I loved being close to her, the zing of her proximity. Simply walking past her at work could be electric. Glancing at her. Having my glance met by hers, knowing she felt the same way; and no-one else aware.

I tried not to think of anything going wrong. I didn't see how the relationship would finish. I saw it somehow fizzling out - and that being okay - when both of us had had enough. I couldn't picture this, but I wasn't sure I needed to. These things unwound in their own ways, and I felt the process unlikely to cause anyone distress.

5. Lewis

billy is a laff, he doant care, his allways of his head. we wos smokeing befor school i went rownt his house, you shud see it theres like a 100 peepel live there, its manky to, theres dogs aswell as peepel, you can see it from miles off

the garden is overgroan and theres all this sh** in there, i thort there wos a baby but it wos a doll with no arms, we wos laffin about that, i kep wanting to laff, we wen and got loadsa munchis from the shop, billy was giveing sum jip to the oaner i sed thats rasist, billy sed thats not rasist thats his name, thats were his from

in school we wos allover all morning, we wos like goasts nowon sore us. one time a teacher did but he made out he hadnt and carrid on walkin on like he wos bizzy as if!!

in the pm we went to town and latr on we got our bikes and we wos at the park haveing a laff

i mist your lesson so im doing my writting now in my room, how abowt that, dad is lissenin to his music punk and regay, this reminds him of wen he wos yung 100 years ago!?!

6. Harry

The weekend promised to be a good one. Not only had I said goodbye to Alice feeling that there was a pleasant equilibrium between us, one that would, in the very short term, be maintained; that we'd both taken what we wanted from each other, and that when we next met up there would be no residues of tension or misunderstanding between us.

Not only that, but confirmation of a loan I'd applied for was currently sitting fat and black in my bank account, and I'd a Saturday - hell, not only a Saturday, a whole weekend - to look forward to with it lounging there, begging to be spent. I'd be able to parade around the shops with Sarah and Eve in the happy knowledge that, if I wished, I could get out my debit card and buy basically whatever my girls wanted; me too: whatever we'd desire for, that day. I could be someone with money. Make that *Someone*. Make that *Money*. Also, as importantly, I could sustain the charade for Sarah that we had enough funds left for this occasional frivolity. "Let's treat ourselves," I said to her as we got into our car on the Saturday morning.

"Harry, that money's for something important, you know it is, not to fritter away. And we've got things to buy for tonight's party."

"Oh yeah. Well, we've got some spare. Anyway, I want to treat you, you deserve treating. Doesn't mummy deserve treating, Eve?"

"Yes," Eve replied from the back, briefly looking up from her doll. "What's *treating*?"

"Being nice to," I told her. "Doing something for somebody that they like you doing."

"I'm treating Jessica," Eve said. "Look, I'm combing her hair, and you can see that she likes it."

"That's lovely," Sarah said.

"See?" I smiled at Sarah. "Eve agrees. You haven't had anything new for ages, nothing for yourself, not since your birthday, and that was aeons ago. A dress or some jewellery or - I don't know - whatever you want. Some perfume. What was that one you were telling me about? You choose. Something for the summer."

"We'll see. If you carry on being nice to me, if you keep this up, I might be persuaded. Why are you being so nice to me?"

"I'm always nice to you, sweet, that's my job," I put my hand on Sarah's thigh. "I've got to be nice to you, else."

"Or else what?"

"I don't know, but there's always an 'or else'. Haven't you noticed that? Isn't that what keeps people going?"

"I might be persuaded then."

When it came down to it, she was. She found a dress in Coast and it looked exquisite on her: she looked like a film star, a film star I was married to. Sarah said, "What do you think?" and I said, "I know what *I* think, but what d'you think?" and Sarah said, "I think it's lovely, I think it really suits me, but I might be wrong." and I said, "No, you're not wrong. You're absolutely right. You look fantastic. You look absolutely bloody fantastic." and Eve said, "Daddy, you said a swear-word. You shouldn't say swear-words." and I said, "Crumbs, you're right too, Eve. I'm surrounded by women who are always right." and Eve said, "I'm not a woman, daddy, I'm a girl."

I got out my debit card: I liked the springy sharpness of its edges, its tensility bound by the solid rectangular shape. I held the card long-ways between my thumb and my forefinger and flexed it gently - there was an advert where the card was muscular and I was reminded of that - before handing it over to the young shop assistant and smiling at her with money in my smile, and signing my name with money in that too, like I was used to making such purchases on a regular basis, and then the dress was Sarah's. She was happy with her new acquisition, she was lifted by it, her change in mood was palpable. She'd been in a reasonable state of mind, but now she was in an even better one, and I was happy for her. I liked to see my wife happy. It made me think I was doing okay; was successful, in some way. There were these boxes, and they had to be ticked. I sometimes thought of her depression as a criticism of me: how come I couldn't keep her safe from it? How come I couldn't protect her? I couldn't even keep my wife happy, basically *happy*, for christssake. Whereas Eve was generally amiable - I looked out for any clues to a disposition that might mimic her mother's -, in a good mood as she was now, having been promised some furniture for her doll's house. To say that you could read Eve's thoughts was an understatement. Her whole body was an index of them, every facial expression and physical movement a manifestation. Sometimes I hoped she would always remain as demonstrative as this; at other times I recognised the hindrance that might be.

Sarah and I held hands as Eve ran ahead of us. I told Sarah that we'd have to go out so that she could wear her new dress. Even though she didn't look forward to doing this, I tried to maintain the regularity of our dates. With a couple of Bacardis in her, Sarah was usually okay for a few hours. A short time later, therefore, when we stopped for coffee and cakes in Caffe Nero, I rang the most expensive, hey, the *best* restaurant in the city - Hart's - and booked a table for the middle of the week after next. "There," I said and I winked at Sarah and smiled broadly at her, and the espresso was good, and the chocolate gateau was good; and the café was filled with a humming hopefulness: people coming and going with important things to do; and the clinking of cups, spoons; and jovial conversations like ours.

By and large, I liked people. My perception was that, for most, life was difficult, fraught, disappointing: not what they had hoped it might be. I saw the existential injustice of this more clearly than, say, social injustice; though I also linked the two together. Consequently, I tended to see the good in those around me - the fact that anyone even bothered to *try* to be good was in some ways miraculous, as

21

far as I could see. Sarah said that I wasn't discerning at all, that some of the people I introduced to her were either wankers or boring or plain fucked-up. My response was that while it was true that most people *were*, at the very least, fucked-up, that facet of their personality didn't appear to be a useful way of categorising them. It was simply a matter of how well they dealt with that state of being, how they negotiated it - that state of being, *the* state of being, as far as I could see: whether they hid it from general view or not; whether it didn't get in the way overmuch once they'd acknowledged it to themselves. It was how well you hid the awful truths you had to face up to in private, I said - that was the key.

"And what am I hiding, Harry?" Sarah would ask me.

"You're complicated," I would say, surprised that she'd asked me this: *c'mon, girl*, "I'm still working on you."

"And what are you hiding, Harry Monk?" Sarah would ask me.

"Oh, only the fact I've nothing to hide," I would reply. "I'm hiding the fact I hope that no-one works that out. Given my theory."

"I think you're hiding the fact that you know your theory's complete tosh," Sarah would tell me, and then the conversation would move on.

Sarah was a beautiful woman. There could be no argument about this. She was slim with pale skin, cropped dark hair and very round, deep blue eyes which were flecked with green. Once or twice she'd been mistaken for somebody French, though her family's roots were Celtic rather than Gallic, and she'd been brought up in the wastes of Coventry. She also had an aloofness about her - actually a shyness - which underscored that English perception. In fact, I was convinced that she was more beautiful now than she had been when we'd first met. She turned more heads now, and I also increasingly noticed the hostile looks she garnered from other women, which always amused me.

Sarah and I sat with our shopping-bags by the fountains in Market Square while Eve rode on the merry-go-round that was part of a small fair temporarily parked there. She waved and smiled at us. Some late-night reveller had put washing-up liquid into one of the fountains so that, every now and again, tiny clouds of bubbles floated past Sarah and me on the soft breeze. I put my arm around her. Even with the breeze, it was a warm morning, the warmest of the year so far. Sarah laid her head on my shoulder. A net of birds spread across the sky above Debenhams. I felt relaxed, expansive. I watched the Goths beginning to congregate at the front of the Town Hall. There was a party of tourists on the steps too, Italians or Spaniards, on the hunt for Robin Hood or a castle that looked like they'd imagined it back in Barcelona or Rome. Eve waved to Sarah and me from the merry-go-round. Sarah had closed her eyes, but I waved back. "It's getting busier," I murmured. "We'd better go soon."

"Yes," said Sarah. "If you don't mind."

"Course not," I replied. "You've done well, we've stayed out later than usual."

I tried to sustain Sarah's connection with the outside world. She hadn't worked since Eve's birth, which wasn't what we'd originally planned. This was one of the reasons why our money problems had spiralled, so that we were now paying off loans we'd taken out to pay off the loans we'd taken out to pay off the initial loans: that was what the new loan was supposed to be for. Consequently there was very little left over from my salary each month, which meant that even food shopping had to be put on credit cards with no hope of anywhere near total repayment. Still, though, I paid for Sarah to visit a psychotherapist, have beauty treatments, buy stuff, all in an attempt to get her well again, or at least keep her cheerful - even if it was a further drain on our resources. I had to help get Sarah right, stop up-the-stairs and down-the-stairs being just about the only journeys she ever made. I'd think of the countries we'd visited only a few years before, prior to Eve being born, enjoying holidays in Eastern Europe, China and Peru. Since then, they'd tended to be more small-scale, in Britain, but away from the crowds. We'd holed up in Devon, north Wales and on the west coast of Scotland, but Sarah became tense after a few days away, so that had to be the limit of it.

The extent of Sarah's affliction was our secret; not even her parents knew how ill she was. Especially not her parents, Sarah would say, her father a car-worker and her mum a secretary, who'd worked hard to support her through university. Hell, especially not her parents. They assumed Sarah was off work to look after Eve as a consciously traditional decision, and neither I nor she said anything to dissuade them of that notion.

I was worrying about Sarah making it through the evening's party when she called me to the kitchen about four in the afternoon. "I can't do this," she said, standing by pallid slabs of fish and other seafood, biting her bottom lip as she often did when she was anxious, so that its skin was rough and sore, and sometimes I would kiss there first, deliberately, to magic it better, to make an effort anyway.

"Course you can."

"No, I can't. I can't do anything. Ring everybody up and cancel. Look at me, I'm all jittery and I haven't even started cooking yet." She held her hands out to show me.

"You just need to get it all going. I'll help," I said calmly.

"No. I can't face it. I really can't face having people round. I don't want people round in my house. This is my house. Why should I want other people in it? Harry, you'll have to do something about it. Find an excuse, make one up. You're good at that, you're good at making things up. Ring them up and cancel."

"Honey, I can't."

"Harry, I'm ill, I'm feeling ill. I can't do it, I really can't. You have to believe me. You have to listen to what I'm saying." I was, but she didn't seem convinced that I was: "I'll have to leave then, because I can't be here when they arrive. You'll have to cook the food, you'll have to be here on your own when they come because I'll be gone." There was a sheen of panic in Sarah's eyes as well as her voice.

"Sweetheart, you always say this and it's always alright in the end. It's only because you're thinking about everything that's got to be done. You've let it get on top of you. It's not the people coming round, I don't think. Come on, I'll help. We'll do one thing at a time, concentrate on one thing at a time. It'll soon be done, you watch."

"You can't cook," Sarah said.

"True," I laughed, "but I can help you."

"But I can't cook now. Look at me, I'm a wreck, I'm trembling."

She was, so I held her, but she continued to tremble, I could feel her whole body vibrate. Behind her was a picture-frame with some of our favourite postcards stuck in. Funny ones like *Things are getting worse. Please send chocolate* and *I've learnt so much from my mistakes. I think I'll make another.* Serious ones like *Only when the last tree has died and the last river has been poisoned and the last fish has been caught will we realise that we cannot eat money.* A few sentences from EM Forster about the aristocracy of the sensitive. A do-it-yourself secular litany.

"Once you get going, you'll be fine."

"I can't see. What the problem. Is. Just you. Being here," Sarah said into my chest, her words and breath entangled, her rhythms all wrong. "They're only coming to see. You anyway."

"Oh yeah, of course they are. What about Claire and Ryan? They're your friends, not mine. Well, they're mine as well, but they're mainly yours if you see what I mean. I'd better get doing it myself then."

"I can't let. You mess. It up," Sarah said to my chin.

"It would be a disaster."

There was a pause, then a snuffled: "That's putting it. Lightly."

"I'd have to nip down the Chinese. They'd never know, they'd rave about my prawn wantons, my crispy beef -"

"Harry -"

"C'mon then, what do we need to get on with first? I'll

25

stick on the football on the radio while we're doing it. Is that okay? A bit of footy? Help me concentrate. After, that is, I've opened this bottle of wine."

7. Lewis

weekends are lush no school. this is what i do, get up late unless my dad shouts me cos mum is allready out, if my dad shouts me i make him his breakfast

my mum works hard, shes a cleaner in the morning and evening and she works in co-op in the day aswell, we used to have more things i can rember that wen dad was ok, but now we doant have so much becos it is mum reelly and sum benfits, but that isnt like it wos befor. like there was more stuff and we whent on holidays like to spane and once we whent to florida, that was reelly the best holiday we whent on cos of disneyland and the kenndy space center but we havnt been away together for years now, dad dunt want to, mum has bin with her friend's on a cruse and went also with them to west indies but not me, im not botherd

but id like to go into space wudnt you. it would be mint i do think theres aliens don't you. i meen there must be wen you stop and think about it, my dad wos telling me the other day how big space is it is big, loadsa stars, there suns you no, and rownd them planets like billions and billions, i meen think how important we like to be my dad says, and yet you no what i meen our lives, he sed, he wos being philosofical he sed

8. Harry

Jon was the first to arrive for the party. He was an RE teacher at school, a bright Oxford graduate who hadn't completely mastered the living-a-life bit. There was something imprecisely deliberate about this: the general forgetfulness, the mess, the raggedy jumpers and oversized unpolished boots. But, until he got too drunk, he was good company - well, I thought so anyway. Sarah wasn't so sure: "Harry, does he have to come?"

"Just this once."

"He's your ugly friend, isn't he?"

"What d'you mean?"

"You know."

"No, go on."

"Pretty *women* often have an ugly friend. It makes them feel even better about themselves."

"Who's yours then?"

"I'm not pretty enough to have one."

"Don't be daft."

"An ugly friend? I'll have to tell him that."

"No, Harry, don't."

Claire and Ryan arrived next, a little after Jon. Claire was Sarah's friend from Nottingham University, who continued, like Sarah, to live locally. She was an accountant, a benevolent, sensible woman who on occasion was a touch too garrulous for me. Her husband, Ryan, seemed content to let her ramble on. I wondered if Ryan actually listened to much of what she did say. He was an ex-policeman who was now something in carrier-bags, I wasn't sure exactly what. A short, solidly-built man with grey hair which was beginning in places to turn white as though paint had been splattered across it, Ryan was a black-belt in a martial art I'd never heard of. There appeared to be a burgeoning number of martial arts I'd never heard of.

Eve had come downstairs to meet the guests. She relished being introduced to them - she was like a celebrity, moving from adult to adult - and Sarah said she could stay downstairs for five minutes. I took her up to her room once Roseanna, a young woman from my department in her first year of teaching, arrived - minus a poorly boyfriend - and Eve had said hello to her as well.

"Daddy, I like your friends." Eve lay in a princess-pink cabin-bed with the corresponding princess-pink canopy over the top half of it. Her heart-shaped face, framed by dark curly hair, peeped out from under the matching duvet. I felt I'd done something right with my life when I saw her like this. There she was, safely tucked in.

"Yes, they're nice friends," I said, standing by the bed.

"Jon's funny," Eve laughed.

"I think he thought you were funny too."

"We were laughing."

"You were."

"He kept saying "Would you Adam and Eve it?" Why was that funny?"

"I've no idea."

"Jon thought it was funny."

"He would."

"Why?"

"He finds lots of things funny."

"Why?"

"Because he's a funny man."

"He is."

"He is." I stroked Eve's hair.

A cloud of seriousness crossed her face. "Why does he shake his words?"

"Shake his words? Oh, he has a stutter. Sometimes he finds it difficult to say them."

"Why?"

"I don't know. It doesn't matter though. Some people have one. It's not a big problem."

29

"I like Jon."

"And he likes you too," I said. "But then everyone likes you cos you're wonderful." I leant forward and kissed Eve on the forehead. Sometimes when I did this I hoped I transmitted something good to her - any good I had inside me. I could *imagine* this happening, if nothing else. "Just wonderful."

"Not everyone."

"They do. Everyone I know does."

"Oliver at school doesn't," Eve said.

"Who's Oliver?"

"He's a boy," Eve told me solemnly. "He's in my class."

"Don't worry about him. Stupid boy," I said. "Boys can be stupid."

"That's right," Eve replied. "Anyway, all the other boys like me, so he will do too one day. That's what mummy said."

Ryan was asking Jon what he meant by *tolerance* in response to a conversation we'd had halfway through the main course of seafood pasta in a lemon sauce: Jon had told the story of a poster of Darren Gough on the school PE notice-board being set alight immediately after England's Test Match win in Karachi a few months before. Jon had tried to put the flames out with a fire-extinguisher, but that had turned out to be empty. Poor Goughy had gone up in flames. Ryan hadn't taken too kindly to Jon's unpatriotic mirth about the incident or the fact we hadn't caught the perpetrators. I jumped in. Ryan's tone was a little aggressive, and I sought to pacify the situation, "It's the sound of the word I don't like," I said. "It sounds like it isn't sure of itself. It's that 'er' in the middle, or something." Quite clever that, I thought, the alcohol beginning to kick in; it had come to me while tackling a particularly tenacious ring of squid.

"Nothing wrong with not being sure of yourself," Sarah said.

"I suppose not."

"Bloody l-liberalism," Jon said. "Too sc-scared to make

its mind up. It'll fail in the end, of course. And to take its place, I suggest fundamentalist Islam. That'd iron out a few creases. You think we'd have the problems in our schools if the M-Mullahs were in control? Would we buggery. And, by the way, none of that either. No arse-b-b-banditry. And at school no bloody crappy little detentions and the like. None of that namby-pamby positive behaviour malarkey. No, a child forgets his homework, chop his b-bloody hand off. Forgets it again: chop the other one off. It'd be like the Black Knight in *The Holy Grail*. Blood everywhere. Tell a teacher where to go, cut the little b-bastard's tongue out. That'd vanquish bad behaviour. Overnight."

"I've a friend who works in a Catholic school," Roseanna said. "He says God's the Headteacher there. If a kid's doing anything wrong, Harvey, my friend, whispers in their ear, "God won't like that. Neither will Jesus. They're watching you." Works a treat every time, Harvey says, they're all so bloody brainwashed. And he's an atheist, it's all a big joke to him. But whatever does the trick, I suppose."

Roseanna was a young woman of medium height and medium build who was not quite pretty. It was difficult to tell why she was not quite pretty; but it was, I thought, undeniably the case. There were angles when she was very nearly pretty and others when she was really nowhere close to being pretty, but mainly it was the not-quiteness which prevailed, even here in the candlelight, with the shadows emphasising her high cheek-bones. She had shoulder-length black hair which was tied back at work, but tonight was down, dark eyebrows arching light brown eyes and a pale complexion; but her eyes were maybe too large and her mouth possibly too small: it was hard to say. She was patently someone who had to watch her weight - five or ten years from now after a couple of children I could see her eventually giving up the fight. But at the moment, what with her gym visits and yoga and vegetarianism she'd a good figure; even if she wasn't, in my view, quite pretty. Not that my view mattered in the slightest, the importance of the looks thing just interested me, you know - how much effect it had on people's lives etc. There had been some research done on this, but I couldn't remember what conclusions had been drawn. I needed to slow down on the wine.

"All order's a trick, you're right, Roe."

"I disagree with that, Jon," Sarah said. "People like order, they like to know where they are, what's expected of them. It's a natural human desire."

"Natural? Desire? Be careful," Jon smiled.

"Why? What d'you mean?"

"There's an argument that n-n-none of those things actually are -"

"Are what?"

"Natural."

"That's an odd argument."

"Possibly. But a lot of people have spent a lot of time arguing it." In the pause that followed Jon's retort, there was a scrabbling noise down the chimney and something landed on the floor close to his chair. "Blood and sand! What's this?" Everybody looked as he bent over and cautiously picked the thing up. It was a dark grey colour and round, marginally smaller than a squash ball.

Ryan immediately took over, "Let me have a look, I think I know what it is. Be careful with it, Jon." Jon rolled his eyes and carefully passed Ryan the ball. "Yeah, I'll show you what we can do with the after we've finished eating. Sarah, d'you have an owl round here?"

"We do sometimes hear one, don't we, Harry?"

"This is a fur-ball," Ryan announced. "It's from an owl. Will, a colleague of mine, showed me what to do with them, we have an owl close to where we work. We'll see what's in it later, if that's okay with you, Sarah. I can show you, if you want."

"Ryan, do you have to?" Claire said. "A fur-ball? Yuk! Not while we're eating." Turning to Roseanna, she said: "He's always doing things like this. Can't take him anywhere."

"No, not while we're *eating*, darling. Obviously."

"It looks interesting," I said. "I'd like to see it."

"It *is* interesting." Bluff bastard. I drained my glass.

"Men," Claire said to Sarah and Roseanna, the word loaded, ready to go off. "Later," she said to Ryan.

"That's what I said." He placed the fur-ball next to his plate.

After a pudding of strawberry mousse, I took Jon out into the back garden for a cigar. Overhead it was clear, the sky dazed with stars, though there were clouds in the distance. "Good idea," Jon said as I helped him negotiate the step out of the kitchen door. "Don't want to dominate too much. Sometimes I can't h-help myself. It's like I'm back on stage fencing with the hecklers. Did I ever tell you about the time when -"

"Too much of a good thing," I said quietly to him, enjoying the cool air, regaining a hint of sobriety.

"Once I get g-going," Jon replied conspiratorially, attempting to unwrap his cigar.

"Absolutely," I said. "Here." Jon passed me the cigar.

"It reminds me of the Fringe, 'ninety-one -"

I gave Jon his cigar back, then lit my own. "I went to the Fringe a couple of times."

"Did you?"

"Before your time. Didn't catch you, I'm afraid. Late eighties. Saw some good stuff. A Spanish company doing Lorca. In Spanish. Couldn't understand a bloody word, but I loved it all the same. The theatre was bloody *it* when I was that age. I loved going. Nice little theatre in Lancaster, where I was brought up. The Dukes."

"Mind if I join you?" Roseanna came out onto the patio. She was faintly unsteady, a full wine glass in one hand, and unlit cigarette in the other. I offered her a light for it. "You've got a lovely house." She wrapped her bare arms around herself. "And Eve is beautiful."

"Thank you. She is."

"Where do you live?" Jon asked her. I hoped Jon realised he had no chance of finishing up there.

"Sneinton. Little terraced house. First actual house I've lived in."

"A traveller! Caravans. Nomadic? Daughter of a tinker? The open road, I sh-should have known!" I assumed that Jon was being ironic, but he was pretty far gone, so it was anyone's guess.

"No. Flats." Roseanna was slightly gawky, I thought, which I'd never noticed at work before; she nervously moved her weight from foot to foot as though she was on a gently rocking ship. Still, Jon was making me nervous too. "Brought up in central London, flats. It's strange living in a house. Can't get used to it. I've a small yard at the back. A small backyard all to myself! I sit out there sometimes and it's well weird. Not like when I was growing up. Used to play football at the back of the theatres, Wyndhams, The Duke of York's. Played football with the actors when they were off-stage. Played with Bill Kennedy, Terry Martin. Didn't know who they were, just adults who popped over for a kickabout."

"Was K-Kennedy a better footballer than he is actor?"

"No he was shit at that too. A real wuss. Terry Martin was a good goalie."

"So you were close to Covent Garden?"

"Round the corner."

"I can't believe anyone actually *lives* there," I said, blowing my smoke towards the moon: that was the tip of someone else's cigar. "It seems a place more for tourists. It doesn't seem like a place where people have ordinary lives. I mean where they *grow up*."

"I loved it," Roseanna replied, "but I suppose it's whatever you're used to, isn't it? That's your life. Everyone else's is peculiar. What *you* do is normal, isn't it? You don't pay any attention to anyone else. I mean, they're just there, in the background. Human muzak. D'you see what I mean? Does that make sense? I can't imagine having been brought up anywhere else. I'm going to bring my own children up there, it's the best place to do it. We used to be in and out of all the galleries, the museums, all the time. Five minutes to

34

the National. I spent hours in there as a kid. The Rubens in particular, Carravagio. Don't know why. Used to sit for hours and stare at those paintings."

"But wasn't it - I mean, weren't your parents worried about you, growing up there? I think I'd be petrified. A girl, a young woman, y'know. Maybe that's me being provincial."

"I don't know about them, but I was more worried when I moved up to Warwick to go to university to be honest. I used to hate walking around the campus late at night, it was so quiet. Back home, there's always people about. The two times I've been approached in London, I screamed and people came and helped straightaway."

"*Approached*?" Jon said.

"Nutters," Roseanna told him. "One put his hand around my mouth. I bit him and then screamed. He ran."

"I bet he did."

"I've got big lungs, I can make a lot of noise."

"Big lungs, eh? I can see that, I mean I can see the v-v-value in that - in those - in that ability," Jon puffed on his cigar like it was oxygen, floundering. "I think I need a slash." He stretched, lodged the Havana on a side of the ash-tray, then shuffled back inside, leaving me alone with Roseanna, who immediately shivered.

"Cold?"

"No, okay."

"Go in, if you want."

"I will," she said. "If I want."

"Okay."

"Somebody walking over my grave."

"Indeed."

"Thank you for tonight."

"Glad you could come."

"Harry, I wanted to ask you something."

"Fire away."

"Why are you seeing Alice?"

"Pardon?"

"Alice." I'd guessed that Roseanna already knew about

this, these things get around, but I was still staggered by her frankness. I was about to make some excuses. I supposed that she couldn't believe that I was willing to risk all this - Sarah, Eve, the house - for Alice. I suppose it did look strange; I suppose it was strange in some ways, though, in truth, I seldom felt I was risking anything, these things seemed so separate. I was about to answer when she said, "Why are you spending time with her, when you could be spending it with me?"

"Harry!" Sarah shouted from the doorway. "Come and have a look at this." I used this opportunity to return quickly inside, with Roseanna, I assume, following.

Sarah, Claire, Jon and Ryan were gathered round the kitchen table, which was in the centre of the square-shaped room. "Watch this," Ryan said. He had a teaspoon of boiling water which he dribbled slowly onto the fur-ball that was placed on a piece of kitchen towel. The fur-ball fell apart, a dark grey smear across the paper like charcoal; then tiny grey-white twigs of bone emerged, and other bits like small fragments of eggshell. "A mouse," Ryan said, "the remnants of a mouse. But look, its skull still intact." There was the mouse's skull, almost unbroken, and, sitting in the middle of it, the red wisp of its tongue.

9. Lewis

dads room is downstairs, it used to be the frunt room now
its dads room, it has a bed in it and that is were he is most
of the day, im tryin to get him up more but he doant reelly
want to, the room still has the 2 samurai swords on the wall
like it allways did when it wos the frunt room.

dad still likes his swords he used to reelly look after them
there genwine Japanese swords, he has knifes aswell but the
swords are the best and mitiest, here are sum Japanese
words for the parts of the sword

tsuba

fuchi

habaki

same

menuki

kashira

dad got the swords sent from Japan wen i wos small, he
used to regly cleen them, i rember him doing that now he
dunt he cleend his knifes to he used to do it on a satday
morning i rember and then he went to Forest the mitey reds!

i sed i wud cleen them for him but he sed he dint want me
to so i dint.

wen dad had a tempa he went red and big, i worrid abowt

them swords and knifes but he has not got a tempa the same no more, he sez i have his tempa, and his rite abowt that, sumtimes i can loose it reel bad, its like you go red inside and outside and evrywere you can see is red, im tryin to controll my tempa im doing pritty well so far

10. Harry

When I woke late the next morning, I didn't give much thought to Roseanna - silly drunk - or even the mouse, now in the bin; I was more concerned about Colin and how I was going to get hold of him. I chose to ring the last number I had for him again. Admittedly it was Sunday, but as I didn't know whether the number was a work or a home one, it was worth a try. If I was being honest, I knew that contact was unlikely. It was simply that I had to keep making an effort, at least until an alternative way forward presented itself. As yet the other solution hadn't occurred to me, so I was left with the phone and ten digits. I keyed them in towards the end of the morning after reading the paper, while Sarah took Eve out on her bike. Colin's phone rang and rang, making the sound of something trapped. Sometimes I would let it ring for minutes at a time, first to my ear and then away and then back again. I listened to the chirr of it at my end of the line, transforming this into any number of ring-tones in any number of empty places where the noise was being made; the noise I'd instigated from my high-ceilinged, cream-walled front room with its two abstract expressionist prints, one by Sam Francis and one by Franz Kline; its display of foreign artefacts; book-parading shelves; and bright stagy sunshine streaming through the bay-window.

I would wonder where Colin's phone might be. My imagination would start off prosaically, somewhere workaday, but now locked-up, shut off, an office gathering dust. A large office, a small office. An office with a hundred workstations, clasped by antiseptic yellow-white light; a small office with one desk: a tiny, barely functional box of a room with bare grey walls. A grand office. Lots of glass. A panoramic view. Or, if at home - what would

Colin's home look like? Again, I wasn't sure. I didn't know how much advice Colin would've been able to pay for. Because whoever's the taste was, if there was any taste involved, it wouldn't be Colin's.

But wherever, there was an unanswered phone ringing in it. Sometimes I imagined that Colin was there, staring at the phone, aware that it was me trying to find out what was going on. I felt sure that Colin would have some way of telling that it was me on the other end; some display on his own phone to forewarn him. Actually, I knew that he wouldn't sit and stare at the phone: he was shameless, he'd pick it up and feed me some smarmy nonsense, seek to make me feel guilty for believing that all my money had vanished. It hadn't vanished, it had been modified. Transmuted. What goes down must come up. Eventually. Hang in there, mate. No worries.

When I eventually did get hold of Colin, I'd all sorts of plans devised for his retribution. Colin was overweight and sweated heavily, always sounding out of breath even when he'd done nothing remotely taxing or strenuously physical, even when he was taking a piss, for instance. The last time I'd met him, Colin had leant against the wall above the urinal, breathing as heavily as if he was fucking not pissing; whereas I was reasonably trim, if not in the Ryan league of Nipponese fitness. I knew I could take Colin, I could take him apart. It was years since I'd been in a fight, but Colin, I felt fairly sure, wouldn't take much - much less than what might be termed a fight - for me to make my point. I imagined Colin's spud-like face squelched with blood, sprouting it somehow. I imagined Colin on his knees begging for mercy, a fat root-vegetable of a man with a blood-sprouting face. I imagined kicking Colin in the head one more time for good measure, then wiping the blood from my shoes as I left him in a pulpy mess on the ground.

I knew none of this would do me any good; and I knew, in any case, that such an onslaught would never happen. I wasn't a violent man, at least not in action. I had violent thoughts occasionally, but I saw those as cathartic, and only sardonically so at that. The real thing didn't interest me. When in the past Colin and I had disagreed, it had been different, we'd been much younger, and the motivation not as important, though it had seemed so at the time. Now, however, Colin had really stitched me up. I'd realised too late my extreme naivety, and so, whatever the game was, Colin was winning, hands down. Colin had always been a cock. I'd known this for a long time, and therefore had only myself to blame: I was capable of unbelievable stupidity. I knew this, and so, obviously, did Colin.

And now the cock wasn't answering his phone.

The cock was doubtless sunning himself on my money.

Colin and I had been friends at school. We were both in the same top class from the age of eleven, and had become involved in various extra-curricular activities as well: sport (rugby in the winter, cricket in the summer), plays, societies, and, when we were older, the school newspaper, which we'd managed to get banned in the space of three issues, each one more scurrilous than the last. (Sample page: headline - 'Everything Mr Atkinson Knows About Science.' Under the title, blank space. Mr Atkinson, science teacher, not happy. And, to be fair, he did know a couple of things - usually involving refraction.) The school was an old-fashioned one, a grammar school with a rigorous work-ethic and rigid standards of discipline, about as far away from Peter Wallingford as could be conceived, but it vaguely allowed intelligent dissatisfaction. And, judging by my own exertions, conspicuously unintelligent dissatisfaction too.

Even at an early age, Colin was full of money-making schemes. He lived further away from the school than the majority of the other pupils, but saved his bus-fare by hitching from home and back, and becoming so well known making the daily journey that he had regular commuters who picked him up and dropped him off, his own free taxi-service. Not that his parents ever found out, meaning he was able to pocket their cash. That was typical Colin, as was the fact that he sold cigarettes, alcohol, pornography, and, later, soft drugs to younger kids. He arranged parties at his dad's bars which he sold tickets for. His dad had a few of these places that Colin worked in most evenings as well as completing his school-work and running his various ventures. He bragged that, like Mrs Thatcher, he didn't need a lot of sleep. When I called him a twat for saying this, Colin said he was being ironic, though I wasn't sure. Colin wasn't big on irony. While both Colin and I made it into the first eleven at cricket (Colin read *The Financial Times* while he was waiting to bat), he excelled at rugby too, playing wing-forward and eventually representing Lancashire Under 18s. I liked Colin, envied his fearlessness; and was also aware of his proclivity for getting what he wanted, come what may. There was a relaxed selfishness about him. It was who he was, it was instinctive - if that's how things can be. Always on the look-out. Colin made friends with boys in our year, for example, who had dads he thought might be able to help him out. Like my dad, initially.

Still, I supposed that I'd used Colin too. He was a passport to regular parties and a way of guaranteeing holiday and weekend work behind a bar either in town or further out in one of the villages nearby. Our last two years of school became a packed schedule of parties, plays, sport and Colin's various scams. Colin was Antonio to my Sebastian, the rugby team was unbeaten and the cricket side reached the final of the local cup competition. In the Lower Sixth, I'd lost my virginity at the after-play party for *Grease*, then slept with a second girl when the first had gone home. There was, I felt, no stopping me. A month later Colin and I shared a girl. What happened was that the three of us got drunk on the girl's parents' whisky. I'd gone to the toilet and when I returned I discovered Colin and the girl, Elaine, having sex on the lounge floor. Soon Colin had finished, but Elaine had not. As Colin rolled off onto his back, Elaine beckoned me forward and I took my friend's place. Elaine's breasts were like two dollops of ice-cream that had fallen out of cones and had melted slightly, each to one side of her chest-bone. I didn't have to fuck her long before she came, and I did too. The three of us lay on the floor giggling. This was the first of a few times we had sex with the same girl.

Colin's dad died unexpectedly when Colin was eighteen, in the spring before we were due to take our 'A' Levels. Colin's first thought was to take over the business. His second was to get as far away as possible from that eventuality. "It's what the old man would have wanted," he told me, "he said it was bloody hard work and on no account was I to join him, he said there were far easier ways of making money. It was alright me helping out now and again, a good way of making a bit of dosh, but I wasn't to think of it beyond that." I had no way of knowing if Colin was telling the truth or not, and it didn't make much of a difference to me either way. "Anyhow," Colin said another time, "look what it did to him. Poor old bugger. Heart attack at fifty-two. He even knew it was going to happen. That's no life. Why work that hard to have a heart-attack at fifty-two? Pointless." As it turned out, Colin's mum and his older brother and sister took over and made a pretty good fist of it; the last I'd heard they'd sold-up and bought a prestigious hotel in the Lake District.

In the immediate aftermath of his dad's death, though, it meant that Colin and I more or less ran one of the bars which was housed in a converted corn mill. There were three bars on different levels catering for three different and distinct clientele: an over-fifties, a thirtysomething crowd and then, at the bottom, everybody else. The bars shut at 1am on a Saturday night, and thereafter it became Colin's private party with a few selected friends.

I had a girlfriend, Abby. My relationship with her was meant to be frivolous, but soon began to seem far more important to me before I was really ready to admit it to myself; it caught me unawares. One late autumn evening as I walked Abby back to her house, I was sure I'd fallen in love for the first time. I grabbed Abby round the waist and pulled her towards me. We stood in the shadows at the end of a sloping street of terraced houses. Our breath mingled in the darkness. I liked that I could see this happening: it was meaningful to me. At that age I saw my life metaphorically, from the smallest to the largest occurrence - every little incident replete with meaning. Meaning that I generated, just by being, well, me. *Me* was in the word 'meaning', after all. The choices that I made mattered, more than I could say. It was a time, in short, of longing and upheaval.

"You know that if I loved you this would be the perfect occasion to tell you."

"What, in the freezing cold?"

"Under the moon, the stars, all that shit." *Sublunary* was a word that came to me, Donne being disparaging; but it was a clear night. "Anyway the cold feels more truthful or something. It gets the truth out of you. Forces it."

"The cold feels more *cold*, you dork," Abby said. "It's freezing. We need to get in." She shuddered to emphasise her point. "But you're not, are you?"

"What?"

"In love with me?"

"No, of course not," I replied, smiling as serenely as I could manage. "What, me?" I said. "I don't fall in love. Love," I said, "is a four-letter word." That last had suddenly come to me, and I was pleased with its asperity: it might possibly save me.

"Good," Abby kissed me next to my mouth. "I do like being with you, we have fun, we don't need to spoil it, do we?"

"Hell, no," I replied, swallowing a little too hard. "Hell. No."

"I mean, we'll be going away soon, you'll be in Norwich and I'll be in Edinburgh, so it would be silly to get too involved."

"You're right. You're absolutely right."

It was only a couple of months afterwards when Colin tried it on with Abby. It was soon after his dad had died, at one of the lock-ins. I'd left earlier as I needed to be up and away at some crummy hour the next morning to travel to my grandparents' house in Inverness for their sixtieth wedding anniversary.

I wasn't back until the following Thursday, but Abby came over to see me pretty much on my return. Her appearance was not for the reason I'd hoped it might be. I took her up to my room and lounged on my bed, while Abby sat in the wicker-chair by the window. Assorted members of REM, Green on Red and Violent Femmes looked down on us from the walls. Michael Stipe, in particular, looked pained.

"Harry, I know we're only having a laugh, but I thought Colin was supposed to be your best mate."

"Well I can't blame him for fancying you." I realised I wouldn't put it past Colin, which worried me. "Look at yourself. You're not exactly unfanciable, are you?"

Abby leant forward in the chair earnestly, "That's not the point."

"I know, I'm being facetious. Look, he's a bit screwed-up at the moment. Everything - it's understandable, isn't it?"

"He *is* screwed-up, but not like you mean. I'm not entirely sure he's that bothered about his dad."

"That's unfair."

"Okay, it probably is," Abby said. "But it doesn't take away the fact that he came on to me. And it wasn't pleasant. And you need to know."

"I'm not trying to defend him, I'm simply saying -"

"You are trying to -"

I saw my chance. "No, what I mean to say is - let's face it, he knows you and me aren't totally serious so he probably thought why not?" There was a pause which Abby didn't choose to fill, instead merely looking away, so I continued, "Was he pissed? I bet he was pissed, wasn't he?"

"That's not the point either."

"So it was drink, and him not thinking that we were properly together." How many times could I make the point without her taking the opportunity to rectify it?

"He said some other things as well."

What more had the dickhead done? He was totally untrustworthy, "Go on -"

"About what you and him have been up to."

I could feel myself begin to go red. I hated the way this happened, didn't see why I should give myself away so easily. I needed to learn to lie more discreetly. "What d'you mean?"

"You and him and some girls," Abby said, brushing at her blonde hair with her fingers, and sliding a few strands into her mouth.

"Colin likes to think he's some sort of pimp. He's watched *Taxi Driver* too many times."

"What about you? Are you a pimp too, Harry? Am I one of your tarts?" Abby said.

"He's such a bullshitter. What? Abby, what're you talking about?"

"Is it true?"

"Whatever he's told you it's bound to be bullshit, it's bloody Colin, for God's sake. Captain Bullshit."

"You and him -"

"Uh-huh -"

"Having - *screwing* the same girl," Abby said, staring straight at me, and me feeling like it was the first time she'd ever done that.

"What?" I knew that my voice had come out thinner, like fruit squeezed.

"Taking it in turns, Colin said. Thankfully he didn't go into all the details, though he was obviously dying to. Elaine, he mentioned, Zoe -"

"Was this part of his chat-up?" I said. "No wonder he's so bloody successful with women."

"Is it true?"

"Is what true?"

"What he said."

"I still don't understand what it was he did say."

"You do."

"It's bollocks," I said, my voice more like my own, but still, I thought, sabotaging me. I stood up, an attempt to rid

46

myself of the nervous energy zipping through me.

"I don't believe you."

"Total, absolute bollocks." I knew my face could light up a street. Sweat pricked my forehead.

"I can find out from them. Elaine, Zoe, they'll tell me."

I had no doubt they would. "You're right, Colin is screwed-up."

"So, he's lying?"

"Yes he's lying. I'll bastard kill him," I said. "He's jealous, that's all. Dick. I'll bastard kill him."

I didn't. But, soon after, there was a House rugby tournament, and my House was playing Colin's. Early on in the game Colin was lying at the bottom of a ruck. I kicked him in the head then stamped on his face. Colin's nose had already been broken a couple of years previously, and it was bloodied again when everyone climbed off him. I skulked round the back of the crowd of players, breathing hard in the spring sunshine. Colin got himself up, jogged over to the touchline where there was a bucket of cold water and poured it over his head. He picked up the towel next to it, slicked his hair back to his skull, wiped the blood off his face and then returned to the match. Towards the end, he scored a brilliant solo try, running half the pitch, to win the game for his team. He said nothing to me during or after this, and I eventually doubted whether he realised who'd caused the damage; but I felt I'd made my point - to myself, if no-one else.

Around Easter, though, as we both sat in the lower bar one Sunday, Colin said, "She was a slag, Harry, it was her who came on to me. She was always coming on to me. It wasn't the first time. I didn't like to tell you, I thought you'd get upset. It was always her -"

"No it wasn't, Colin," I replied.

"It was, I swear. She had that tiny red skirt on -"

"Forget it," I said. I'd actually felt happier since my relationship with Abby had finished, but I wasn't going to tell Colin that. Likewise, I knew I wouldn't ever trust him again. Not properly. Not with important stuff. Whatever that was.

"Hey, I can't help it if your girlfriends have the hots for me."

"Yeah, yeah, yeah," I said to him. "Get me another pint, you devious little fucker."

11. Lewis

i seen you in town miss stiles satday pm, you dint no that did you.

i woz with Brett and kris we woz lucking in game and jjb, kris wos wanting sum stuff, me and tyrone wos with him then we went to Maccydees, you no we wos outside, there a grupe of us and the police came for no good reson, Brett sed pigs and they sed we can arrest you for that so be carefull?! pigs

then i seen you, you were with sum friends you wos all laffing abowt sumthing, i cud see you, i dint want to say nothin so i dint say nothing, you lucked nice, your hair lucked nice, it was all flowin wich wos diffrent from what you normly hav.

i like other things to but i woant say what? it wud be inapropepreeat

wen i askd you how old you are you laffd, you dint say, i no your not old, i think your 22 am i rite. that is only 7 years diffrence, 22-15 ect

12. Harry

I hadn't seen Colin in nearly ten years, not long after Sarah and I were married. Every now and again there'd be a photo in the local paper which my parents might mention they'd seen or even, on occasion, cut out and save for me. I remembered one in particular of Colin leaning back on the bonnet of one of his five Porsches; or another: a low-angled shot of Colin with his arms folded, standing in front of some tower block, which I assumed must have been Colin's offices. Whatever it was, Colin had obviously *done well*, though I hadn't been shown any more newspaper evidence to corroborate this for some time. Even so, when Colin rang, I was intrigued by the thought of seeing him again. We hadn't actually had time alone since I'd been at university. Colin had visited in my final year. We'd got on well enough, but there was a sense in which it was the finish of things rather than the re-animating of our friendship, however much Colin drunkenly promised he'd join me on my proposed travels once I'd graduated. "I love you, man." "Yeah, yeah, me too." "No, man, I mean it." "I know you do."

"Bloody hell, Colin, how are you?"

"Me, Harry, I'm sound."

"That's great."

"It is."

"You're looking good."

"You too, my man."

Colin had rung and told me he was in town visiting clients and he reckoned he could do something for me too. We met in a bar in the city-centre. It was early evening and the place was devoid of any other customers. Colin had aged badly, it seemed to me: it wasn't Colin, it was Colin's dad; Colin's dad, yeah, somehow back from the dead - but no, it wasn't Colin's dad, it was, in fact, Colin. I wondered if he was thinking in a similar vein about me. We were both only in our early thirties, after all, yet Colin seemed to me to look ten years older. He was much heavier and the lines on his face were noticeably pronounced; even the dimple in his chin seemed more distinct, presumably because of his increased jowliness and extra flesh. His head gave the impression that somehow it had melted into his neck, like its bulk had caused his neck to collapse, or like a thick candle whose wax had guttered around itself. He reminded me of Brando playing Kurtz. He certainly didn't look like a millionaire; but then again I didn't know what millionaires were supposed to look like. There were so many more of them these days, it was hardly a big deal: I supposed they came in all shapes and sizes.

"Listen," Colin said after a short time when we'd caught up with news of mutual friends, "I'm not going to bullshit you, Harry. We've known each other long enough. I'm not going to pretend or dress this up. What's the point? We're old friends. This is me and you. We're mates. What's the point in wasting breath when this can be sorted out quickly? Sorted out to our mutual advantage. You know what I'm saying, don't you? You feel the same way, I can tell." Colin's accent inhabited a strange Lancashire/Estuary English hinterland, some words veering one way, some equally the other. "There's something more here, and that's what I want you to bear in mind while we talk. I want you to bear all that - that historical stuff - in mind. Because if we can't escape it, and we can't, we might as well make the most of it - which we can. You see, I've got this question for you, Harry. This is a question solely for you. This is the one which seems the most important for you to answer, given what I do know and also what I don't. Harry, what do you not have enough of in your life? What is it that you *lack*? What is it that you could do with more of?"

"I dunno, Colin."

"I'm sure you do."

"I don't, to be honest."

"Think, Harry, think -" Colin's eyes were close-set which seemed to emphasise an almost hypnotic concentration about his face when he spoke. I felt the strength of that now, but refused to submit to the pressure that was being exerted. I relaxed further back into my brown faux-leather armchair and ignored the rays.

"I dunno."

"There must be something."

"I suppose there must be," I replied.

"Y'see."

"I can't think."

"It'll come to you," Colin said, with a smile like a scowl.

"I'm sure it will."

"I know it will."

"I just need time."

"Is that what you need?"

"What?"

"Time?"

"Yes," I admitted.

"That's a good answer, Harry."

"No, I mean that's what I need now. To answer your question. Not as an answer to it. Sorry."

"Right."

"There's always chocolate, I guess," I said.

"Chocolate?"

"I find a nice bar of chocolate - a Kit Kat or a Mars Bar, for example - keeps me going, yes. It's something I look forward to most days. I'll have something in the morning, and then something in the afternoon too. Like stabilisers, to keep me upright and moving along. I think I might be addicted. But only in a good way. There are good addictions, I think. And chocolate is one of them." I didn't know how far I should push this, but I couldn't take Colin's probing as seriously as I supposed I ought - or, at least, as seriously as he wanted me to.

"Okay," Colin said. "So what buys you more chocolate, Harry?"

"I can answer that."

"Good." Colin stuck his bottom lip out hopefully.

"I think I can."

"Go for it."

"Money, I guess, Colin."

"You don't have to guess, Harry."

"I don't suppose I do."

"Money. I knew you'd get there in the end. And you name anything. Anything at all. I've had people tell me all sorts of things. As many different things as there are under the sun. They might say houses or cars or holidays. Sometimes people think they're being clever with me and they do say *time*. That's what I thought, y'see, when you said.... Time itself. Colin, they say, I don't have enough *time*. They think they're being clever, which is fine. Not that I thought *you* were, obviously, you were being thoughtful, but *they're* trying to catch me out. That's how people are. Clever, clever. But, strictly speaking, *what* buys you time, Harry?"

"Is the answer money, Colin?"

"The answer *is* money, Harry."

"I thought it might be. I'm on a roll here. Ask me another." I raised my glass in salute of myself, but before I was able to enjoy my moment, Colin had already replied:

"The answer is *always* money, Harry."

"Maybe it is," I said. "Maybe you're right. If that's the way you want to think about things. I guess the answer can always be more or less what you want it to be. We're all pretty good at self-justification. Though my friend Jon was recently explaining to me what would happen if we decided to abolish money. It was pretty interesting. If what we valued didn't rely on money to value it. If there was no such thing as monetary value at all."

Colin ignored me, "Now, you're doing okay - more than okay, in fact: you're doing well. You've got a good job, you've got a nice house, a decent car. What car d'you drive, Harry?"

"A Peugeot 406. Don't ask me anything about it though

cos I won't know the answer. Sarah's dad sorted it out."

"Okay. And your house?"

"It's a nice house."

"Detached?"

"A semi," I said. "Victorian. Three floors. Four bedrooms. Fourth bedroom in the attic. More like a dumping ground up there. I'd like to change it into a study eventually. That's the plan. Decent-sized garden. A small pond at the bottom. Some fish. What about you? Somewhere plush? You married yet?" I'd been wanting to ask. Sarah had always had this theory that Colin was actually gay. Repressed or in denial. That sort of thing. "You haven't said."

"Me? No, I lead a sad, lonely bachelor's life," Colin laughed. "I'm not like you. I'm a selfish son-of-a-bitch. At the moment settling down with someone would lead me to be dishonest. And that's about as honest as I can be about the situation. It suits me. I get bored too easily, Harry. Seen that, done that. Can't see the point in seeing it and doing it again. Or again and again. And again. Also, y'know, I think I like a bit of chaos in my life, if that doesn't sound over-the-top, some *uncertainty* anyhow. Just a bit, y'know, keeps me on my toes. Wide-awake.

"But your life, it sounds great. It sounds like you. It sounds like the Harry Monk I remember. You've got those things. You've got a beautiful wife and a beautiful daughter. You've got a beautiful home. Those things are sorted. How to make the most of what you've got, that's the question. Time, Harry, time. Time to do all those things you've always wanted to do. Time in your day-to-day life. Time. You're a teacher - you go to work, what, eight till four? Is that about right? Eight till five? But it doesn't end there, does it? It never ends there, does it? I've spoken with other teachers. There's all the other rigmarole. There's meetings - how often do you have meetings? Once or twice a week, I'll bet. Am I right? Once or twice a week after school. On a good week, I'll bet. Then there's marking. Marking, I bet that takes forever. All those essays. There's preparation for the next day's lessons, there's reports - those reports now, they're like books, aren't they? Not like when we were at school. I was always *Quite good*, that was always my comment in everything. *Quite good*. But what the hell did they know? Excuse me, I'm not being rude about teachers per se. But in my case they knew bobbins. *Bobbins*. They thought I was good at sport and that was it. Acting maybe. But - enough of that. The point is: where's the time, Harry? Where is it?"

"It does seem to disappear."

"Disappear? Too right. It vanishes. One minute," Colin clicked his fingers. I noticed the barmaid glance over, semi-alertly. I wondered if this was a good shift because there was bugger-all to do, or a bad one for the same reason. "The next. Last time we saw each other was, what, 'ninety, 'ninety-one? Seems like last week."

"You're not getting philosophical on me, Colin, are you?"

"The point is this, Harry, the point is - with *money* you can create *time*. With money. That's the secret. That's what money unlocks. I know it's never been the most important consideration in your life. I remember how anti it you were when you were young. I remember how almost *religious* you were in your antipathy towards money. And a lot of people treat money as if it is almost sacred, so if you're going to hate it, you might as well hate it with that intensity, that zeal. But we're different, you and me. We have a lot in common, but we're different in many respects. I realised a long time ago that all the - and I don't mean *you* here, I mean other people - all this - *snobbery* - about money was preposterous. Money doesn't have to be the central motivation in your life; there are other important things - more important things - in life; it doesn't have to be your only motivation, and yet it can still be liberating, having it, making it. It can help you in your life. Take time, Harry, to look at what it can do for you," Colin said.

"Okay," I replied. I glanced around the bar. It was still empty. The barmaid was chatting to a newly-arrived barman. Behind them the bottles of spirits stood in front of a white fluorescent wall. For a few seconds, I wanted to believe in that bright arrangement of liquid and light. Briefly, I thought that I did. If I could believe in anything, it might be that. That might be the closest to belief that I could come.

"What d'you think? Colin said. There was a skein of sweat across his forehead. He found a hankie and quickly wiped it away.

"I can see your point," I told him.

"There you go. I knew you would."

"Yes."

"Because of that and because of who you are, Harry, and because we go way back, because of all that - to be frank - strange bullshit; because I am not ordinarily a sentimental bloke, I don't hold a great deal of store by sentiment: it's too easy an emotion, there's something superficial about it. But because of all that, because I know I can help you get more of what you want, I'm going to tell you a way, a *piss-easy* way, of making money. Which is not to say that I won't be making it alongside you. I'll be making it as you're making it. I wouldn't pass up an opportunity like this one, and I wouldn't want you too either. And this, Harry, is the way that you'll buy time. This is the way that you'll get your time back."

So I invested the inheritance from my uncle in Colin's scheme - in essence a land purchase, involving buying a large area of countryside outside of Huelva in Spain - without mentioning it to Sarah. I wanted to knock her for six. Thinking about it now, that was how I rationalised it anyway. That and the fact that she was ill. Daft obviously, but I'd wanted to be able to walk in one day and let her know I'd quit my job, then show her the cheque which had allowed me to do that. Actually, I didn't know if I would be able to completely quit, but that didn't matter - I might stay on for two days a week; I would wallow in that, I would put everything into those two days, I would teach as I once had, with freedom and creativity, because I'd no longer be knackered or have to rely on the salary. Early in my career, I'd been a star turn. I'd pushed things as far as they would go, made them memorable. The man who'd taught me to teach, Mike Whittingham, had sent me a card on my first day. In it he'd written, 'Remember: if it isn't risky, it isn't teaching.' I'd held that maxim true to begin with, and I'd enjoyed myself doing it. I wanted to get back to that. Meanwhile, I could invest a large portion of what we'd made elsewhere. Everything would be fine. It would be so easy. And that was what I required: ease. At last my chance had come, and I was convinced that if I didn't necessarily deserve it, I didn't actually *not* deserve it. Thus it was good that I had a friend in Colin who'd long known the truth about money, about life, the two being so symbiotically combined - the sixth sense, Colin called it - and who'd allowed me to profit from that knowledge.

But then, some months later, around the time that I'd begun my affair with Alice, planning permission for the land had not been granted. Instead, as I understood it, though I was still a little confused, the land had been designated the Spanish equivalent of green-belt, and, in terms of the developments Colin had in mind, it had become worthless overnight. And now Colin - the cock - wasn't answering my calls.

"Are you cross, daddy?" Eve said when she returned from her bike-ride.

"No, darling," I replied.

"You have a cross face."

"I've been thinking," I said.

"Does thinking make you cross?"

"I suppose it depends what you're thinking about."

"You had a cross face on."

"That's his normal face," Sarah laughed. "You know how he's always grumpy."

"My daddy's not grumpy, are you daddy?"

"I was only joking," Sarah said.

"There, there." Eve patted my head.

"You two," Sarah said. "Thick as thieves."

The phone rang, and it was mum, as was usual on a Sunday afternoon. She and dad would have their Sunday lunch, then she'd load the dishwasher while listening to *Gardeners' Question Time* before talking to me. I cherished my weekly conversations with her - they were, on the whole, only with her; dad would occasionally be steered to the phone. Though mum had retired she was happily involved in her local community - from a wine club to running the library reading group; she liked talking to me about their latest choice of book. It was mum's love of reading which had been one of the major influences in my life. I'd always read. Even in the earliest photos I had a book in my hand. It was mum, ahead of anyone else, who had made me what I was. It was all her fault! I could blame her! Today, she asked me what I was reading, and I told her I was still working my way through Kingsley Amis, and how I was glad I'd only recently discovered him as I wouldn't have appreciated him before now. "I thought he was a misogynist," mum said, "and you a New Man."

"No-one uses that phrase any more, mum, you're so out of date, I dunno," I told her. "And anyway, unlike you, I don't have to agree with everything in a book to enjoy it."

"Excuses," mum replied. "You're just pretend. I know you!"

"What's dad doing?"

"Pottering."

"I love it when he potters."

"Me too." Then without missing a beat, "Do you potter yet? Have you reached that age?"

"All the time. My whole life is one big potter, I think."

"It's your genteel, dilettante upbringing."

"Thanks to my genteel, dilettante mum."

We'd always been like this with each other: kind of open, bantering, to the point. It was clear to me that I relied on the mooring of her phone-calls, the routine of them, their humdrum love.

13. Lewis

we wos haveing sunday lunch, always 2 o'clock i never miss my mums sunday lunch, you wud not beleaf it, we have beef, mash, roastis, sausages, vej like carrots, collyflower, peas with gravy, horseraddish, apple sorce, man your bulgd with it, it is mint, our plates are pild high like mountins, it takes hours to eat it, the tastes are amazeing everything like amazeing in your mouth, you see what i do is put diffrent things together, diffrent comboes like 1 mouthfull will be beef and sausage, 1 mouthfull will be beef and peas, 1 will be mash and gravey so you can have loadsa tastes, 1 after the other, then there is mums pud it mite be

> apple krumble
> ice-cream
> jam spunj

she dus it herslf and afterwoods we are so stuffd we carnt move and we are all in a gud mood, i do the washing up thats only fare, mostly it goes in the dishwasher

were all laffin laffin laffin. ha ha ha ha

mum lets me and dad have a smoke, she dunt

dad watches the football, ill play on the computer, mum dus the crossword its peacefull

sumtimes my sister comes to from skeggy, she has a husband (my uncul) and 2 dorters (my neeces age 5 and 2), wen they have lunch with us its abit more sirius but still gud.

then its evening and then its night, and your thinkin ogod school next morning no more fun and happiness, sumtimes i think this, sumtimes i on purpose forget or i do not on purpose, and its a shock Monday morning sh**

14. Harry

In the evening I decided I had to see Alice. Had to. It was crackers, I knew that logically, but the need was overwhelming. Sarah said she'd a prescription which could do with picking up, and as it was seven o'clock the only chemist open would be the all-night place in town, and would I mind? I could pop in for a pint somewhere on the way back if I wanted, make the trip more worthwhile. It was only that she really could do with those pills, and she'd been meaning to fetch them for days, but hadn't managed to get round to it, and sorry to be a pain, darling, but would I mind? I pretended to be a bit fed-up, I'd work to do, why couldn't she sort it out herself etc etc, she could have told me earlier, but I finally acceded to her request.

Town was a large detour from the direction I wanted to go in - Alice lived across the city and further out at the beginnings of the suburbs, but I knew this was my opportunity. I drove first to the chemist, picked up Sarah's tablets and then started towards Alice's, keeping my eye on the in-car clock which, as I paid attention to it, flickered the time forward, but each second staccato somehow too. I realised I'd maybe an hour from the moment I left the chemist's. It was approximately a twenty minute drive to Alice's, then fifteen minutes from there back home. That would give me twenty-five minutes with her. Twenty-five minutes with Alice. What was it Colin had said about creating time? Well, this was it. This was what it came down to. This was the alchemy I required. Not concentrating on what I was doing, I'd marginally jumped a red-light, seemingly one of the few sets in the city centre which didn't have a camera pointed at them. These were everywhere now, sinister yellow birds perched on metal branches whose squawk was a bright light. I checked my mirror to make absolutely sure, but nothing had flashed.

In the split-second I did this, a car was coming directly towards me, headlights on, its horn blaring, doing sixty or seventy. It took me a moment to realise what was happening, that the vehicle was heading straight at me, on my side of the road, like the driver thought he was driving abroad. *Shit!* I swerved to the left out of the car's way, slammed my brakes on and skidded, turning into it like I'd been taught all those years ago, banging over the kerb and climbing the pavement towards a lamp-post, which I narrowly managed to avoid.

Then: wall! Wall! Stopped!

I looked behind me and saw a pursuing police-car coming over the rise I'd been heading towards. I watched that shoot past, then checked that everything seemed to be okay, that I'd somehow avoided hitting anything, before backing slowly onto the road. I parked up, got out of the car and double-checked the front of it was undamaged. A skinny middle-aged man with grey cropped hair and ice-blue eyes, which must have been enhanced by coloured contact-lenses, walked over, "You alright?"

"Yeah," I said. "It was coming pretty quickly."

"Kids, looked like," the man said. He was wearing jeans and an Eels t-shirt. I quite like them and was going to mention it, but it didn't seem the right time, so I just nodded. "Four or five of them. A couple of girls in the back. Lads in the front. Having a whale of a time."

"Right."

"Feds took a wrong bloody turn past you."

"You're joking."

"Kids went right, they went left. Bloody useless. How's your car?"

"Seems alright."

"That's something. Could of gone straight into you."

"Yes, I guess so. Lucky no-one was on the pavement."

"If you're alright then," the man shrugged his shoulders.

"Yeah, fine, thanks."

I got back into the car and set off again. Drive. Partly I

wanted to laugh: what if I'd been in an accident because of this? What if the other car had finished up headlong into me, because of this? This - whatever it was? What was it? Tomfoolery. Monkey business. I ought really to turn round and head back home. I tightened my grip on the warm steering-wheel, then relaxed it again like I was engaged in an exercise routine. I looked at the sunlight on my forearms and at where the shadows hollowed behind the knuckles on both hands. I wound down my window and stuck my right hand into the vortex of air which cradled around it, held it up, balanced it in the travelling space. I opened my fingers out as if I was about to perform a magic trick: look, nothing there. The air was heavy and cool like a stream. I drove on with my hand out like this, continuing to notice the pulse of the clock's colon, even after the near-accident. Watching the seconds, the minutes, working out how long, reasonably, it would be before I arrived at Alice's: one second, then the next, then the next after that.

Her house was midway into a large puzzle of an estate put together as though it had grown organically over a number of decades - all twist and turns and unforeseen cul-de-sacs. It looked less than ten years old. The road names enjoyed a British animal and bird theme: Otter Drive, Fox Close, Robin Avenue. Alice's house was on Heron Walk. Did herons do a lot of walking?

I approached the front door, having seen Alice's car on the drive, then knocked; and a boy whom I assumed to be Alice's elder son, Nick, answered. "Is your mum in?" The boy was bigger, older-looking than I'd expected; his resemblance to Alice wasn't readily apparent either. He was nearly as tall as me with longish wavy brown hair over his ears and down to his collar. Most of the boys his age at Peter Wallingford had their heads shaved, so it was quite a surprise for me to see a fifteen year-old who wasn't bald.

Nick shouted, half-turning, for his mum. "Someone to see you!"

"Who is it?" The question came from up the stairs at the end of a small hallway.

"It's Harry," I said to Nick, "Harry Monk. From work."

"Somebody from work," Nick shouted up the stairs with what I recognised as a teenaged boy's studied insouciance, "Harry -"

"Monk," I said.

"Monk," Nick repeated.

It sounded as though Alice's voice came from the landing: "I'll be a minute, Nick." It was Nick. "Ask Harry in."

"Come in," Nick said, as though he'd thought of the invitation some time ago, but only now had energised himself enough to act upon its impulse.

"Thanks," I followed him to the living-room door.

"In here. Sit down if you want," he held his open palm of his right hand towards one of the two large black leather sofas. He left me to it and soon after I could hear him rummaging around in the kitchen, choosing items from cupboards, doors slamming.

The living-room had a beige carpet and peach walls hung with a couple of Da Vinci cartoons and lots of photos of the boys - skiing; with some dolphins; at Disneyland; walking in hills -, a black widescreen tv, chrome spotlights, numerous herbs growing in pots on the window sill, a carriage clock on the mantelpiece. Looking at this, I realised I had fifteen minutes if I was to keep to my schedule.

Alice arrived, looking quizzical. "Hiyah. What are doing here?" She was wearing jeans and a gingham blouse. Her mid-brown hair was brushed back into a short pony-tail. She looked younger, extra alert. We stood facing each other.

"I wanted to see you," I told her, more apologetically than I'd intended.

"Why?"

"I'm not sure - I don't know. I mean I do. I wanted to. That's it, I guess. I just wanted to. The be-all and end-all. Dumb, huh?"

"Dumb," Alice said.

"Told you. But life's too short, Alice. I've decided."

"When exactly did you work that one out?"

"Only recently. Momentous. A piercing insight. You know I'm a bit slow."

"You said it." She smiled with her mouth closed, as though that was all she could permit herself.

"I wanted to come over, so I did. Why shouldn't I do what I want? I'm sick of not doing what I want." Now I was petulant too.

"I didn't know you didn't."

"As a rule, I don't think I do. But I have now."

"I'm glad you're here," Alice said. "I'm glad you're here." She shut the door quietly behind her. We were alone in the room. We heard Nick running up the stairs. "But what are you here *for*, exactly?" She sidled over to me, hands behind her back like in a fifties Hollywood musical, the beginning of a number sung by the coquettish lead, and kissed me lightly on my lips. "Was *that* what you came here for?" I smiled. She kissed me again, more intensely this time, reaching up and holding the back of my neck. I responded to her. We kissed for a short while. She smelt different, felt different. None of the weekday in the way. More her. I felt different too. More me. More just us. Just. Us. Nothing else. We held each other. I felt the warmth of her body against the warmth of mine. I kissed the top of her head. I didn't want to let her go.

"This is the effect you have on me," I whispered into her ear. "This is why I had to be here."

"Good," Alice murmured.

"Very good," I said. "Very, very good."

"Yes," Alice replied. "I like the effect I have on you. It makes me happy. It's like I'm doing something right without even trying. Which is unusual for me."

I kissed her. "What about the boys?"

"Don't worry about them. Nick's upstairs playing some dreadful computer game and Tim's not back from his girlfriend's yet."

"Well trained," I said.

"Not that this happens every night of the week, you understand," Alice said. "My various lovers. Not every night anyway. Sunday, I do like to have a rest. Most Sundays. Turns out tonight's an exception."

There was something teenaged about the way we sat on the sofa and kissed. We took our time over this. If kissing was all we were going to indulge in then we were going to make the most of it. The nearness of our breath, of each other: breathing in each other. Eyes, hands, lips.

Twenty minutes afterwards, we stood in the doorway while Nick charged past us down the stairs. "Thanks for that," Alice said, "it'll give me something to think about."

"That's okay," I smiled, "if you think it'll help."

"It will. I'll get working on it."

"Good," I replied. "It's like *Are You Being Served?*, this conversation. 'You're all doing very well.'"

"Maybe we are."

"Maybe."

Then, as Nick went into the kitchen, Alice kissed me again. "You can surprise me more often. I like surprises. I like surprises like this."

When I arrived home, Sarah said to me, "Thanks, baby. Did you stop for a drink?" She'd just finished some ironing and was folding the board up. Natalie Merchant was on the mini-system.

"I tried the White Hart, Jim was in there. Had a couple with him."

"Good," Sarah said, "so it wasn't a wasted journey then?"

"Not if I'm doing something for you, sweet," I replied, taking the ironing-board and putting it in the cupboard under the stairs. "No. I quite enjoyed myself in the end."

"How was Jim?"

"Jim was fine. Well, when I say *fine* - Jim was Jim. Everything's shit, but his strong sense of irony will see him through."

Sarah laughed. "I'm feeling much happier at the moment, have you noticed? These new tablets are helping."

She picked up a small brown bottle from the side table next to the sofa she'd sat down on.

"That's good," I said, sitting down next to her.

"It is. Have you noticed?"

"I think I have," I said, "yes. Yes, I would say I definitely have."

"Look," Sarah opened the bottle and took a tablet out, a little white oblong of happiness, put it in her mouth and swallowed it, then smiled as if it had had an immediate, exaggerated, zombie-like effect. "See," she said, lolling her head. "I'm okay now."

"You're funny, I know that," I replied, holding her hand. The room was genial with light from two lamps with Henry Moore style holes in their bases.

"I suddenly remember what it feels like, and then I see how I've been behaving and I can't believe it. I feel normal again. I'm trying to think why, but I don't know why. It must be these," once more holding the bottle up, "that's all it can be."

"It might be. New tablets have sometimes done it for a while in the past, haven't they? But don't worry about why, it's good that you're happy, don't worry about the reasons for it."

"I'm not worried really, I only want to know the reasons so I can continue keeping it going. The tablets must be helping, mustn't they? They must be doing something. It's definitely since I started taking them. The trouble is if it is just these, like you said, the effects never seem to last, do they? It's only temporary. There must be something else, there must be something that can wipe the depression away, you know, for ever and ever. That's what I need to find."

"I guess," I replied absentmindedly, thinking for a millisecond of Alice and of being at her house and kissing her.

"You're getting bored with me," Sarah said.

"No."

"You're getting bored with all this, me never getting better," Sarah said, glancing at the floor then back at me.

There was the tiny flicker of a frown across her forehead, but her eyes were firmly on me, so that my defensiveness was more than a little strident:

"You're better at the moment, and that's great, it's bloody brilliant."

"No need to be sarcastic. I mean it."

"I'm not being sarcastic, love. I think I'm tired. It's getting late." I tapped at the arm of the sofa in time to the music, a ripple of fingers against the fabric. I remembered seeing 10,000 Maniacs support REM in 1989. The first time I heard Natalie Merchant sing. "What's the point in me being sarcastic? There's no point, is there?"

"You sounded it," Sarah replied. Her pale skin was pixellated with only the slightest changes in emotion, so that now, in her increasing distress, there was redness around her eyes, her nose. Any colour blemished her face with the severity of eczema.

"I didn't mean to."

"It doesn't matter whether you meant it or not. You're fed up with me, I can tell you are, I can understand that, I really can. *I'd* be fed up with me. *I'd* have left me ages ago." This is how these things spilled out of her sometimes, with unpredictable rapidity and abruptness. "Go and find someone else if you like. Go and find someone who's always happy, someone happier than me."

"Don't be daft."

"I'm not being *daft*. Don't patronise me. I mean it. There are plenty of women out there who'd love to be your wife. Go and find one of them."

"Sarah, I don't want to."

"I bet you do."

"Sarah, I don't. Give me a break. It's late and we're tired."

"I'm not tired."

"Well I am."

"Just an excuse. You always say you're tired when you don't want to talk to me."

"Alright, let's talk."

"Don't sound so cross."

"I'm not being cross, but if you want me to be honest about it, all this - yeah, it does get a bit wearing now and again, if I'm being truthful about it. If that's what you want. Let's talk. You know it's been going on for quite a long time now, five years on and off is quite a long time. And sometimes I wish it hadn't affected you, you know, that we hadn't had to have it in our lives." As I said this, part of me wished that I hadn't, but I also felt a release in the words, an unknotting.

"For richer and for poorer," Sarah said steadily, her words dipped in a colder anger.

"Fine. And I believe that. I totally believe that."

"Do you?"

"Yes, I do. Totally. There was no reason doing it otherwise." Then, though I knew it wouldn't help, "Anyway, we'll soon be poorer, that's for sure."

"Don't bring this up."

"I'm not bringing anything up."

"It's not my fault I can't work."

"I never said anything about that. What did I say about that? Did I mention that? Of course it's not your fault. I don't care if you can't work. There's nothing clever about working. It's basically a waste of time. It doesn't mean anything. Work," I said, as though it was the most offensive word I could rustle up.

"You said we were going to be poor."

"We are, but that's not your fault."

"Well, it's not yours, so who else's is it?" Sarah said. "Is it Eve's? No. It must be mine."

"Maybe it *is* mine. Maybe I should be doing something better paid. Bloody teaching, the pay's shit," I said. "But I never thought about money ten years ago. Hopeless, I wish I could go back in time and choose something different."

"But you wanted to teach. That was what you wanted."

"True."

"Don't you anymore?"

"I do, I suppose. No, I like it. You know I like it."

"I don't know where the money goes," Sarah said.

"No."

"I know I spend money I shouldn't."

"Everyone spends money they shouldn't."

"I'm more guilty than most."

"No, you're not."

"I think I probably am."

"Fuck it," I said. "Fuck money. Fucking money. Let money go fuck itself. We're both as bad as each other. We only have to look at it and it disappears."

"I'm worse than you," Sarah was biting the inside of her mouth, the front of her cheeks sucked in.

"Not really. You buy bigger things. I fritter it away. Books, CDs."

"We'll have to use our savings," Sarah said. "There's your uncle's money, isn't there? There's all that money sitting there. Silly, worrying."

"Maybe. Maybe you're right. Come here, you," I replied, patting my lap.

Later, after Sarah had gone to bed, I thought that, failing all else, suicide might be the solution. I'd thought this through before. For life-insurance purposes, I would have to make my death look like an accident. But a plan properly carried out would solve all my financial problems. Alive, I was worth about £30,000 a year before tax. Dead, I was worth about £250,000, money which would sort out my debts and help set up Sarah and Eve. The house would also be paid off, while I had an inkling that a tax-free lump-sum was paid to Sarah by the LEA too. All in all, my death made unsparing financial sense.

The processes involved didn't scare me particularly, though it did seem nicely absurd that, at a blink, like that - a click - it would be all gone, the colour, the noise, what my senses were quick with, that lucky pulse. I liked being alive; but *I* would be all gone. Lights out, as Edward Thomas - a favourite of mine - had it. Like sleep, and a completely dreamless one at that. Everlasting death; at least in my present state. If I understood correctly, the molecules that

70

made me up would then be modified into soil, plants, worms, birds. At the very least, I hoped my corpse could be reasonable compost.

15. Lewis

a conversation i had in the easter hollydays like what you
sed to do, this one is all trew, not made up the fax

what do you want to be my dad sed to me

i dunno i sed

you dunno.

i dunno

you need to no.

yes.

your leaveing school soon and you need to no.

yes

have you thort abowt it

no.

what wood be gud?

a footballer.

you doant like football

no

he laffs.

but luck at there money and women.

he laffs.

yebut youv got to be gud to be a footballer. youv got to like football at leest

yes your rite, he wos rite i like animals i sed i cud be a vet.

you like animals he sed.

yes.

do you

there allright

what abowt computers

computers

your on your games

yes

you cud make games

is that a job

yes

dunt sownd like a job

nobut it is

sownds like fun

yes

so thats what im goin to do, be a game makker for computers, and what do you think to that

a thing i did wos on my bike with Billy, we did that a bit and computers to

few

16. Harry

"I got took f' a dick by Darren, then I got took f' a dick by Jamie," the tall girl said. She was walking past me on the way into the dining-room.

Smiling at her, I said, "Thanks for that, Layla."

"That's okay, sir," the tall girl replied. "Anyway, it weren't meant f'you."

"No, it's just with your voice half the school hears it whether they like it or not."

"Y' right there, sir," Layla's friend, Keeley, said.

"Sherrup, you!"

A voice behind me, Balshaw - alongside Alice, the other Deputy Head - shouted that the girls needed to take their caps off. He was right, of course: according to the school rules, I should have been reminding kids of this as they came in, caps off and their hoods down, hoods which many still wore up even though it was the beginning of the summer term. I always forgot rules like that because, in truth, I didn't deem them to be particularly important. That was one of the reasons why I'd ruled out ever moving into senior management - I couldn't be doing with having to remember caps, coats, chewing-gum and then having to make such a public display of their removal. Balshaw, on the other hand, did think the rules were important, which was one of the reasons why he was a Deputy Head at thirty-five. He was a small, sharply-dressed man with a crew-cut and eyes that were never still. It was like there were bees in his skull, and, perhaps, buzzing around the rest of body too. I didn't know how many cups of coffee he drank in a day, but it was, without doubt, three or four cups too many. There was always something slightly frantic about him. An idiosyncrasy of his was that he licked his forefinger and thumb as though about to turn the pages of a book each time he had something vital to impart. He invariably had a lot that was vital to impart: he would lick his forefinger and thumb and then put his hand back on the table or down by his side with the regularity of a speed-reader. Balshaw always knew best.

In essence, he ran the school. After a couple of years Whitehurst had effectively given up and Balshaw had taken over in everything but name. He'd come down hard on the pupils, and, after a while, his policing had begun to work. Once other staff had taken their lead from the Deputy Head and realised that control could be wrested back from the children and their parents, their sense of purpose had returned too. Balshaw's philosophy was simple: children, ultimately, liked control, they hated the vacuum of freedom; they hated *having* to mess around (because they could), as it was an added pressure - it was something else to have to think about, sidetrack them or, perversely, live up to. It was another added *stress*. Therefore, Balshaw would maintain with the few who continued to challenge him on the matter, keep everything black-and-white: this bad behaviour meant this punishment; that good behaviour meant that reward. Children liked to know where they stood. And so, for that matter, did the adults in charge of them, whom Balshaw often treated as children too.

I could see some merit in this starkness in particular contexts, and the school had definitely enjoyed a period of greater stability than it had managed in previous years, but there were dangers in the rigidity too. I wondered if a system which merely cowed pupils in the short term rather than educated them for the longer was wholly beneficial. The other problem was that there were plenty of teachers in the school - including myself, I'd be the first to admit - who didn't always obey Balshaw's holy writs. This was the in-built deficiency, Jon would say, of a graduate profession full of lefties and self-styled mavericks who didn't like being told what to do. Likewise there was a hard-core of kids - say ten per cent in each Year group, about fifteen children - who wouldn't respond *whatever* anyone threatened; even, to an extent, Balshaw. They were unbound from whatever it was that eventually meant most other people did what was expected of them. Often their parents were too: they were all part of the same families that neighbours or Housing or the police had problems with, so why should their children be any different at school?

Balshaw was haranguing one of them, Billy Edwards, now. This usually finished with Billy walking off the premises - he couldn't give a toss if he was at school or not, preferably not really - and Balshaw phoning home telling whoever answered that their son/ stepson/ grandchild/ brother/ friend's kid had been excluded for a few days. Billy would then return after his stint away, and carry on from where he'd left off. Balshaw was a one-man exclusion machine, but the problem was he couldn't do it all himself, and it wasn't the whole answer anyway. Meanwhile, though Alice was a competent Deputy, she was competent in her own way, which tended to be very different from Balshaw's. Kids generally liked Alice and just about did as they were asked. She was quietly firm with them, believing that temper didn't work with Peter Wallingford pupils: many were shouted at much more explicitly at home; the teacher who relied solely on that mode of communication had no chance. Alice felt that you only made headway if you were able to communicate properly with the individuals who were causing the problems. Give children no reason to hate you, she would tell staff new to the profession.

The difficulty for the school was that with Whitehurst locked in his office or away at meetings, and with the two Deputies barely on speaking terms, the school's leadership functioned as an expression of contradictory personalities rather than as a focused and cohesive system of shared values. Thus, for all Balshaw's hard work (and, for that matter, Alice's), Peter Wallingford had recently begun, I thought, to feel fragile again. There were small indicators - the number of fights, the number of smashed windows, the manner in which the kids behaved moving between lessons - but all these hints added-up. Over the years, I'd developed an acute feeling for this: I could sense the school tipping first one way, then the other. If there was one useful thing I'd learnt, it was that inner-city schools had to be constantly moving forward. In some regard, the destination was irrelevant, it was the sense of resolve and momentum that were crucial. No matter how well run, they could always, very quickly - once again - get out of hand.

At its worst, four years previously, Peter Wallingford had, at times, been almost lawless in places. It was not uncommon to see forty or fifty kids in the corridors, in small or larger groups, refusing to go to lessons or disturbing the other ones taking place. I learnt to gauge what time it was by the sound of breaking glass, the frequency of which increased as the day wore on. (Exchange of this period, to exemplify what was taking place - Kid (to teacher): "You Scottish wanker!"; manful retort: "How dare you? I'm Welsh.") The Headteacher before Whitehurst, Askew, had no idea what to do: he kept permanently excluding pupils who kept returning to the school on appeal. They were then, naturally, worse than ever, having escaped the strongest sanction the school could muster. They saw themselves as untouchable, and many of the staff began to believe it too, wondering what the point of attempting to discipline them was if, somewhere further down the line, their authority was going to be undermined.

I'd been a new Head of English at the time; thankfully, my department didn't fare too badly. Most of the pupils liked and respected most of the teachers who taught the subject, and my team built on this to develop lessons which maintained their classes' interest. So when a firework was set off in a lesson or when whole classes went on strike, it was invariably elsewhere in the school. The fun and games had been going on at a similar time to the disruption at the Ridings School in Yorkshire which had made the national news. The teachers at Peter Wallingford had joked how leafy and serene that school looked. I'd wondered how many other places were at Peter Wallingford's stage: back then, word didn't necessarily have to get out as long as visitors were handled carefully. I couldn't face it slipping back into that stew again. It'd been exhausting, even in a more temperate area of the school. I wondered whether what I needed was a job somewhere comfortable: some cushy job in the county where I could sleepwalk through my lessons, where I might teach children who could actually read and write at something like their chronological age. In Peter Wallingford, more than half of the twelve-year-olds had reading ages of eight or under.

Some of them would grow into the fifteen-year-olds like Mark and Adam, kids who couldn't keep up. "Who is it, Mark?" I'd strolled outside as part of the lunch duty.

"This kid, sir." Mark was of medium height, with red cheeks and the look of somebody who was permanently shrugging.

"Yeah."

Mark had begun to explain something to me, but was faltering, "He's in our Year. Maybe."

"Maybe?"

"Maybe," Mark said. "It's difficult to say."

"Why's that?"

"I don't know. But it is."

"Right. Well, is he white, black, Asian?"

"White."

"And he *is* a boy?"

"I think so, sir." Mark glanced up at the sky as if the answer might conceivably be scrawled there.

"You think so?"

"Yeah, he is. I'm sure. I'm fairly sure. No, he is, sir. Yeah, that's right. He is a boy. For definite."

"That's a start then," I said. "That's about fifty per cent of the school we're left with: only four hundred more to whittle away now, Mark. Should be a doddle."

"Adam might know."

"He might, but let's not forget we're talking about Adam here. Adam," I shouted to a skinny kid with unkempt brown hair, "come here!"

Adam looked around himself for a few seconds before

finally understanding where the shout had come from.

"Come on, Adam!" Mark said.

Adam came over slowly, as though he wasn't entirely convinced which direction he was supposed to be travelling in. Kids ran around him, but he was oblivious of them. As he came nearer, he said to Mark, "You've told im, aven't you? You av, aven't you?"

"I'm not answering that question."

"Mark," Adam said.

"I'm not saying nuffin."

"He 'as, asn't 'e?" Adam said to me.

"Don't answer that question, Mr - Mr -"

"Monk -"

"Monk. Damn, forgot again!" Mark exclaimed. It was true, he did often forget my name. I kept meaning to ask Jon if it was only my name Mark forgot or everybody's. "Don't answer that question, Mr Monk."

"I think I'll have to."

"Oh." Mark was despondent.

"He has," I said to Adam. "He has told me, I can't lie."

"Don't you ever lie?" Adam asked.

"No, never," I replied. "Do you?"

"All the time."

"Is that a lie?"

"No, it isn't."

"What about that?"

"You're confusing me."

To be fair, I was confusing myself. "I'll have to watch you, Adam," I said, "now you've told me that. That's made me think totally differently about you."

"Has it?"

"Yeah." Adam looked downcast. "No, I'm only joking," I said. "Anyway, Mark was right to let me know. Mark did the right thing. Good lad, Mark. What's going on, Adam?"

"Nuffin."

"Adam."

"Tell him, Adam," Mark said.

"No, don't wanna," Adam replied, sulkily.

"Adam," I said, "if someone's taking your money, I need to know."

"Why?" Quite often, like now, Adam didn't seem properly engaged in the conversation. It was like he was talking to himself rather than anyone else. There was a permanent distractedness about him.

"To stop it happening."

"You don't stop it. I'm gonna tell me brother, he'll stop it."

"I'll stop it, if you tell me who's taking it. If I don't manage it, then you could get your brother in," I suggested, not meaning what I'd said - Adam's brother was in his early twenties with a history of GBH - but merely trying to prompt Adam into telling me more about whoever it was taking his money.

"It's this lad," Adam said.

"That's that confirmed then," I told Mark, who didn't appear to notice that he'd been spoken to, but then nodded hurriedly.

"What?" Adam said.

"Doesn't matter."

"Dunt matter," Mark agreed. "Honest, Adam, it dunt. It were something we said earlier."

"I think 'e's new," Adam said.

"He is, sir, he's new. That's right, Adam, he is. He's new." Mark was breathless with excitement. He raised his hand in a high-five, and Adam responded clumsily. They giggled together after completing it.

"Small?" I asked. "Big?"

"He's bigger en 'im," Adam said of Mark.

"Yeah, but everyone is, Adam."

"Yeah, that's right, sir," Adam replied; then to Mark, "You're small, you are."

"He's not really," I said. "He's not really that small, is he? Anyway, the lad, what's his name, Adam?"

"'Is name's not Adam, that's my name."

"No. What's *his* name? The new boy's name. D'you know? His name, Adam. Not yours. I know *your* name.

Your name's Adam. His name. Have you heard anyone say it to him?"

Adam thought for a while. "It might be *Louis*. Is that a name?"

"*Louis*, maybe. What about Lewis? And you say he's new?" I'd an idea who they might be referring to, Lewis Tuckwood, a child permanently excluded from another school in the city who'd recently arrived at ours. What happened with kids like Lewis was that they went on a merry-go-round of the local 'bad' schools (the 'good' ones wouldn't let them anywhere near), picked up usually unwillingly and then invariably dumped as quickly as possible, while the LEA ignored the fact that there might be a wider problem that only they had the resources to help solve. Lewis was a sneery, spotty-faced youth with a large nose, and, as the stories already circulating the staff-room had it, an even larger temper. It was doubtless claimed he had ADHD or something. None of it would be his fault.

"He's definitely new," Mark said, becoming excited now, "isn't he, Adam?"

"I think so. I aven't noticed im before." Which coming from Adam didn't mean a great deal, bless him.

"D'you know him, d'you know who he is, sir?" Mark said.

"Possibly."

"Sir's gonna get him," Mark smiled at Adam. They high-fived again; this time almost successfully.

17. Lewis

why i like computer games

there fun
the grafics
im skillfull at them
im better than kris at them
Billy thinks his gud but his not
there exsiting!
the shooting and that
it doant make me want to kill peepel tho like you sed
wen you get to the next levell you have dun sumthing
im thinkin abowt how i can do it like im walking arownd
school and im thinking abowt it it takes my mind of all the
sh**
if you doant do gud start agen
dad likes them to sumtims i let him win, doant say nothin

this is why i like them, you want to keep playin them

i want a ps2 for my birthday

i no your first name, its Roseanna isnt it. i herd another
teacher say it to you,
mum sezs are you still on that computer its time for your
dinna, i say no im writting. she dunt no what to say to that
then she sezs writing

yeah

what about

its homework

bloody hell Lewis are you feeling allright, laffing, dave did you here that

dad sezs he did

its a gud teacher

must be

well done teach

she a looka?

i didnt even say you wos a she

both of them laffin but its ok, i suppose it is funny reelly

hahahahahahahaha

18. Harry

The two boys and I stood at one end of the Yard, close to the dining-room door, watching the pupils come and go (not talking of Michelangelo.) (Ho ho.) After a few minutes, I saw Lewis, who I'd already bumped into briefly, but without aggravation, walking towards us. "Is that him?"

"Yeah, it's him," Mark replied. "Yeah, it's him, it is, isn't it, Adam?"

"I think so."

"Yeah, it is, Adam."

"Yeah, if you say so."

"Yeah, I do say so."

"Right," I said. "Leave it to me."

"Hey you!" Mark shouted across to Lewis. "Sir's gonna get you."

"Mark, leave it," I told him, "let me sort it out."

Lewis ambled towards us, his head gently nodding in time to some invisible music, "Oh yeah, what for?"

"Our money," Mark said.

"What about your money? What money?" Lewis looked flatly at him.

"The money you took."

"Don't know nothing about it. Your money! Don't mek me laugh. What money?" Everything about Lewis was still now. I quite liked lads like him. They usually had something about them - an intensity, a strange charisma - even if it wasn't always channelled in the most productive ways.

"Ourn," Adam joined in, feeding off Mark's batty confidence.

"You're special, aren't y'?" Lewis said to Adam, up close to him. "You're a special kid, aren't y'? I feel sorry for you. I think you're confused. Y' know, I think it's all got a bit much for you. Your 'ead's in a spin. You need someone to look after y'."

"Lewis," I said, "it is Lewis, isn't it?"

"No, I'm not Lewis. Who's Lewis?" Lewis asked, swivelling round to face me. "Lewis? Never 'eard on im."

I smiled coldly. "Well, whoever you are, son, let's say you ever think about borrowing Adam or Mark's money in the future, you won't, will you?"

"For fuck's sake, I never took their fuckin money. Might as well say they took mine. It's the same, cos I never took theirn."

"And I'm not saying that you did, I've no idea one way or the other. I wasn't there. What the hell do I know about it, Lewis? Nothing. I didn't see it. No, I'm simply mentioning the fact that you won't in the future, will you?" I knew that Adam and Mark were telling the truth about what had happened - they were incapable of making anything up - but I needed some other people to back up their story. I needed written statements and the like, which was the way it had to be followed up to prevent parents complaining. And, given Adam and Mark's propensity for keeping only each other's company, statements were going to be difficult. "I'm checking that with you, and, with you being new to the school, I thought you might like to know. I'm looking out for you, I suppose; think of it that way."

"Fuck that," Lewis said. "This fuckin school's shit. Like every fuckin school." He began to walk away into the main building.

"Lewis, I haven't finished talking to you."

"I've finished," Lewis said over his shoulder.

"Yeah, but I've not."

"So fucking what?" Some kids around Lewis stopped and watched. "Dick." There was disbelieving merriment from the audience. Fun could ensue.

"Lewis, back here, please," I said more firmly. Lewis looked behind himself and then started to jog away. "Lewis, come back here, now."

"'E's gone," Adam said. "See, you don't do nuffin. Told

y'," he said to Mark. "I'll get Alan to sort it. Alan'll get our money back."

I pursued Lewis into the building, shouting after him. He bobbed along the tide of the corridor, drifting with some children, while others moved aside. I gained on him gradually, mainly because no-one wanted to be in my way, a gorilla surrounded by chimpanzees, and when Lewis went up the stairs, I took those two at a time, faster than him. I was going to catch him, and then he was going to finish listening. *Dick.* I was going to catch him. I rounded the corner at the top of the stairs and found him lying on the floor in the middle of the corridor, a few feet away from Jon.

"Y' bastard! Y' tripped me!" Lewis sat up, held onto his knee and stared at Jon. "Y' fuckin bastard!"

"I've no idea what you're talking about, young man," Jon said, hands in his pockets, a sticky grin on his face. "From my p-perspective you seem to have fallen over your own feet. All that charging around, always a risky business. Asking for trouble."

I ignored Jon and stood over Lewis, "When I ask you to stop, Lewis, you stop."

"Looks like he has now, Mr Monk," Jon said.

"Looks like he has, Mr Ward."

"Divine intervention."

"God is good."

"Ah, yes."

"My fuckin knee, I'm gonna get you for this, I'm gonna tell me dad, I'm gonna fuckin av y', y' fuckin puff."

"Has a pr-problem with his knee, Mr Monk," Jon said.

"Fuck you, y' fuckin puffs."

"Has a problem with you, Mr Monk."

"And with you, Mr Ward."

"Seems to think we are of the homosexual, er, b-bent, Mr Monk."

"Mmm."

"A foul calumny," Jon said. "A slur on your good name. Yours, at the very least."

"Shouldn't ignore me."

"Always a mistake, young man," Jon told Lewis. "Mr Monk isn't someone you should ignore. Now, do you require any assistance g-getting up?"

"No I fuckin don't, not from you."

"It was only an offer," Jon said.

"Shove it up your arse, y' stutterin twat."

"Given what you've insinuated about me, I'll shall p-probably enjoy that."

Later, after I'd finished talking to Lewis and he'd then hobbled away, I said to Jon, "I don't think you should have done that really. I'd have caught up with him in the end."

"Done what, Harry?"

"Whatever it was you did do."

"He tripped, Harry," Jon replied. "Like I t-told you. You know, at that age, all arms and legs."

"Okay. Sorry. I was only saying. I didn't want you to have compromised yourself on my behalf."

"An unlikely scenario, I'd have thought."

"True."

"The wrong angle for the cameras, unfortunately, so I can't prove to you what happened. Entre nous, something of a blind spot at the top of the stairs."

I went to see Alice. I'd a free lesson in the afternoon and was pleased to discover her alone in her office, an unusual situation, working at her computer. She was looking tanned and relaxed. I hadn't seen her over the Easter holidays as she'd taken Nick and Tim to Cyprus. "Have you got five minutes?" I said. "Or are you busy?"

"I'm fine. Make yourself a coffee and me one too. I need to finish this. It won't take long."

"I can come back later."

"No, no, put the kettle on, this is very nearly done."

I filled the kettle up. I chose a couple of clean mugs from a small cluster of them on a school-desk parked against one wall before taking a carton of milk and some ground coffee out of the fridge in the corner. I shook some of the coffee into the cafetiere and then sat down at the opposite side of the office from Alice's desk and waited for the kettle to boil. The office was in a quiet corner of school, backing onto playing fields, an area of those that were seldom used. When I got back up to pour the boiling water into the cafetiere, I looked across the fields to the estate that bordered the furthest limit of them. The helicopter chugged across the skyline. There was smoke in the distance, which worried me, but which might have been from anything, a bonfire, something industrial, anything, and wasn't necessarily the consequence of the untoward. I didn't like the way that my first thought was increasingly hostile or pessimistic. I felt contaminated, almost, and though I knew that my response was unfair, I was becoming worn down. Still, the constituency the school served was reputedly the one with the highest youth crime rate in the country - though I was sure there were any number of other constituencies who likewise believed themselves to be top of that particular table.

"There. Finished," Alice said.

"What was it?"

"Next week's training on learning styles. I've prepared some material on multiple intelligences as well."

"*Multiple* intelligences?" I said. "I'd be glad of *one*. Not even that. A smidgin, a trace of an intelligence. A *rumour* of one. That'd do me."

"You'd do fine in self-awareness. It's all the latest theories, I say 'latest', I think a lot of it's been knocking around for a while, but, you know, visual, auditory, kinaesthetic learning, all those things. We've got a lot of kinaesthetic boys. That's my new word for this term."

"What, *boys*?"

"Yes. But you know how a lot of them are, they're always up and down, aren't they? They want to be *doing* things, not sitting behind a desk, writing or whatever. So much physical energy that we don't burn off. That's part of the problem, I think; more than part of it."

"Sounds about right." Although Alice knew that I thought our profession had a tendency to over-complicate everything. Education was, intrinsically, a simple exchange.

Alice came over and sat down next to me. We were away from the door and couldn't be seen through the thin strip of glass that partly occupied its top half. Alice placed her right hand in my left and began running her middle finger along each of my fingers on that hand in turn. I wished I wasn't wearing a wedding ring, but Alice spent as long on that finger as on all the rest and didn't appear affected by its presence. I put my coffee down, kissed my fingers lightly to my lips then touched Alice's forehead with them. I curled my arm around her and she rested her head on my chest. We sat like this in a broad, relaxed silence for some time. I could smell Alice's perfume: it was light, understated. I kissed her hair, her neck. All good. "Stop," Alice said softly after I'd done that for a few seconds. She got up, walked over to the door and locked it, leaving her key inside the hole so that no-one could use it, then returned to my side of the room, pulled the blinds down on the windows overlooking the playing-fields and the other one directly behind her desk. I watched Alice. She was wearing a dark grey fitted jacket and skirt. She continued to say nothing, walked over to me and stood above me. "Now," Alice said, "now." I reached for her arse as she leant down to kiss me. As we kissed, Alice hitched her skirt up while I pulled her knickers down. They were black and the material between my fingers seemed hardly there. Alice stepped out of them while I undid the zip on my trousers and released my cock. Alice sat over me and guided my cock into her. Her cunt was hot and buttery: it felt hot and buttery around the length of my cock. I leant back and closed my eyes and we began having sex sitting like that on the chair, me holding Alice's arse with both my hands, a buttock in each one, my fingers feeling the edge of her anus, while she held onto my neck, the back of my head, kissing me. "Got to be quick," Alice said. I stood up, still inside her, her legs wrapped around my lower back. I liked the weight of her in my arms, my upper body: I liked the featheriness of our interconnection. As I lay her down on the floor my cock slipped out of her but I re-entered quickly and smoothly. I knelt above her, her legs up against my chest, then around me and everything was harder and faster, her orgasm sparking mine. I lay down next to her on the floor. I put my cock back into my trousers and did my zip up. There was the sound of our breathing and the sound of the zip. Everything else was quiet, as though whatever went on outside the door no longer functioned. The door opened into nothing and nowhere. Alice reached over for her knickers and put them on. She lay back down, her head next to mine. We lay like that for a while. Occasionally we kissed each other with gentle affection.

There was a knock at the door; the handle juddered. "Shit," I said.

"Quick," Alice said. We both got off the floor. I rolled up one of the blinds while Alice smoothed her skirt and hair as she walked slowly to the door. I smartened myself up too, then sat back down on an innocent chair. My shirt was sticking to my back. I pulled it from there and leant forward a little. Whitehurst, an emaciated, pink-faced man with a full and thick beard, entered with a boy I recognised but didn't know the name of: he had a mouthful of blood caused by a badly cut lip. The boy spat blood onto Alice's carpet close to where she and I had just had sex. "I can do without that, Richard," Alice told him.

"It were in me mouth. What were I meant to do?"

"Swallow it," Alice replied. "It is your blood. It's not going to do you any harm is it?"

"Whereas the rest of us -" I said.

"I found this boy wandering lonely as a cloud in the corridor, Mrs Hibbert," Whitehurst said, "one for you I think." He smiled at me, "And how are we, Mr Monk?"

"We're very well, thank you, Mr Whitehurst. Yourself?"

"Good, good."

"I'll leave you to it then," I said to Alice, excusing myself past Whitehurst, who made to depart at the same time, causing me to stop.

"No, after you, Mr Monk," Whitehurst said, "might be a

landmine out there." He smiled at me. He'd a slightly piscine mouth, pushed forward from the rest of his face. I smiled back - very funny, Mr T - then left the room first. As I walked along the corridor I was tempted to laugh out loud - at what had happened, at Whitehurst's expert powers of delegation - but common sense got the better of me and I smirked at the nearest available camera instead. I wondered who from the site management team might be watching me, the gurning idiot.

Arun was walking towards me. Arun was a Northern Irish lapsed-Hindu maths teacher with whom I'd a relationship based solely on mutual abuse. It seemed to console us both. "Buttmunch," Arun said.

"Dickbreath," I replied.

Back at home, as I took my trousers off while getting changed out of my suit, I noticed a stain around my zip from the earlier shenanigans. I took my trousers into the bathroom and scrubbed at the fabric, then washed my cock, balls and pubic hair as well. Next I brushed my teeth and splashed water on my face and hair. I was cleared of the deed, of the work day as a whole. I put clean boxers on as well as my jeans, found a white t-shirt in my wardrobe. Then I was back at home, properly at home; and work, and what went on at work, ceased to exist for me.

It was when I went back downstairs, changed, that I saw Eve playing in the dining-room. I sat down and watched her, and then she asked me about Father Christmas. "Father Christmas?" I said. "It's the beginning of summer, he's not coming for a long time."

"I know," Eve said, "but I was thinking about him."

"And what were you thinking?"

"He must be way old." Eve skipped over and sat on my knee.

"I suppose he must be."

"I mean, he must be older than you and granddad and grandpa," Eve said.

"That's very old indeed, you're right."

"Told you."

"You did."

"Something else I was thinking," Eve continued, kissing me on the cheek.

"Blimey, two things," I said, smiling at my daughter and hugging her close to me. She was so small, she fitted into my chest. "Two things you thought about."

Proudly, Eve said, "I did a lot of thinking about him."

"I can see that."

"Can you?"

"Yes, I can. I can see where your brain has been whirring round."

"I thought you might be able to."

"I am your dad; dads know these things."

"I was wondering," Eve said, "who cuts his hair?"

"Good question."

"I know."

"I guess," I thought for a moment. "I guess Mrs Claus does that."

"Or one of the elves," Eve said.

"Good point."

"Yes, cos all the elves will need their hair cutting as well. There must be, like, an elf hairdresser."

"True."

"That's quite interesting, isn't it?" Eve said.

"It certainly is," I replied cheerfully.

19. Lewis

whose this dickhead calld word, his a fat stutring battyboy bastard and his ded. theres the other 1 to, the 1 who fansys himself thinks his the big man. his no big man, his nothin. on the street his nothin, see him on the street wots he gonna do, he cums up to me it was in lunch with these 2 spaccas, there sayeing i tuk there money like i did, they doant no me, so they grassd me up, i doant need there money f**k them, so he starts playing the big man, why shud i lissen to that, no thanks i doant need that it dus my head in

so i walkd away thats what dad sez walk away that is the number 1 rule, dad sezs count to 10 walk away, so thats what i did and i had your lesson next to so that wos another reson to leaf, i walkd away, dint do nothing leaf me alone thats all

but the big man teacher follows me, im running up your classroom wen bang the fat battyboy bastard trips me, i no it wos on purpose he was laffin. peedo puff like ha ha ha, like an evil laff. he stuck his foot out and i went flyin my knee wos killin, sorry i dint cum to your class but i was to pissdoff, i wos beter of takin time owt

i went round to billys insted, we smokd sum weed and then i was chilld and now my knees ok, but im gona batter word

its gud to have freinds

20. Harry

Alice and I went away for a weekend to a five-star hotel close to Chester. It was a large, corporate one we could get lost in, with nobody paying us any attention unless we required it. As we drove up the road towards the hotel, it looked like some vast façade, or an optical illusion, far too big to be a single building, more like a massive liner or a swollen series of country houses all rammed together. It went on and on across the skyline, with fountains, striped lawns and a gravelled drive in front of it - after the proper road had run out just enough distance away to suggest that it didn't actually exist. It was nearly a surprise to discover that the building was three-dimensional and not a film-set we could look around the side of, find stanchions holding the thing up and people bustling about with cameras, sound equipment and scripts. Inside, there was also a sense of inflation and fakery about the place, the reception bigger, the main bar at one end of the building stupidly immense, sailing over the placid sea of the lawn.

Our room was large too, but this pleased us, and our sardonic commentary stopped once we'd shut the door. It seemed like a room we temporarily deserved. "I'm so glad we're here," Alice said, looking around. "I haven't been away like this for a long, long time. Thank you for bringing me here."

"Thank you for coming," I replied, "for accompanying me." I took out a bottle of champagne I'd brought in a cool-bag. I opened the bottle carefully, holding onto the cork as I released it, the effervescence genieing into the air, then poured us both a glass. "Cheers."

Alice clinked her glass against mine. We drank these quickly. Alice had asked me to take my ring off for the weekend, a request to which I'd complied. I noted the lighter skin where the ring should have been, but felt surprisingly unconcerned about this: I told myself that it was merely the result of wearing a ring; it was like having had a plaster on for an extended period of time. The comparison was reassuringly facetious. "We should live like this forever," Alice said sitting in a Georgian-style chair. "Live this kind of life. I'd be good at this kind of life. I think I could do it. I think I ought to be given the chance."

"We could stay here till the money runs out."

"That'll have to do," Alice said. "How long have we got?"

"Till Wednesday," I told her. "Provided we don't eat."

"As long as we can still drink."

"We can manage that."

I kissed Alice. Her lips were fuller than Sarah's. I relished kissing Alice more. Whether this was simply the frantic novelty of her lips, her mouth, her tongue, I didn't know. It was more than anything, I thought, another example of Alice's greater fleshiness, her solidity. I was reassured by Alice, her presence, her corporeality, in a way I could never be by my wife. I didn't feel Alice might evaporate, as I sometimes thought of Sarah: she was such a lean, flimsy thing, I might wake up one morning and she might not be there. It was as though her body was only an extension of her moods - it was brittle-seeming, all angles and bones: the jut of her hips, the knots of her spine, the imprint of her ribs. Sarah's stomach was almost concave, Alice had a proper one: it was there, at the top of her trousers in the middle of only a slightly definable waist. Alice was altogether more substantial. I liked the capability this superficially suggested to me. I didn't feel she needed me, that was the crux - she didn't rely on me. There was always a happy distance between us, a mutual satirising of each other which meant that transactions between us were, I felt, uncomplicated. We both gave as good as we got.

Afterwards, Alice said, "I'm going to use the facilities, I'm going to try the pool and the gym. According to the promotional material they're both places where you can leave your cares behind and utterly unwind. I think the rhyme's deliberate. You want to come?"

I shook my head, "I'm going to use the facilities in here, the tv and, oh, I dunno, the mini-bar. My cares are going to be left behind right here without me even having to move. And guess who'll have more fun?"

"And guess who'll die of a coronary at fifty?" Alice said.

"I won't make it to that age," I laughed. "Fifty? No chance. The big five - oh? Forget it."

"It's your funeral."

"It will be."

"I do look good in black."

"I'll expect quality couture."

"It'll be cheap and cheerful. Well - cheap."

Once Alice had left, I rang Sarah on my mobile, "Hello, love, how are you?"

"I'm okay."

"Good."

"What's your hotel like?" Sarah asked.

"Yeah, it's alright. Got a well-stocked mini-bar in the room."

"You're there to work, not drink."

"True. But, y'know, later, when I'm bored. But we're working till nine."

"Poor thing," Sarah said.

"Ah, well. It's been good so far. Lots of information. The people running it are pretty good. Know their stuff. Might make me more marketable, I'll be up on all the latest ideas - well, the latest phrases anyway, and they usually do for ideas. Is Eve there?"

"I'll give her a shout." I could hear Sarah calling our daughter, then a gleeful response in return.

"Hi, Daddy," Eve said.

"Hi, sweetheart." Talking to my daughter, I felt a small tremor of guilt about where I was, but I finished off the champagne and tried to ignore the sensation. It fluttered momentarily.

"What are you doing?"

"I'm staying in a posh hotel on a course."

"What's of course?"

"It's when daddies and mummies learn things," I said.

"But you know lots of things already."

"I suppose, but there's still lots I don't know about. Lots and lots."

"What like?"

"Oh, I couldn't begin to tell you, darling. There's so much."

"Like who builds houses for giants."

"Like that. Just like that."

"Who does?"

"I'm sure I'll find out while I'm here. I'll tell you on Sunday."

"Okay."

"What you doing?"

"Playing with my doll's house. Jessica's been naughty, so she's not allowed to go with the others to the seaside. She's got to stay at home."

"Oh dear."

"Yes. I'm very cross with her. Bye, Daddy. I love you."

"I love you too, honey."

Sarah came back on the line, "Okay, darling, have a nice evening. Speak to you tomorrow."

"Will do," I replied, relieved to have got the conversation over with, the nerves kicking in now it was done. I got a beer out of the cooler-bag. I ran myself a bath. I lay in the bath drinking the beer.

When Alice returned from the gym, I grabbed and held her and wouldn't let her go though she tried to escape. I kissed her neck which tasted salty. She said that she needed a shower. I demurred: I wasn't going to stop. I liked the taste. It reminded me of being in the sea as a boy. It reminded me of licking the salt off my skin after leaving the sea when we went abroad, my skin warm like Alice's. I had her in my control now and she gave up struggling and started laughing instead. "Okay," she said, "you win." I bent her over the bed, her head and upper body flat on the duvet. I pulled the tracksuit top up her back and traced my tongue down her spine to the top of her arse, the cleft there which I licked, and then all the way back again to her neck. I ran my fingers across her back and she bucked a little and laughed again, more lightly this time. I peeled off her tracksuit and knickers and put my fingers into her. I licked around her arse and then right in the hole, which she always liked, then moved my tongue to where my fingers were. After this, I entered her cunt from behind. I stood tall behind her, holding onto her waist, and thrust quickly; and, in part, I felt like I was punishing her: punishing her for being with me like this. I slapped her arse once, twice, three times as I thrust. Alice's arse was bigger than Sarah's, each cheek rounded, globular, soft and spongy, her hips wider than my own. She had light hairs running up the bottom of her spine. Most times I thrust, Alice moaned a sharp, tight moan and her head jolted to one side on the duvet. "Fuck me harder," she said, "harder." So I did.

When we'd finished, Alice relaxed into the bed and I stood by it, looking at my shrunken cock and the gossamer of come dangling from it, before lying down beside her. My face was inches from hers. We kissed again. "We should get away more often," I said. She nodded like she'd just woken up. We grinned recklessly at each other. "How happy are you?" I said. We sometimes asked each other this, on a scale of one to ten.

"Nine point five," she said. "That's high," she said, in case I didn't know.

"That's the highest ever."

"It is." We laughed at the fixed idiocy of our mouths. "How about you?"

"Nine point nine," I said, "and I don't do ten. Ten's impossible. Ten's for God."

"And you don't believe in him."

"Exactly."

She began to stroke the stubble on my chin. "You feel like one of Tim's lizards."

"Thank you."

"No, it's nice. I like it."

"I thought lizard skin was smooth."

"Not Tim's lizard. I don't know about other ones, but Tim's lizard is rough." She stroked the stubble some more. "Nine point nine, that's not bad. How long will this last, Harry?"

"For ever, with compliments involving lizards."

"Seriously."

"As long as we want it to."

"Yes," she said.

We were booked in for a meal in the restaurant on the first evening. Both of us dressed up for the occasion. We were drinking as we got ready. There was a giddiness about Alice that I hadn't seen before. She was girlish, sweetly excitable. She sung to herself as she put her earrings and necklace on, but I didn't recognise the tune. It was as though Alice had forgotten I was in the room with her, but then she turned and saw me again. She smiled in a way that was new to me, like I was seeing her smile properly for the first time. Previous smiles had seemed fine. Decent smiles. But this one, this one: it was as if her whole body was smiling at me, her whole body, her whole self, who she - undeniably - was. "You know," she said, "this is the first time I've got dressed up like this in a long time. It feels good."

"You look good," I replied. "You look good enough to eat. I might forget dinner and eat you instead. More than usual. All of you. You're a very sexy woman, Alice. Look at you. *Look at you.*"

"I don't want to," she said, turning her face away from the mirror in front of her.

"Mmm," I said. "Uh-mmm."

"Stop it," Alice replied, closing her eyes.

"You can't see what I can see. How can I stop it? How can I do that? I get to look at you all of the time. I get to enjoy you the whole of the time. You look beautiful."

"I don't."

"You do."

"Don't embarrass me."

"I don't want to embarrass you," I told her, "but I want you to know how beautiful you are. How beautiful and sexy you are. Men are going to envy me tonight. Men are going to wonder how it is I'm here with you tonight. Look at you." I meant what I said. I was staggered by her, her hair put up which emphasised the smoothness of her neck and bare shoulders, her good skin; the way her peach dress caressed her body, her hips, particularly around her hips, her arse; she had grab-her-and-do-her hips and arse, there-and-then hips and arse; and high heels: I'd never see her in high heels before. She was more my height in them, and I liked that: it further emphasised our physical equality, our equality generally. "Hell," I said. "Woah! See what I'm reduced to. I can't even get words out." I stood behind her and lightly kissed the nape of her neck. That perfume again - I needed to check what it was. We were in a large, well-furnished room with a king-sized bed, and maybe this was our bedroom in our house, our mansion; and maybe this was our life.

"Have I still got it?" Alice asked, into the mirror.

"In spades," I said, back at the glass.

"I'm hungry," Alice said.

"All that working-out."

"Of one sort or another."

"Let's go and eat."

Over dinner, Alice told me more about the break-up of her marriage. She told me that she'd got over the betrayal much quicker than initially she'd thought she was going to. Much quicker, in fact, than Simon had; which was mildly ironic, seeing as Simon had instigated the separation. Though Alice would seldom admit it to anyone (so she confided to me) she'd settled into her new life - her second life, she called it - with ease. It had certainly seen a new impetus in her career, though she'd already been successful enough even prior to the breakdown of her marriage. At home, she brought up her two boys with an energy and briskness that she was known for in her job. The boys, Nick and Tim, were aged fifteen and thirteen, and didn't, she told me, need the looking after they once had. Alice was increasingly proud of their growing independence, though naturally it tugged at her too. She loved her sons fiercely, but she had strong and set views on how they ought to turn out; how they ought to turn out, precisely, as men. She knew the type of men she wanted them to be. She talked vehemently to me about this: not the faintly bilious, vacillating specimen her husband had often been. Not that kind of man at all. He'd never appeared happy with who he was, never satisfied with the way his life had turned out. Or, should she say, *their* life, as it also was, his and hers. She was happy enough: why couldn't he be? What was it about men? she asked me. Why was there always something else? That grasping after something which almost certainly didn't exist.

It was like Simon thought that all the choices he'd made had been wrong, so that he was miles away from where he should have been. He was constantly looking back and reviewing each of his decisions through contemplation of their opposite. (Did he have nothing better to do with his time? I'd asked Alice in return. Surely with you he had something better to do. "Like what?" she'd said. "I'll show you after this," I told her.) Alice was part of that, she was part of that sequence of mistakes, she said; and though Simon never intimated as much, it seemed to Alice that she couldn't avoid drawing that conclusion.

Funnily enough, she still didn't really know how Simon *had* wanted his life to turn out: he never made that clear to her, and she doubted that she could. "Little boys," she said to me, and I nodded. She doubted that he understood it himself. It was purely that anywhere else was better, and that perception of his had infected everything. Anywhere else. It made her laugh. Because, of course, anywhere wasn't - as he'd since found out, she said to me in a voice flecked with a sort of spiky joy. It was just different choices that led to marginally different places. It all added up to the same thing: it was still *him*. But then *he* was probably her fault too. She was to blame for everything.

But now Simon had been ringing her occasionally and had been trying to talk to her for longer when he picked up and dropped off the boys at weekends. "Like last night," Alice said. "He came over and, I don't know, but it's as if, sometimes, he thinks we're still together. I mean, he left me. How can he still think that? How is that still in his head? You're a man, you explain it to me."

"I've no idea. I suppose when he sees you he's reminded about what an idiot he's been."

"Do you mind if I talk about this?" she said, drunkenly.

"No," I replied. I really didn't. I liked listening to people; and particularly I liked listening to Alice. "Whatever you want to talk about, go ahead, that's fine by me. I'll sit and stare at you, as long as you don't mind that. Don't get miserable though. I'm having too good a time here. I can't be coping with misery."

"I won't be miserable," Alice said. "I've done all that, I'm past that. It makes me laugh to think he thought he could leave me. Look at him now, the washed-up bastard, and then look at me."

"I am," I said.

"I know," she replied.

"It's good."

"It is."

After getting up late the next morning, we went for a walk in the grounds of the hotel. It was a mild day. We took a path into the woods behind the main building. The trees - oak, beech, ash - cathedralled around us, a swoop of branches and green light. We held hands as we walked: we were completely at ease. We put our arms around each other's waists and continued on our way. It was quiet in the woods, though at one point a gang of children raced past on their bikes, which startled me: as if anyone else could be here. Alice told me about some of the flowers in the wood. She picked me garlic mustard and showed me its small white flowers, its green leaves like hearts, toothed. She got

103

me to sniff the one she'd picked and told me that the smell was the same as mustard gas. "I'm an old romantic, me," she said and laughed. "But then these," she said, pointing at a vast number of other white but even smaller flowers, "I like these, wood anemones. My dad stole some from a wood near us a few years ago, and now they're all over his garden and mine. Their petals close up and droop when the sun goes in. They open up again when it comes out. It's all rather magical."

I remembered this a short while later when we were furthest away from the hotel and the weather began to change. I wanted to see the petals close en masse. The sky wrinkled, the green and brown colours of the wood deepened, and, after a few minutes, rain was falling. "It's only a shower," I said, "let's stay under this tree." We stood under a large oak and watched the rain, but it was heavier and more prolonged than I'd expected, so we decided we needed to get back, and gave up trying to stay dry. We ran, and then we stopped running, and by the time we reached the hotel building we were each laughing at how soaked the other was.

On returning to our room, I saw that Sarah had been ringing me. While Alice changed, I went out into the corridor and called back, "Hi, sorry, I had the mobile off in the last meeting. Are you alright?"

"No, I've been trying to reach you for ages," Sarah said.

"What's the matter?"

"I'm not feeling very good."

"Okay. How?"

"I'm feeling shaky. I've been crying again for no reason, there is no reason. But I cry and I can't stop."

"D'you want me to come home?" I said quietly, as though I wasn't sure how those words had escaped from me; hoping in that instant for the answer that I wanted.

"You can't do that, your course."

"I'll have to, if you're feeling poorly."

"I'll be alright, I'm sorry, I shouldn't have rung you, you've got other things to think about, I'm sorry, you don't want to be worrying about me. It's Eve though, she's been a problem all day. Never stopped yapping at me. Always wanting something. Never leaves me alone. I told her I wasn't feeling well, that I needed some time, but she never let me alone."

"Sarah, she's six. She's six years old. That's what six year olds do. They want their mums."

"Don't you start criticising me too. I've been criticised all day by Eve. I ring you because I think I'm going to get some support from you, but then you start on me too. Everyone is always criticising me. I might as well not be here. It'd be better if I wasn't here. Your lives would be so much better. You could go and find someone else, you'd be so much happier. Eve could have a different mum, she'd be happier as well. You'd both be better off."

"Sarah, don't -"

"You go back to whatever you were doing. I'm sorry. Concentrate on that. I'm sorry, I know you've got lots to do. I'll be fine."

"I'll be home tomorrow morning," I said, wincing a smile at a couple who passed me in the corridor.

"Yes."

"Are you sure that's okay?"

"Yes."

"Where's Eve now?"

"What d'you mean 'Where's Eve?', she's upstairs," Sarah said. "What's Eve got to do with it? Why d'you think about Eve all the time? You don't want to think about me, do you? It's only Eve you care about. You collude with her all the time. You never criticise her, you never discipline her. That's always me who has to do that. You don't care about me."

"Sarah, don't be stupid, I'm only asking after her."

"It's true. You don't think about me, you never think about me. Everyone else, but not me."

"You know that's not true. You know it's not. Don't say that. It's not fair."

"I'm sorry."

"You don't have to be sorry. I'm worried about you, that's all," I said.

"I know you are. I feel so low. I wish I could make it go away. I don't know why I can't make it go away," Sarah said. "I feel desperate."

"I'll come home."

"No. I'd feel worse."

"One day, it'll get better. You'll see."

"Do you really think so?"

"Yes."

"Do you believe that?"

"I really believe that," I said.

Alice and I went to the pool. I sat on the side reading *Q* magazine then went in the Jacuzzi and sauna while Alice swam lengths. She was an accomplished swimmer - had swum at county level as a teenager - whereas I wasn't, and I didn't want her to see quite how woeful I was. My dad didn't swim at all, and I hadn't started to learn till late, so I'd never felt particularly confident in water. I didn't see how it could keep me up. Alice, though! She cut through the water with seemingly little effort and in a range of strokes. She swam lengths for half an hour and didn't seem particularly tired by her exertions. I sat and watched her for the last ten minutes. I liked her being my friend. I felt better when I was with her: more as I would like to be.

21. Lewis

my mum sed who was that.

i sed that was billy.

mum sed whose billy.

i sed his a mate

i doant like him

you doant like him

no

you doant no him

i no him enuff

what dus that meen?

that meens he doant cum rownd here no more

he wosnt

wen do you see him?

only sumtimes

doant

why not.

his trubbel i doant want him draggin you down

he woant, his all rite

did dad meet him?

he was havin a showa most of the time

i doant want you seein him you unnerstan

i can luck after me self

she laffs

you worry to much

i have to worry, if i doant who will

tea soon

22. Harry

After midnight, the phone in the room rang. It took both Alice and I a few seconds to realise what it was, and that we could respond to it. I muttered to her not to answer.

"I better had," she replied, switching on the bedside light, "it might be something important."

I had my right arm over my eyes, sleep clogged my head, my words slurred: "It won't be. It never is. It'll be a mistake, a wrong number."

"I'll have to. We can't just let it ring and ring." Alice picked up the phone, "Yes? Yes. Yes, he is." She gave me the receiver, holding her hand over the mouthpiece.

"Who is it?"

"It's reception," Alice whispered, "they've got Sarah on the other end."

"Oh," I said, clumsily sitting up into my pillows, as though carrying them on my shoulders - like they ought to weigh more but didn't - and then taking the receiver wholly from her. "Hi."

"Harry, is that you? Did I wake you, I'm sorry? I had to ring, I've something I have to tell you. Harry, I've something bad to tell you. Are you awake properly?"

"Yeah, yeah, I am." I was now. Well, awake enough. I felt jetlagged. "What is it?" My first thought was of Eve. "What?"

"Your mum, Harry."

"My mum?" I felt, at almost the same time, relief and shock. "My mum? What d'you mean? What's happened?"

"She's collapsed, had a stroke we think. She's been rushed to hospital, your dad's there. She's in intensive care."

"Which hospital? The General?" I felt Alice move beside me, but I continued to stare straight ahead, at the large, shadowy hotel room, at the crimson and blue-striped curtains, at the crimson and blue-striped chairs. It was more and more like a stage-set. Open the curtains and what would be there? An audience? "Is that where she is?"

"Yes, I think so. Your mobile was off again. That's why I rang the hotel. Silly girl didn't seem to know much about your course."

"It's okay, you got through to me," I replied hurriedly. "Right. Okay. Thanks for telling me. I'm sorry you had to do it like this. Thank you. I'll set off as soon as possible. It shouldn't take me long to get sorted here."

"I'll come over, and we'll go up together."

"You can't. You stay there with Eve. You get some sleep. It's nearer from here anyway. It's only an hour or so, maybe less."

"I want to be with you."

"I know you do," I said. My voice was deep in my throat. I liked the feeling of it: it was rich and crumbly. "Thank you, but it's okay. I'll go there now. You and Eve stay where you are. I'll go up and find out what's happening. I'll phone you once I know. Who did you speak to? Who rang you?"

"Your dad."

"Dad." It couldn't have been anyone else, but still it seemed like a surprise. "How was he?" Alice looked at me with concern. I shook my head at her. She held my free hand. She put her other hand against my face. I leant gently against it. It felt cool. It was like she was my wife.

"He told me what had happened," Sarah, my real wife, said. "He sounded okay, I don't suppose it'd sunk in really. She collapsed in the hallway, he said. They'd been for a walk and had just come back."

"When was that?"

"Tea-time, I think. Early evening."

I sighed: "Why's he only rung now?"

"He didn't want to worry us."

"Jesus. Dad. Right, I'm putting the phone down and I'm going to go up there."

"Be careful, Harry. Get yourself together first. Take your time. Work out what it is you've got to do. Don't rush. Have a coffee. Wake yourself up. Drive carefully. Ring me as soon as you've got something to tell me."

"Yes."

"I love you."

"Yes," I replied. I wondered if Alice could hear what Sarah had said. She didn't appear to have done. She'd closed her eyes, while still sitting up.

"No, I mean I really love you," Sarah continued. "And I miss you, I can't tell you how much."

"Thank you," I said. "I'll speak to you soon."

While passing the phone back to Alice, I explained to her what had happened. She reached out to me and I held her next to my upper arm. She put one arm across my stomach.

"I've got to go to the hospital. It's Lancaster, where they live."

She looked up at me, "Of course. Go."

"What about you? How'll you get back home?"

"Don't worry about me. You go. I'll sort out everything here in the morning. It shouldn't be hard. Go on. Go. Now."

I arrived in Lancaster in the early hours. After entering the main doors of the hospital I remembered my ring and had to return to the car to get it out of the glove compartment. I slipped it on my finger and it was as though it had never been off. I played with it as I was directed down a maze of corridors, the early morning light as grey as the surroundings. I had to ask if I was going the right way to passing staff, all of whom seemed to be foreign - East Europeans and South Africans, as far as I could tell: like the South African supply teachers working at Peter Wallingford, though we hadn't yet started recruiting in Eastern Europe. It wouldn't be long.

The intensive care unit seemed too sparse and dimmed, the technology horseshoeing each of the four beds too plastic, too wiry, too boxy to be keeping mum alive. I couldn't in fact quite trust I was there, that this was happening. It was like I was watching a different life going on, one that I'd somehow materialised in. I should turn around and walk away - back myself out of it. Then I saw dad standing at the end of mum's bed, saw him before he noticed me. In the bed next to mum's, a nurse was trying placate a man who was having a fit. I didn't want mum to be there. Even unconscious. Why should she be there next to him doing that, for crying out loud? "Dad," I said.

"Hello, Harry," he turned towards me. I gave him a stiff-armed semi-hug. "How are you?"

"Well -" I opened my palms towards mum. "What happened? Sarah told me, but -"

"Did she? Did she pass on the message? Yes. Yes, I did tell her. Well, as I said to Sarah, your mother was about to go upstairs to have a bath. Fortunately, as it turned out, I was behind her. I was listening to a telephone message on the answering-machine. I stopped her fall, I stopped her banging her head, I think. Could've been quite nasty. I thought she'd slipped, silly girl, but she hadn't. She'd collapsed. Keeled over. They say they think it's a stroke," he told me, as if Sarah wouldn't have passed on that information herself, "but they don't know how bad a one. There's all different sorts. They're doing more tests later today. We'll have to wait and see."

I walked over to mum who was lying on her back, her arms down by her sides with tubes and electrics growing from her. She looked pale and old, properly old for the first time; and I was stunned by her sudden transformation, her shrunkenness. I put my hand to her face, which I half-expected to feel cold, but which wasn't, then softly touched her fingers, whispering her name. Sitting down next to her and the machinery which monitored her, I thought how it was my job to do the same.

Dad sat on a chair opposite, upright, his hands in his lap, churchy. "How was your drive?"

I played along: "Fine."

"Nothing on the roads."

"No. The odd lorry, but that was it. No police-cars,

thankfully, the speed I was doing."

"Got all those cameras now, son."

"Yeah, I guess I was hoping they wouldn't be working this time of night."

"Wouldn't be too sure. Not where there's money to be made."

"You're right. Ah, well. Too late now. Not to worry."

We sat for a time in silence. The patient in the next bed had also gone quiet. There was some murmured conversation between the nurses at their desk, interwoven with an almost comforting hum and beep from the technology, the weak light soothing as well. I could feel my eyes growing heavier and a couple of times jolted myself awake. I had to look after mum. I had to *monitor* her, that was it, remember. Dad was still sitting as though he was in the middle of a sermon. He was lost in thought, staring in my general direction, but not seeing me. I slipped lower into my seat, stretching my legs out and huddling my arms around myself, resting my chin on my chest.

The next thing I knew Sarah was with me. "Alright?"

"Yeah. What are you doing here?" My head was fuzzy and I wasn't quite sure where I was, the light around me smeared and blistered, the hotel maybe, or home. But no: I remembered. At least, I thought I remembered.

"I had to be here." It *was* Sarah.

"You shouldn't have." Things were still a little dizzy around me.

"Well, I am."

"Thanks," I said, rubbing my face. "What time is it? How long have I been asleep?"

"Not long," dad said from across the bed. Dad? Oh yeah, *dad*. "Half an hour. Not long."

"You should've woken me up straightaway."

"You were tired. There was no point you being awake."

"D'you want a coffee?" Sarah asked me.

"Please," I was still annoyed with dad, in avoidance, I knew, of being annoyed with myself. There were times when I was next to useless. Christ, give me a simple job. I

113

looked at mum and silently said sorry. For all the good that would do.

"Robert? How about you? Would you like a coffee?"

"No thank you, Sarah, I'd one before you arrived. And that was unusual for me. But it's been an unusual night, all told."

"Yes," Sarah replied. "Anything else?" She said to me. "Biscuits or chocolate? I'm sure I'll be able to find a vending machine if the shop's not open."

"No, love, no thank you."

"No chocolate. Are you sure?"

"Not even chocolate, thanks. Not at this time of the morning."

Sarah left the room. I watched mum for a while, watched her breathing, listened to the machines around her, their bleeps and sighs. I looked over to dad, "You look worn out. Go home and get some sleep. I'll call you a taxi. Me and Sarah'll stay here. Or one of us could drive you. We'll ring you if there's any change. You could be back in no time."

"No, Harry," dad said firmly. "No. I want to be here when your mother wakes up. And they're doing the tests in the morning, and I want to be here for those."

"Okay, but if you want to -"

"I'll let you know." We both knew he wouldn't. We sat in silence for a minute, then he said, "I always thought it would be me that something like this happened to first. Not your mother. That was the one thing about being that bit older than her, it seemed inevitable. We'd talked it through. All planned."

"She'll be fine," I said. "You watch. You know mum. She doesn't give up."

"True."

"People make full recoveries from strokes."

"Yes, I'm sure you're right."

I didn't know if I was and I was sure dad was unconvinced too; when I spoke it was like I was pressing play on a recording of my voice made days, weeks before.

114

Sarah brought the coffee back, touching the top of my head with the palm of her hand when she brought mine over to me. She sat on the opposite side of the bed, next to dad, drinking her coffee, looking at me forlornly from time to time. I supposed that was all she could do, and I felt sorry that she had to be there. She would have been better staying at home with Eve. I closed my eyes again, this time not through tiredness, but more through a desire to shut out where I was, if only for a few moments. I thought about Alice. I thought of her asleep in the hotel bed. Involuntarily I sniffed at my shirt and smelt Alice's perfume very faintly there.

The man in the next bed began vomiting blood. Two nurses rushed over to him and pulled the curtains around his bed. I was nearly glad of the distraction. It occurred to me that I hadn't seen mum asleep like this - was she asleep? Was that how it could be described? Unconscious, anyway - for twenty-five years, since the times I used to climb into bed with her and dad in the early hours. I'd had bad dreams, I would tell both of them as I did so, though I could never remember what the dreams were about when I awoke in the morning. It was dad who would respond when I arrived in the bedroom; he would pick me up and put me between himself and mum, who was seldom aware of my arrival. I would lie in the half-light facing her before rapidly dropping off. In the morning, mum would always say, "Hello, my little soldier, what are you doing here?" as if it was the first time I'd ever appeared in their bed like that, "When did you get here?" And I would reply, "Only a minute ago, mum. I crept in when you weren't looking. Didn't you see me?" Then mum would congratulate me on my stealth and bring me close to her, kissing me on my forehead; and I'd have happily stayed there next to her for the rest of the day. What was it Alice had said? *Little boys.* Little boys and their mums.

But my nearness to my mum now no longer made any difference. She was sealed up somehow, and there was no way through.

23. Lewis

today wos anger mangement, it wos with a gud techer culled miss blake do you no her do you talk to her. i had to tell her who my faverite teacher wos and i told her it wos you she werent suprised.

in the boys bogs there is a rate miss stiles arse competition, i tried to cross it out i did manage it, by the way there where lotsa 10s (outta 10) top

so this is what we did fist, we sat in a circle there wos 4 of us and miss blake, 4 needin the corse

we sed what made us angry?

we talkd abowt a time we wos angry and wat had set us of, this is confidentel, noone can tell noone, noone can laff or nothin, its like a secret thing, these things wich make us angery are triggas we have to avoide our triggas, the goth boy sed people, we all laffed but then we sed sorry for laffin, he told us to p*** of

sumtimes it is becos we carnt say what we want and this makes us angry and frustratd

we have to be assertif

we have to say how we are fellin

it wos intresting but funny to, like serius but like also what?! as if

but sumtimes my tempa is bad i recugnise that, this is a gud start miss sed

it wos beter than being in lessons anyrode

24. Harry

Leading-up to the GCSEs was the time of the year when I usually enjoyed teaching the most, and currently it was a decent diversion from what was going on in Lancaster. When mum first regained consciousness she could neither speak nor use her arms or legs and things looked particularly bleak. At the hospital, I was making sure she was comfortable, chivvying staff along. I stayed with dad and showed him how to use the microwave and washing-machine, the spin-dryer. Meanwhile at school it was all about getting Year 11 through their exams. There was nothing like teaching poetry about bored, aimless, semi-literate, working-class young men to a class which included a number of bored, aimless, semi-literate, working-class young men. It added to the spice. These were times when I was bloody good at my work; when I was teaching these kids something difficult and they understood - they got it; I'd helped them get it! - and then that was a great feeling, one of the best: when I knew I'd helped them make a discovery about things in general, about themselves. There were bright lads too, like Kieran, who was determined to be the first in his family to make it to university. I gave whatever extra help Kieran needed, and he was going to be fine.

Anyway, I wanted success for all my class because I believed there were many who would not genuinely wish this for them. Whether or not this was true was largely unimportant: it afforded me the impetus I required, it pricked me into action; it reminded me why I did what I did, why I worked where I worked, and with the children I worked with. I annually rediscovered an extra zeal on their behalf. In particular, at this stage, my arch-enemy was the exam-board. I did everything in my capability to undermine the power of this organisation in order to improve the prospects of my leavers. It was my mission. For example, as Head of English I could inflate as many of the cohort's coursework marks as possible, thus giving them more of a chance to achieve a decent grade overall even if they performed badly in their exams. In any case, most of the coursework had actually been written by the teaching staff, often in the style of a grade or so above what the student was capable of. I knew that this didn't merely go on at my school. It went on everywhere. From schools like Peter Wallingford to the most middle-class (whose children also had their work completed by their parents or private tutors). And not merely in English, but in every subject; a vast educational impersonation: teachers awarding themselves a variety of grades. "There was even one school," I told Roseanna, "where the Head of English burnt his own office down to avoid sending the sample in. A masterstroke, but only a once-in-a-career masterstroke. I'm saving it up for a later date. Some time towards the end of my glorious rise to power." At lunch, Jon, Roseanna and I would sit together either in the cramped, untidy English office or in a corner of the larger but just as untidy staff-room. Roseanna would eat her daily home-made salad - her first meal of the day. She didn't do breakfast, she said, she'd been "a bit of a heifer" as a teenager, and had worn glasses: "I'm long-sighted, but I don't need glasses anymore. I've trained myself to see. I look at photos of myself then, and I think 'Who is that person? Who is that huge-looking, ugly girl?' Because it isn't me," and she wasn't going back to that. She was again explaining to Jon why she'd become a teacher. She'd apparently always wanted to do it, "one of those sad little girls who used to arrange her dolls into a class in my bedroom. I even had a register. The dolls sat in alphabetical order. How weird is that?"

"So was anyone ever absent?"

"Oh, we had our problems at the Mark Owen High School."

"Splendid n-name."

"A couple of the Barbies had issues. Anorexia, bulimia. Skinny as rakes. Enormous tits though. Lots of single parents - I only had one Ken. It was a tough neighbourhood."

Ray strolled over to the three of us. He had a problem: he was taking a trip to London the following day, and Julie Brudenell, the Head of Art, was no longer able to go as she was absent with illness. "Harry, how about you? Why don't you join us? Roseanna's coming."

"One of your trips?" I said. "You've not signed up for one of his trips have you?" I said to Roseanna. "Fatal."

"I did tell you, Mr Monk."

"Yes, I remember now. You did."

"They're not usually quite that bad," Ray continued merrily. "There haven't been any actual deaths, as yet. Not *death* deaths."

"*Death* deaths? As opposed to - ?"

"The collapsing bridge wasn't my fault, as you well know," Ray said. "Anyway the emergency services were very quickly on the scene. Only joking, Roseanna, don't worry. You *are* Roseanna's mentor, Mr Monk, it's your professional duty, you can show her how a trip should be run."

"I'm not running it, Ray, you are. Let's make that clear. And especially if I choose to join you. You're in charge. I'm the rookie along for the ride."

"Coming from a man whose favourite Dylan album is *Nashville Skyline*, I'll take that as a yes." Ray said.

"I'll think about it, Ray. That's making the numbers up. That's *think* about it, Ray. And yes, Zimmerman's country phase was indeed the pinnacle of his career."

The Year 10s went with Roseanna and me to the National Portrait Gallery, as arranged by Julie Brudenell. While we were there, the Year 9s visited the London Dungeons with Ray and Liz Hopkins. Ray did explain the educational purpose of this, but, for the life of me, I couldn't remember what it was. We all met two hours afterwards at the entrance of Downing Street, where it had been arranged that we would be allowed through the gates and down the road itself. It was strange, but I did feel like I was walking on a film set. I'd visited the Downing Street at Granada Studios in Manchester the year before - and, as I said to Roseanna, the real thing was, if memory served, a decent copy of that mocked-up version. Even on a grey, cool day it did the fake justice. Griddled with excitement, the kids were having a whale of a time. Firstly they pretended to shoot the armed policemen at the end of the road, then, as soon as they were allowed through the gates, they ran off to find the section of it a few of them recognised from the news, some knocking on the other big black doors and standing on the railings to peer through the ground-floor windows. I was too relaxed from looking at portraits to do much about this and I sauntered behind the group, trying to take the street in. Anyway, it wasn't my trip, it was Ray's, as I'd made clear to him at the outset, so as far as I was concerned Ray could sort it out.

Which is what Ray did. He began shouting and the kids started to calm down. Ray organised them all for a photo in front of Number 10, and the mood of the children was in the process of settling when the door behind them opened and the Prime Minister emerged. At once, the cry went up, "Blair! It's Blair!" The children surrounded him in a matter of seconds - there was no way back for Tony - mobile phones thrusting in his face as though he was being checked for radiation; phones which managed photos of his neck, his nostrils, "Eh, Tone!"

"This way, Tone!"

"Tony, look at me!" Frankly, Blair looked scared. I felt like saying something jovial to him, possibly "Education, education, education" or asking him when he was going to call the General Election, but Ray had got there first, pushing past the scrum of kids to shake Blair energetically by the hand, "Good day, Mr Blair, Ray Chiltern, Head of Humanities, Peter Wallingford School in Nottingham. Pleased to meet you."

"And you," the Prime Minister said hurriedly, his smile

blooming like an over-fertilised flower. "An enthusiastic bunch you've got here."

"That's one way of putting it."

"Hello, everyone!" Blair said, like a children's tv presenter more than anything.

"This'll be something they'll never forget," Ray said.

"Eh, Tony," one of the Year 10s was saying to him, "I've got me mum on the phone - no, I'm not fuckin lyin, mum - it's FUCKIN TONY BLAIR right in front on me -."

"What's your name?"

"Glenn - f' fuck's sake! Sorry, Tony, that's me mum, not you."

"Hello, Glenn's mum!"

"See!"

"Everyone's very excited to meet you," Ray said. Blair was obviously angling for a way out, but Ray wouldn't let go of the Prime Minister's hand. He was also engaging him in one of his Chiltern stares, a look of extreme interest he'd developed over long years of teaching, which could, on occasion, appear a little manic in its intensity. Like right now. Ray looked as though he was trying to hypnotise Blair. It was then that I noticed that a small percentage of the year 9s had fake blood smeared around their faces courtesy of their London Dungeons' visit. No wonder Blair's agitation seemed to be increasing by the second: he probably thought he was in the middle of some yet to be announced protest, probably something about foot and mouth - perhaps the kids were impersonating dying cattle. Ray was still talking at him and still shaking his hand. The whole occasion was a triumph. I watched as Blair finally pulled his hand away.

"Ere, Tone," Daniel, a Year 9 boy, said, "Can I come in and av a look?"

"I don't think that would be possible today," the Prime Minister replied. "Perhaps we can arrange that for another time."

"That'd be marvellous," Ray gushed, continuing to be oblivious of Blair's desire to escape. "If it was at all possible."

"Yes, well then," Blair said, beginning to back into Number 10, "Enjoy your visit to London. Goodbye." And with that the door was shut in Daniel and Ray's faces.

"Outstanding," I muttered to Ray as we led everyone back out of Downing Street. "You told him the name of the school, didn't you? I heard you. You did, didn't you? You actually told him the name of the school. Expect an Inspection within the week."

We walked the kids over to Covent Garden, advised them where we would be for the next couple of hours, then took it in turns to wait there. I told Roseanna to go and call in on her parents while I did our shift on my own. She asked me if I was sure and I said I was, so she left me to it. Even though it was cloudy, I sat outside and enjoyed a pint, thinking of what I might do. I got out *White Teeth*, but couldn't concentrate on it. I rang Alice and we had a short chat in which I told her about the meeting with Blair. I watched a juggler in the square in front of me. The bloke was entertaining; funny as well as skilful. He juggled his three skittles in different styles as suggested by the audience who'd gathered around him. He took his shirt off while continuing to juggle. He then moved on to juggling five skittles. After successfully doing this for a minute, he shouted, "Bugger, I've just realised I don't know how to stop!" I laughed out loud. His grand finale was juggling while balancing a pole on his forehead with a tea-set on a tray on top of the pole, a challenge he somehow managed to complete. I marvelled at his dexterity. When he'd finished, he shouted, "I did it, and I'm alive!" At the end of the performance, I gave the bloke a fiver, then went and sat back down at my table. The money reminded me of Colin, whom I'd thought to ring before the juggling caught my interest. I was relaxed with the beer I was drinking, and I thought I'd nothing better to do now that the entertainment had finished, though there was an escapologist setting up while I tried Colin's number. I watched the preliminaries as I listened to the phone ring. The phone rang. Colin answered. A part of me thought I'd either entered the wrong number or that Colin's voice was the beginning of an answer-phone message. But it was neither: it was Colin. After this initial disbelief, I said, "Hey, Colin, it's me. Harry Monk."

"Harry, howdy! Everything okay?"

"Fine, Colin, how about you?"

"Can't complain."

"I'm pleased to hear it."

"Family okay?"

"The family are fine. Mum's not so well at the moment."

"Sorry about that. Nothing serious, I hope."

"She'll be okay," I said. "She's on the mend, had a stroke, but she's doing okay."

"A stroke? Poor Jean. She's okay though, yeah? It must be difficult for you, you were always so close. Send her my regards, won't you?"

"Of course. Anyway, listen, I needed to talk to you." The escapologist was being tied into a straitjacket by two young volunteers from the audience.

"Why's that, HM?" Colin said.

HM. Colin hadn't called me that for years. We'd had a flurry of referring to each other by our initials when we worked on the school newspaper. *HM, CP* or *H, C.* I've no idea why we thought that it was funny. More eighties mockery. "I'm concerned about the money, the money I gave you," I said, "I'm concerned that I've not been able to contact you for - months - now."

"Didn't you get my message?"

"No, Colin, I didn't. What message was that?"

"Harry, I'm sorry. I thought everyone I'd dealings with had been contacted. I can only apologise if that hasn't been the case with you. I'll have to speak to a couple of people about it. I'm very sorry. You see, I've had some time off. Been away. No, wrong phrase - not like that. Not banged-up or anything. Not yet, anyhow! Finally got round to doing what you did. Travelled. Been off and seen the world. The last few months. Properly this time, not from the inside of airports and hotels."

"I'm very pleased for you, Colin," I replied, sitting in a sudden burst of sunshine: Christ, Colin even controlled the weather. "Glad things have worked out and suchlike. You know that's really, really good. But at the moment I'm more concerned about my money, to be honest."

"I need to get back on track with that. There's been a few difficulties over there, you're right - but they're not insurmountable. What's involved here is a long-term investment, and in the shorter term it can seem disturbing, but you've got to hang in there, I'm afraid. Can you leave it with me for a while? I'm sorry if that sounds like a cop-out -"

"It does, to be honest -"

"I can understand your feelings, Harry, I really can. But everything has its ups and downs. Bear with me on it, will you? I need to make a few calls and see exactly where we are now. It takes an age for them to make decisions over there, it's all *manana, manana,* and I need to find out which part of the appeal we've reached. I need to speak to an associate of mine pronto. Can you wait a touch longer until I have some firm news?" Colin's voice was so blandly authoritative, I felt like throwing my mobile at the nearest wall: I pictured Colin trapped inside the mobile as I did this. "It won't be long before we know something," Colin said. "Can you hang fire?"

"I suppose I'll have to. I can reach you on this number again now?"

"Course, goes without saying. Any time. You don't need to worry. I wouldn't have brought you into this if I didn't know it was going to be a huge success. You know that. Where are you now? Work?"

"Yeah, but I'm in London. A school trip. I'm in Covent Garden."

"You should've told me before. We could've met up," Colin said.

"Maybe another time. When you bring me a suitcase of money. You can tell me all about where you got to."

"Yeah, nice one."

And, bloody hell, my own personal metaphor of hope - the escapologist was already free.

25. Lewis

billy sed cum in this house

i sed whose house is it

billy sed this mans

we went in the backdoor it wos open, billy was lucking in the hall, the man wos in the frunt room wachin tv it wos on reelly loud, we went upstairs billy went first he went into this bedroom, i stud in the doorway, he luckd in the draw, in the draw wos money he tuck it out

i sed what you doin

billy sed he ohs me money

what for.

sh** I did

what sh**

doant mater

tell me

ill tell you later

what sh**.

hello a voice sed.

f***

whose there

f***

we leggd it downstairs, the man wos at the bottom of the stairs, he wos old, white hair like small

what you doin

billy pushd him over, the man fell backwoods into the wall, there were a crash i stopd.

f***ing move you f*** billy sed, the man wos on the floor f***?! billy came back to get me stud there, wen he got me he kickd the man in the hed, f***

we leggd it out the house, we legd it down the street, then we startd walkin all carm pretendin we wos carm whisslin

heres your tenner

i doant want it

why not

i doant

doant have it then, then he went f***in have it you twat, he shuvd it in my hand, you woant say nothing will you

im not a grass

beter not

im not a grass

you want to bye sum booze and fags

yes

money innit

we went and got bladderd, then sum girls came over and they helpd us with our stash, and then we had sum fun

26. Harry

"Spoke to Colin the other day, remember him?" I asked dad as Eve and I sat with him in his garden, having returned from our latest visit to mum. It was strange her not being with us sitting in the sunshine - it was odder in some ways than the process of visiting her: the absence, the gap, where she ought to be; but we did our best to ignore the fact, though it was obvious that we each half-expected her to reappear, from shopping or a trip out with friends.

"Your pal from school?" dad said. "Big lad. Did well for himself."

"That's the one."

"Good rugby player. Wing-forward wasn't he?" Dad had been a Rugby League fan until I'd started playing Union at school. He watched me whenever he could, would stand on the touchline, all silvery and immaculate, occasionally shouting advice in his firm baritone. Whatever was going on, I could always hear him, from the bottom of a ruck or running free with the ball.

"Yes."

"Does he still play?"

"Wouldn't have thought so, dad, he's the same age as me."

"Yes, but he was a *serious* player," dad said, without rancour, "he was more serious than you about most things." I thought this unfair, but let it pass. I could live with the rebuke, far worse things had been said about me. My favourite, on the boys' toilet walls: *Harry Monk is a cunt.* Everyone had a point of view. "You always lost interest after a while. You had lots of things you lost interest in. Which didn't matter, that was you when you were growing-up. A lot of nine-day wonders, that's what your mother called them. You'd be enthusiastic for a week or two, and then you'd lose your enthusiasm. You'd get fed up. Trying things out. Testing them. So where did you see him?"

I shifted in my seat: "I didn't actually see him. I spoke to him on the phone."

"How is he?"

"He's fine."

"I remember him. Didn't he lose his father when he was young?"

"He did. Colin was seventeen."

"I remember him. He was a good wing-forward. Quick and strong. Very determined."

"Granddad," Eve said, leaning forwards towards dad as though in mid-bow, "do you want to see a dance I made up?"

"Yes, please, Eve," dad replied. "That would be lovely, darling."

Eve looked very solemn as she began, first pushing her hair from off her forehead, looking momentarily at the sky, then traipsing from the left to the right on the patio and back again on the front of her toes, like a ballet dancer, I thought, though I knew bugger-all about ballet, apart from clips I'd sometimes seen at Christmas or occasionally on BBC2 when I was looking for something else. After twenty seconds of this, the dance changed into a routine that was more contemporary, including little jumps and struts and the placing of her arms in criss-cross fashion over her chest then her stomach, before finally leaping round one hundred and eighty degrees and wiggling her bottom in our direction.

"Very good," dad said, clapping. His voice was sometimes reedy now; he would clear his throat to counteract the problem when it occurred, though, for the most part, the resonance was still there.

"Where did you get that last bit from?" I asked, also clapping.

"Laura at school showed me it," Eve replied proudly.

"Oh. Is Laura in your class or is she older?"

"In my class. Why?"

"No reason. It was really good. Laura must know her stuff." Her mum must be a lap-dancer.

"That was very good," dad said, beaming at his granddaughter.

"I know," Eve said, running up to him and hugging him round his neck in a haste of adoration and limbs. "I love you, granddad," she said.

"I love you too," dad leant back and grappled with her as if to prevent her from kissing him, making her laugh.

"Tea's ready," Sarah called to Eve through the kitchen window. I thought of mum shouting the same thing to me at Eve's age. I saw her there, and then it was Sarah again. And all that time had gone, and I was grown-up and a little deflated and far too often sidetracked. From what? And how, precisely, had that happened? "Do you want it inside or out?"

"Outside," Eve released herself from dad, then said, in a sing-song voice, "Outside! Outside!"

"Please," I said.

"Please," Eve repeated, running over to sit at the round, matt-blue patio table.

"Good girl. She's a good girl."

"She is," dad said, smiling at Eve. Eve grinned at us both, a dark space in the centre of her mouth where a tooth had recently fallen out.

"D'you want a drink, dad?" I started to get up out of my seat, then sat down again, not quite able to make it.

"No, I'm alright. Maybe later."

"Can I get myself one?"

"Help yourself, son. You know where it is." Dad always had an air of blunt generosity.

"Might have a G and T."

"It's all there. Bottles of both. And there's ice in the freezer. Your mother makes the best gin and tonics. Her colonial upbringing. Doesn't taste the same when I make one." Dad's mouth was bracketed with deep-set grooves. The whole of his face increasingly seemed to be held together by the stitch-work of these lines.

"Sarah's good at drinks too," I said, not meaning it to sound as crass as it had come out.

"What's that?" Sarah asked as she bought Eve's tea to the table.

Guiltily, I said, "Mixing drinks. I was just saying you were good at it."

"Was that a hint?" Sarah was happy, her eyes smiling, a sort of tra-la-la about her.

"No," I laughed, relieved.

"Do you want one? I can do you one if you want."

"I'm making them." Finally, I managed to get up. "How about you?"

"I'm fine," Sarah replied. "There, love," she said to Eve, "how's that?"

"Delicious," Eve brushed her hair behind her ears then picked up her knife and fork, ready to attack her spaghetti bolognaise. There would be a bloodbath of sauce. "Dee-licious."

Later on that night in the spare room, my old one, as we were getting ready for bed, Sarah said, "Sometimes, does this happen to you? I have to look in the mirror to remind myself who I am. I know it sounds silly, and mostly it's enough to do that - to look into my own eyes and see if there's anything behind them, anything I recognise, anything at all. There's usually something. Do you do that, or is it just me? I bet you know who you are all the time, don't you? You're so secure in yourself, that's what I love about you, that's one of the reasons I love you. You're so solid. But me, I look in a mirror and uh-oh! Who are you? Who?

"Remember when Eve was a baby and she was too young to realise that the reflection was her? She tried to play with the baby in the mirror, but when she reached out all she touched was glass. When I was about Eve's age now, maybe a bit older, maybe six or seven, I used to imagine that other worlds went on in mirrors, that *we* were bits of *our* reflections. I used to think that one day I'd look into the mirror and see something of the real world going on, get a glimpse of it, y'know. But another part of me said that that was stupid, said that if it ever happened I'd be scared half to death. I really didn't want to know about it. This world was more than enough, I think. I wouldn't have been able to cope. So it was never going to happen." Sarah was looking in the mirror, turning herself around, examining her body from different angles, "I feel fat." She squeezed some flesh at her waist which wasn't really there, ghostly flesh.

"You *feel* fat?" I watched her from the bed, stretched out with my hands behind my head. There was a flat patch at the back of my skull and I smoothed my fingers over it. My hair felt wispier there. I wasn't going to have dad's luck.

"I'm not thin -"

"You're fine."

"You agree I'm not thin, you see you do agree with that -"

I immediately realised my mistake and shuffled uneasily on the bed: "You're thin."

"Now you're just saying it." Thankfully there was still a trace of the afternoon's happiness lodged in her voice.

"Well, thin? Thin's bad, isn't it? I mean *thin*?" I threw a pillow at her. She picked it off the floor and threw it back, hitting me in the face. "Good shot!"

"Thin's good."

"Oh. Okay. It sounds bad. To my untrained ear."

"Men know nothing," Sarah shook her head.

"About all that, I can't disagree, it's beyond me. I don't know why you allow yourself to be pressured in this way. It's bloody weird. Why be bothered what men think?"

"It's not for men, it's for me." Sarah was looking at her buttocks, "My bum's definitely fat, you can't deny that."

"Your bum's great, I know that. I can say that without any fear of reasonable contradiction. I love your bum." Sarah had a high, spherical arse; a proper woman's arse.

"It's still fat. Just because you love it doesn't make it any less fat. You're biased. It doesn't diminish it in any way."

"I'll check it out if you like," I said, crawling across the bed towards her. "It'll need a closer inspection as it's obviously important to you. A proper examination, every inch of it. Intense, y'know." I grabbed at her waist. "I think I ought to take my time."

"Perhaps you ought," Sarah said, falling back onto the bed next to me.

27. Lewis

i had bin smokeing sum weed with dad and he sed theres this theery that wen the universe finishes growin, gettin larger and larger, wen it can do that no more it has reechd its limits, then it will get smaller and smaller

and wen this hapns, wen this is hapning, time will run backwoods, like evrything that has hapnd will hapn agen, only it will hapn backwoods. imagin that he sed. so well do this agen backwoods well be talkin like this

ill get my legs back, ill get back on my bike and ride away

instead of geting olda and olda, well get yunga and yunga

i sed will we go to Florida agen?

we will

sound i sed, wat will hapn wen you die.

you woant die will you, youll cum back to life and then be all the way back to a baby, think abowt that, people will walk out of there graves and sh**, there coffins will go back to there houses, theyll be placed in them theyll get up wereever they fell, i mean there house the street however it was, think about eatin, all the food will cum back out of your mouth, doing a sh** itll go back up into your arse, he pulld a funny face wen he did this like it was happnin to him

thats wierd

your rite it is, i cant wait to get my legs back though, top banana, theres a few things i need to sort.

but itll be the same only backwoods

thats trew maybe not tho, maybe ill be able to change sum things, ill worry abowt that later, ill be doing that aswell

ill have to do school again skank

me to but doant forget itll get easier as you go along

youll forget how to read and rite

you never learnt them in the first place! dad sed is there anything you want to tell me, anything wen the world go backwards you doant want to do again

you meen like school

like that but not like that anything else

no nothin

you sure

nothin

your not lyin

no

28. Harry

I received a call to go into a Geography classroom at break where Lewis Tuckwood and Carl Talbot had smashed a globe to pieces. Ray had Carl with him, explaining to me that the boy had admitted the vandalism while also implicating Lewis, as had three others in the class, but that Lewis was having none of it. I took Lewis to the English office to question his account of events.

"I din't break the globe, I wan't even there."

"Lewis, you were. Why would four people say you did it when you didn't."

"They don't like me. And the cost on it. Carl'll only have t'pay half, won't he? It's fifty quid. Half on that's a big difference. That's why, innit?"

"Come on, just admit it."

"If I'd done it, I'd admit it."

"My problem is these witnesses. I can't understand why at least three of them are lying. I can see what you mean about Carl, that makes sense. I'm not saying I don't believe Carl, but your argument does make sense. The other three though, no. They've bog-all to gain. And you, you see, you've also got something to gain by lying. I can understand why you would. You made a mistake. You don't want to pay for the globe. We all make mistakes, Lewis, and none of us really want to pay for them. That's not a problem. I've made enough of them in my time. I've made plenty of mistakes. But the thing is, I'll admit it. I'll hold my hand up. I'll say I'm sorry, and I'll try and learn from it. That's the thing. So I'm saying, come on, have the bollocks, pardon my language - but have the bollocks to admit it." Lewis shook his head. "Okay. Right. I'll have to ring your mum then to explain why she's getting a bill from school."

"Ring her. She won't believe y'."

"She might not, Lewis. But I need to explain why she's getting the bill. It can't suddenly appear and she doesn't know what it's about. That wouldn't be right."

"She'll not pay you."

"That's up to her." I dialled the number.

"She'll not pay y' 'cos I din't do it."

"Is that Mrs Tuckwood?"

"Yeah, who's this?"

"It's Mr Monk, from school."

"Uh-huh."

"I've got Lewis with me."

"What's he done now?"

I explained the situation to Mrs Tuckwood, who listened to what I had to say, then asked who the witnesses were.

"They're three people we can trust."

"People *you* can trust."

"Well, yes, okay."

"It were definitely Lewis?"

"Yeah."

"D'you want the money tomorrow?"

"As soon as you can manage it, Mrs Tuckwood, it doesn't have to be tomorrow -"

"She's not payin y'," Lewis said. "I'll pay y'."

"You'll have it tomorrow."

"Thank you."

"She's not payin you."

"I don't want him endin up like the rest on em, Mr Monk. He's a bright boy."

"He is, Mrs Tuckwood."

"Tell him, I'll be havin words when he gets in."

"I will. Thank you for your support, Mrs Tuckwood."

"Alright, duck."

I put the phone down. "I like your mum. She's a good mum, your mum."

"I'll pay the money. She's not payin y'."

"You know, I'd not bill her if you'd admit it."

"Nothing to admit."

"Go on."

"No."

"Just for me."

"Not f'r anyone. I'm not a liar, whatever you say."

"I didn't call you a liar."

"No, but you think it."

"I think lots of things, Lewis, but most of what I think is neither here nor there."

At the end of the day, I went to visit Alice in her office. Since our weekend away, we hadn't managed to see as much of each other as I'd hoped might happen. There was the week when I was away in Lancaster, and since then Alice had appeared distracted by work. She worked much too hard as far as I could see. Much harder than was good for her. Work was important for me, but only insofar as I had to be there; and if I had to be there, I wanted to make a decent fist of it. Alice needed to get out more. Get out more with me.

"Hello," she said. "And how are you?" She was sitting behind her desk, paper in half-a-dozen neat piles, yellow and pink post-its patching them.

"I'm okay. How about you?"

"I'm fine," she replied, though the words were abraded by something that suggested she might not be. I chose to ignore that. I doubted it had much to do with me. I'd used to think that everything had something to do with me, that the moods and attitudes of those around me were totally dependent on my own. So much easier to adopt the opposite, and, I thought, saner position. I had no proper effect on anyone, and no-one had any proper effect on me. Each to their own etc., etc.

"Good. Want to go to the pub tonight?"

"Can't do tonight, got a meeting. Tomorrow?"

"No, I can't, sorry," I said, though I might have been able to, had I made the effort. Tit for tat.

"The beginning of next week?" Alice said. "How about that? Are you away at the weekend again?"

"Yes."

"How is your mum?" This was more like an old family

friend asking, but again I ignored the implications of her tone. Plough on. Always the best way. Clichés kept me sane.

"She's getting a bit better. I mean, very slowly. She's trying to say the odd word now. And when I say 'odd', I mean it. She's coming out with the most peculiar stuff. She's not herself at all, she doesn't seem like her, y'know, the doctors do say her personality could be permanently altered by it all. Which is horrible, isn't it? I mean your personality's *you*. And she still can't move her left side. But at least the right side has improved, and, as I say, she is doing some talking."

"That's good."

"Yes, it is." I had my hands in my pockets, my feet quite wide apart. I swayed slightly, as though about to strike a tee-shot. "There's so much going on, Alice."

"There is. And, actually, Harry, you've been looking a bit poorly. Tired, I mean. Pale. Have you lost weight?"

"You know I'm always having to chase up that things are being done as they should be, I can't expect dad to be worried about all the details, he's got enough on his plate, so it's keeping an eye on everything really. You know, a word here, a word there. They have so many people to look after, you've got to try and remind them about your person, the one that matters to you. Things seem to happen so very quickly. They're making decisions about her all the time. So many things, very, very quickly. Whizzing up and down the motorway. And then I get back here and it's hardly calm, is it? Busy, busy, busy."

"You need to look after yourself."

"I will try."

"I do miss you," she said.

"I miss you too."

"Do you?"

"There's not much I can do about any of this."

"No, I understand that."

"Be better soon."

"Course it will."

The following weekend, I drove Sarah and Eve up to Lancaster again, then went alone to visit mum in hospital. It was a private place on the edge of town, a single-storey, flat-roofed building set in large, well-ordered grounds. Mum's room was halfway down a corridor of shiny, squeaky lino, with dried flowers on the walls, the blare of tvs from open doors and the compulsory smell of food that had been overcooked. The room itself was a small but smartly functional space with a bed, a specially-adapted chair, a built-in wardrobe and a television high up on a bracket in the furthest corner - which always made me think of my local Chinese takeaway - while a room to the left of the main door contained a disabled-shower room and toilet.

Mum was sitting up in bed, supported by a wall of thin greyish-white pillows, pillows that were a similar colour to mum's complexion. Attempting a smile, she managed to croak my name when I came in. When I asked her how she was, she shook her head and closed her eyes. "At least you're sat up, that's good. Are you comfortable? Do you want me to do anything for you?"

"'Kay."

"You are okay?"

"Yes."

"You look a lot better," I said, though this wasn't true. She looked, if anything, a month further on, worse. These changes in her dumbfounded me. How they came out of nowhere - although a crisis like this had been building up, had been waiting to happen, for years, as I understood it: the tear in her brain suddenly getting too much. But it shocked me nonetheless. Briefly I considered it: what some fucker giveth, some other fucker taketh away. The world appeared increasingly fragile, given over to shifts and explosions, to an inconstancy that, though I'd recognised it previously, had never threatened to up-end me quite as now. We really were on the edge of an abyss, however much we pretended or played about or fooled around! And what to do about that? What could anyone do about that?

Possibly just carry on with the pretending and the

playing and the fooling around. Possibly, that was it. But then possibly that wasn't it at all.

Mum had always been someone concerned with the way she presented herself to the world. Now, however, her hair had been badly cut in the hospital and she had no make-up on. My other mum, my previous mum, would have died rather than look like this. My other mum, my previous mum, would have died rather than be like this. Her arms were curled-up, her fingers stuck together, making her hands seem paw-like. Her legs lay uselessly in front of her, like false legs, like the legs of a hand-puppet. She wore a greyish-white hospital gown. Mostly everything about her seemed greyish-white: pallid, washed-out. Her eyes were dull, coated over. It was as though there was something dusty about her.

The mum I remembered was one half of a luminous couple who always seemed to be hosting parties or going out to them. As I reached my teenage years and dad rose higher in the manufacturing firm he worked for and eventually helped buy out, so the frequency of these evenings increased. Mum always liked me to take a photo of her and dad before they left the house or before their guests arrived. She kept albums with these photos in, alongside invitations, menus or other mementos. When she and dad entertained she recorded who had been invited and what she'd cooked - she was a brilliant cook, it was universally agreed - all with short comments about the successes of the party: the food, the drink, a funny anecdote someone had told. As a child, during these evenings, I would sit at the top of the stairs, listening and watching. Occasionally, dad would come up and see me, his face florid with hospitality, a cigar and thick smoky hair, his neat beard and large, dark eyebrows that appeared owl-like, feathery. Downstairs would be an adult confection of talk, laughter, the smells of good food, smoke, women's perfume. I would go to sleep with these sounds and smells seeping gently into my room. I would feel blessed by this. I would feel that I was at the centre of the universe, and no

142

other boy was as lucky as me. As an only child, that certainty was further amplified: I, and I alone, was witness to it all.

And later, whether the party had been at home or elsewhere, I would always awaken fleetingly - though long enough to remember the next morning - when mum came into my room to kiss me. I would hear the rustle of her dress, the creak of the one loose floorboard in my doorway, feel her lips graze my cheek, breathe in the scent of the party on her too.

My parents had a sunny, easy-going relationship. Dad had, of course, been married once before. I'd never met dad's first wife, Kathleen. She had, apparently, turned up for the funeral of my grandfather when I was eight, but I'd no recollection of her being there. So whether dad had learnt from his first marriage or whether it had been as equally harmonious as his second until whatever had caused its demise, I'd no idea. I knew, simply, that I always thought of my parents as happy in each other's company - I could barely remember a cross word between them -, as being good parents and a good husband and wife; and I was grateful for that.

"Sarah and Eve are coming along later with Dad, but I thought I'd come on my own for a while." A nod. "You've had your haircut." Another nod. "Dad's going to bring some more of your things over. Some photos, some CDs, I think. Sarah's brought you two new nighties. They're in the bag, look." I placed the carrier-bag on mum's bed then took the nighties out. Mum looked at them and then mouthed something that I didn't catch. "I'll hang them in your wardrobe," I said. "Oh, and look, a new school photo of Eve. She looks beautiful, doesn't she? So grown-up. I'll put the photo on the window-sill by the flowers." There were flowers, chocolates, fruit and audio-book cds from her friends. "She looks a bit like you, mum, don't you think? Your eyes, cheek-bones. There's a photo of you as a small girl on the beach in Scotland, that place you used to go to, that fishing village, d'you know which one I'm thinking of?

143

If you put those two photos next to each other -" I trailed off. Mum seemed to be in pain. "What's the matter? Are you alright?"

Mum shook her head. "Hurts," she said. Even in pain there was something as unreponsive as botox about her face.

"Have you had your tablets?"

Mum nodded, "Fucking hurts." In all my life, apart from a mild *bloody* now and again, I'd never heard mum swear. "Fuck," she said, with venom. She was patently making up for lost time.

"I'll get a nurse," I said. "Shall I get a nurse?" There was some shouting from another room close by; shouting and the sound of running in the corridor.

Mum shook her head. "No good," she said, grimacing, "no good." Breathing through the difficulty, she closed her eyes. I stood by her and held her hand. She clutched me tightly for a long minute, then something left her as quickly as it had come, and she released me. Her face hinted at the makings of a smile.

"There, mum, there," I said, running my fingers across her forehead, her temples.

"Don't want you to see me like this," mum said slowly and with difficulty.

"Don't be silly."

"Not."

"No, okay. But, it's fine. It's fine," I said.

"No."

"Yes." There were tears in mum's eyes. "Hey," I said, "hey," I said. I bent over her and kissed her on the top of her head. I wanted her to feel as I'd done all those years ago. I wanted her to be able to realise. I knew that this wouldn't happen, but even if she knew I was trying it would be a start.

29. Lewis

the thing about mum is this if im bein honest she lucks out for me, but if she dunt beleaf me then she sez so and then she expexs me to tell her the trewth. if i tell her the trewth and im like sorry shell be like ok with me again, she expexs that i tell her what she wants to no.

like she says you only have 1 mum, that is the 1 mum who gave birth to you, thats pretty awsum wen you stop and think abowt it, i sed yes allright i had sumthing to do with the globe i carnt lie mum but it was trew it wasnt only me.

carl wos there to he had as much blame as me only he wantd to blame me

so why did you do it mum sed

we wos only messin i sed, we wos only havin a laff, we dint meen to brake it, it wos no biggy, it dropt and it broke, it smashd easy, youd think they shud have made it stronger but they dint it wos like they wantd it broke

the teachers allright in there, mr chilten his safe, i shud pay harf no dowt

mum sed she wud pay the harf and i cud pay her back, i sed ok

doant tell dad i sed

no.

30. Harry

At the end of school one day, a kid shouted to me down the corridor that there was a problem in Miss Stiles' classroom. I went along there to find two boys in the corridor. "C'mon, Lewis!" one of them was shouting into the classroom, off-stage, somehow, in the wings.

"What you two doing?" I asked as I approached.

"Waitin fr'im," the one that had called Lewis said, pointing into the doorway.

"Wait in the Yard, Dean," I said.

"In a bit, Lewis!" Dean shouted, and he and his friend left.

Roseanna was standing in the doorway with her back to me, trying to prevent Lewis Tuckwood gettting past her. As I arrived, Lewis was right up in Roseanna's face, "Fuckin get out of my way."

"No, Lewis, I won't, I want to talk to you." Roseanna had her hands up at shoulder level, making it clear that she wasn't going to touch Lewis, while at the same time refusing to move out of the doorway.

"FUCKIN GET OUT OF MY WAY, BITCH." Lewis's face was screwed up like a fist.

"What did you say?" I asked in a tone of measured boredom, moving alongside Roseanna, then edging her out of the way so that I became the barrier to Lewis's progress. Though the windows were open, the room was hot and smelt of fifteen year olds, something peppery and canine mingling with the hint of cheap deodorant.

"Not fuckin you again." It was true - you got into cycles sometimes: certain kids seemed to become unavoidable.

"'Fraid so, Lewis, and another thing, because I'm the Head of English I'm going to tell you that you need to watch your language." My amusement at my own officiousness almost leaked out into laughter, but I managed to restrain myself. "That's one of my jobs, you see - language police."

"Fuck off," Lewis was having none of it: he attempted to barge past me, but charged into my chest instead.

"Watch it," I said, taking a step backwards. Lewis charged again, this time with his head down, towards my stomach. My good humour dissolved. As he came at me, I pushed him backwards into the classroom, then kicked shut the door behind me. He looked at me temporarily nonplussed, then charged again; I moved to one side and put my left arm out straight as a turnstile barrier so that it was the arm which took the full force of him at the top of his stomach; then, in one movement, I swung him round into the wall by the classroom door. The wall, made of MDF or some-such, shook like a soap-set. Lewis was facing me with the wall behind him, a usual suspect, then straightaway, trying to punch me. I grabbed both his arms and, after a quick struggle, turned him round against the wall as though I was going to frisk him. It sometimes helped being a big bastard. Make that *Big*. Make that a - etc. Anything John Prescott could do, I could do better. "Miss Stiles, lock the door, health and safety." I revelled in the hex of those words, as ludicrous as they were, "We don't want you smashing the school up or hurting yourself, do we? Do we, Lewis?" My breath was rapping out of me quickly. I didn't like having to do this, it seemed to me more trouble than it was worth, but there were times, like now, when I thought it obligatory. This kid needed to learn.

"Get the fuck off me, motherfucker, I'm gonna bang y' out," Lewis attempted to donkey-kick me, but failed.

"Don't you ever push into me again," I said quietly into Lewis' left ear. My shirt was sticking to me with sweat, but I couldn't remove my jacket, the sweat garlanding my neck, my shoulders.

"I'll fuckin 'ave you done, get off me, GET THE FUCK OFF ME!" Quivering with anger, it was like Lewis was having some sort of fit while still standing upright.

"No. Not till you calm down," I said, my face sheeny. "I'm holding you - please note that I'm telling him this, Miss Stiles - I'm holding you because you're a danger to the people you're with and you're a danger to yourself. Understand? When you're calm, when you are calm, when you calm down -"

"I AM FUCKIN CALM!" Lewis tried stamping on my feet.

"No, Lewis, you're not," I replied, doing a kind of tribal dance in response, lifting my feet out of the way as Lewis's came down in the spaces between. We were dancing in a pool of light, and our shadows were strong on the floor, the wall.

"Fuckin *am*."

"I'm not sure you are, Lewis." The dance continued. "Look at you."

"You don't know me."

"Don't I?"

"No, y' don't."

"You're right, I don't," I said. "You're right. But if you control yourself, we can start to sort this out."

"Let go of me then."

"I will, once I think I can," I told him. "But at the moment I can't."

"You don't fuckin know me!" Lewis again tried to kick me while facing the wall, and I briefly felt as though I wanted to slam his face against the wall or kick his legs from under him, and get it over and done with. Why put up with all this shit? There had to be better things to do with your time than all this shit. "Y' can't fuckin do this! Get the fuck off me!"

"Shall I get help?" Roseanna said. "Would that be best?"

"No, not yet," I replied, "leave it a while, I need you here really. Wait and see, but I think we're getting somewhere now, aren't we, Lewis?"

"I'll 'ave you fuckin done, both of y', I'll tell me dad," Lewis said, the rage in him beginning to subside, giving

148

way to something more plaintive.

"Yeah, fine. Tell your dad."

"I fuckin will, I mean it, I fuckin mean it. You're fuckin dead and so's she."

"Yeah, yeah. Miss, remember the threats that have been made, in case I end up dying in mysterious circumstances, y'know, drowning after going for a walk by the river, that type of thing. And I'll do the same for you." There was quiet for a while, then I said, "Lewis, you're getting calmer - which is really good - well done - and I'm going to let you go. Don't make it worse because we can sort this out."

"I don't care."

"Neither do I, I really don't, Lewis, but it would be good if we could put a stop to this. I don't know about you, but I would really like to go home."

"Fuckin go then."

"Right, can I let you go yet? That's what I'm going to do. I'm going to let you go." I slowly released him and he immediately made to escape me. "Hey, no," I stretched my arms either side of him, forming a triangle with the wall.

"What y'doin?"

"Listen, Lewis," I said icily, my breath now settling down into its customary rhythm, "I can wait hours till you're ready to go. We can still be here tomorrow morning if you like. We can go to first lesson together. Frankly, I couldn't care how long it takes. But you, you need to think - you're going to calm down and then you're going to apologise to Miss Stiles and to me. And then, when I've decided, and only then, you'll be able to go. Think about it."

"Me dad'll 'ave you," Lewis said.

"Whatever," I replied, not quite believing that I'd used that word in the way I had. "Fine." That was better. An adult disinterest.

"Motherfucker. Y' can't keep me 'ere."

"Funny, that."

"Motherfucker."

"Christ, you're dull. Call me something else. Use a bit

of imagination, be a bit more adventurous, you're boring."

"So are you."

Lewis had tears in his eyes, I thought. But it might have been hay-fever. "I do know I'm *bored*. That's one thing. I do know I am very bored. You wouldn't be able to believe how very, very bored I am. If we lived in the country of Boredom, I'd be the king of it. Look, apologise. Simple. Done. Finished. At least for now. You'd have done enough - for now. Then I'll let you go. Jesus," I turned to Roseanna, "this is tedious. Ask the little boy to apologise, Miss Stiles. He might accept it from you."

"Come on, Lewis," Roseanna said, "say sorry and then it's all over and done with, we can all go home, I know I want to and I'm sure you do too. No point prolonging this, is there?"

There was a long pause before Lewis mumbled an apology.

"Sorry who?" I asked him. I wanted this finished properly, the boy had hurt me, and I was hot and tired, and I wanted to be happy with the outcome.

"Sorry, miss," Lewis said.

"And?"

"What?"

"Me."

"Sorry." The word came out like it was stuck between his teeth.

"Sorry what?"

"Sir."

"Put them together."

"Sorry. Sir."

"That'll have to do for now." I let go of him. "Right. Go." Lewis ran for the door as Roseanna unlocked it, then shouted some obscenity as he made off down the corridor. "How are you?"

"I'm okay."

"Sure?"

"Yeah," Roseanna replied. "Yeah, I am. Thanks. Thank you for helping."

"That's okay." I pulled my right hand down the side of my face like I was smearing greasepaint on it. I'd helped Roseanna out before, of course. That was what you did with NQTs. That was what you did if you were a Head of Department. This time had been more feverish than usual, however. "Knackered."

"I'm sorry," Roseanna said, biting the right-hand side of her bottom lip - making me think of Sarah, though Roseanna held her lip like that longer, I'd noticed - and looking past me, "that was my fault."

"It wasn't your fault. How was it your fault exactly? What did you do wrong?"

"I should have let him go, I suppose, but I only wanted to talk to him about his behaviour, he'd been such a pain, showing off. Will he complain?"

"About what?" I said, wiping my forehead with the back of my hand. I leant back onto one of the desks, then stood up and took my jacket off. My shirt was sealing itself against my skin. I put the jacket on a desk then undid my tie and two top buttons and pulled the fabric away from my chest, my stomach, all to little avail: the heat was inside my skin. "Too much exertion for one day, I had to chase after a kid earlier the afternoon, halfway round the bloody school. That nearly did for me on its own. Little sod was pretty quick."

Alice came into the classroom, unhurriedly, like she was in an exam-hall, I thought, which was how she always walked. She looked directly at me. "What's gone on in here then? Bit of a rumpus was there, Mr Monk? You seem to have got yourself a tad overwrought."

"These summer days. Too much for me. Not enough ozone or whatever it is. I'm very delicate."

"Lewis isn't best pleased with you," Alice said to me. "Mouthing off when he left. He's said he's going to get his dad."

"Lucky his dad's banged-up then, isn't it?" I replied, to Alice's evident surprise. "Didn't you know that? I thought everyone knew that. It's not often I know something you don't." I smiled at Roseanna, "I quite like it."

"His mum's scary enough," Alice told Roseanna, "forearms like Popeye."

"Me and Mrs Tuckwood get on well, so that'll be fine. Nothing happened, anyway. Nothing to worry about," I said. "He was pissed-off because Roseanna kept him back at the end of her lesson, during which he'd been a prat."

"I see. How are you?" Alice asked Roseanna with a wildly apparent lack of interest.

"I'm fine," Roseanna replied, plainly understanding the dismissal in the question.

"Have you got a moment, Harry?" Alice said.

"For you, Mrs Hibbert," I said sardonically, "of course." As I followed Alice out of the classroom, I winked at Roseanna, who had moved over to the board and begun to wipe it slowly.

Once a short way down the corridor, past the cleaners hoovering up, Alice asked me what had happened. I told her.

"You didn't do anything you shouldn't have?"

"Course not."

"Good. You know what the boss is like."

"A pathetic wimp, you mean."

"He's got to keep everyone happy."

"Does he? Why's that?"

After this, I went back to Roseanna's classroom. Roseanna was sitting at her desk, arms around herself, trembling slightly. "Thanks," she said.

"Hey, c'mon," I said. "Don't let that little prick get to you, he'll be out of here before long. He can be with me every time you've got the class from now on."

"No," Roseanna said, "it's not me, it's not bloody Lewis, it's everything. The whole lot of it. I don't know if I can do this any longer. I don't know if I want to, more to the point. It's too much. It's shitty, isn't it? This isn't what adults should have to put up with." There was redness around her eyes.

"Hey," I said, walking over to her. She looked up at me

and tried to force a smile; it was nearly there. She'd a tiny line of acne up the right hand side of her jaw that was more noticeable because she was upset. I remembered how young she was, how inexperienced. "It's your first year. Everyone feels like this in their first year. It's all something of a shock after university, and teacher-training's hard, but it's not the same as this. I felt pretty much stunned for my first *five* years, but, y'know, after a while - the next five were a lot better, much improved. Comparatively. All things considered." She did concoct a proper smile this time. "Come here," I said, "look at you." I reached towards her and gently brushed a tear away from her face. Roseanna leant forwards into my chest and I held her with one hand lightly behind her head. I was careful that the vague comfort I was offering remained that. I didn't want anyone to walk in on us like this. People were always ready to come to the wrong conclusions - it gave them something to do; until it became their turn to have the wrong conclusions drawn about them. I did tense my stomach however. Unwittingly, I put my other hand to my mouth and realised I was tasting Roseanna's tears on the edge of my lips. I held her more loosely for a few moments then let her go, "Okay?"

She nodded, "Sorry. I'm sorry." She was laughing and crying at the same time. "It's all too much at the moment, it's getting the better of me. I'm very tired. I'm not usually so weak."

"Weak isn't a word I'd use to describe you."

"Sorry," she said again, sitting on her desk.

"You must stop apologising to me," I told her. "I see that as a step in the right direction. I think it might help." Roseanna nodded, crying and smiling. "It's a crap job," I said. "But there's plenty of those out there. They're shit in different ways. This one's explicitly crap, you can't escape its execremental qualities, they're self-evident from the moment you consider them. My guess is that other jobs are full of hidden crap. Crap that rises around you after a while, till suddenly you realise you're mired in it, and there's no

153

way out - you've got to keep your head above it. At least everyone knows how bloody awful teaching is, you hear that intake of breath when you let people know what you do, especially when they find out you're not Primary. And the other bonus is it's quite amusing at times. That's the other thing in its favour as far as I'm concerned, it's better than the telly most days. It's what keeps me going, if the truth be told. How many funny stories d'you think accountants have? You know stories about how their sums didn't add up or something. A play on the word 'percentage'. And there's some quite nice people in teaching. So I've heard. On the grapevine. So someone said who once worked at a school in Exeter. Apparently the staff there were a laugh-a-minute, absolutely spot-on. The school closed though. Poor results. Being a public servant is a serious business."

"I like it really," Roseanna said. "I think."

"There you go."

"I'm tired, worn out. I go home, fall asleep in front of *Neighbours*, wake up, have tea and then I go to bed early and I'm still shattered. I wake up every morning wondering how I'm going to get out of bed. Then things like this happen. It was a good lesson apart from Lewis kicking off. But that's the problem isn't it?"

"No, it's not - you had a good lesson; twenty-five kids got something out of it. Just because one idiot didn't because he deliberately set out not to."

"I suppose. But what d'you do about that one? Why do we waste our time with that one? And then when I was trying to talk to him, the little bastard was staring at my tits. Not looking at me at all. Looking at my bloody tits. I wouldn't mind, but there's hardly much to occupy his attention for long. Anyway, in the end, I'd had enough so I stared at his willy."

"Did you?"

"Actually, no - but I wish I had."

"Even less to occupy your attention. Anyway, go home, have a couple of drinks, forget about it. Or better still, go

154

out and get pissed. That's the advice of a cynical hack."

"And what d'you think I should do?" Roseanna said.

"Sweet," I replied.

31. Lewis

you no rite now i f**king hate you, why do you think you can do that, why did you have to get that no all bastad involved, f**king pervert monkey man

that wos between me and you

that wosnt abowt no-one else, we wud have bin fine but then that peedo cums along and its all sh**, whenever his around its all sh**

he wos tryin to showoff, he wantd to impress you, dus he fansy you, i think he fancys me to, f**kin peedoh

he thinks he can f**king do that to me

he carnt do that to me, his ded

im sorry if i p**sd you off, i wos only messin i wos board

32. Harry

When I arrived home, Sarah told me that Alice had phoned, "I said you weren't home yet. She said she needed to get in touch with you, if you could ring her back. I got her mobile-number off her, she said she didn't know if you had it or not."

"Thanks, love," I said, "I'll ring her in a bit. I'm sure it's not as urgent as she thinks it is. These things never are."

When, after playing with Eve for a while, I rang Alice from the master bedroom, she said, "Before you say anything, this is about school."

"Fine. I wasn't going to say anything."

"I wanted to make it clear."

"You have."

"We've had Mrs Tuckwood on the phone alleging all sorts, how she's going to phone the LEA and the press and God knows who else. Says Lewis has got a red mark on his neck where you tried to strangle him."

"Oh," I looked out of the bedroom window at the street in front of the house: children were running up and down, in and out of the parked cars. Eve had joined them. I watched as she chased after her friend, Poppy. Eve had a flat-footed run, like me. "And?"

"Did you?"

"No I didn't, Alice, don't be ridiculous. Read the statement I wrote you." I pulled a face at the phone.

"I have, but I still have to ask."

"Do you?"

"Harry -"

"How long have we known each other?" A silver BMW drove into the cul-de-sac slowly. It was the couple who lived at number seventeen, I didn't know their names. I always meant to find out what they did, they seemed to have plenty of money, new gear arriving in lorries from Jessops and the like. The older kids shouted at the younger to be careful. I watched Eve stand still on the pavement, watching the car go by. I liked living in a cul-de-sac. It reminded me of a line in *Adrian Mole*, which always made me smile. "I mean, how long have we known each other?"

"That has nothing to do with any of this."

"I restrained the streak of piss because he was getting out of control and I thought he was going to have a pop at both me and Roseanna. I told him what I was going to do before I did it, I did it by the book. Eventually, he apologised, off he went. That's it, end of story. Till you exclude him, of course. Which you'll have to do. Permanently. The union'll love it. Roseanna was there the whole time, she saw the whole thing. We wrote our incident reports and left them in your tray."

"How's he got the mark on his neck?"

"On his *neck*?"

"Yes, apparently."

"No idea. Not from me. Nothing to do with me. I can't actually believe you're suggesting that it might be, but there you go."

"I'm not. I'm merely -"

"Probably did it to himself later. Look, Roseanna was there the whole time. She was the only other person there. She's my witness. Ask her about it."

"I already have."

I was taken aback by this. "Thanks."

"What's that supposed to mean?"

"You might have waited to talk to me first." I turned away from the window and sat down on the bed. There was a new quilt cover on I didn't recognise: big red roses on a white background.

"You weren't home. And you weren't answering your mobile."

"What did she say?" Matching pillowcases too. I laid down and stared at the ceiling.

"Not a great deal. Similar story to you," Alice said. "As

158

I'd've expected."

What did she mean by that? I wasn't going to respond. "So tell Mrs Tuckwood to go fuck herself. Ring up who she fucking likes."

"You know it's not as simple as that, Harry. The local press are gunning for us at the moment, you know that, that new education correspondent trying to make a name for himself. He'd love to get hold of this. I'll try and placate her. I'll do my best for you."

"It's not for *me*, Alice, let's get that clear. It doesn't bother *me* what she does. Call the police. Suspend me. I could do with a holiday."

"I'm sure it'll be fine, but I thought you needed to know."

"Well - thank you for your concern." I yawned; because of the bed or the conversation I wasn't completely sure. "It's really appreciated."

"Don't be like that."

"I'm not being like anything."

"I'll see you tomorrow."

"Uh-huh." First she was ignoring me. Now this. Ah well, all good things, da di da di da. I needed a drink.

It was a fine early summer's evening. Sarah and I ate our tea on the patio, the French windows wide open and *Murmur* by REM playing from the dining-room. Eve was playing on her bike with Poppy and a few of the other children. From time to time, she'd cycle round the back to pick up something - a doll, some crayons, a cup - and then be gone again. Sarah and I were soon quickly through a bottle of wine. I began to relax; I got myself a cigar and opened another bottle of Syrah. The sun softened behind the trees and birdsong prettified the stillness. 'Perfect Circle' was playing. There were the distant sounds of traffic and, closer, overlaying this, the noise of other people in their gardens: laughter and the purr of adults talking, a rare shout. A light breeze gently played around my face and midges shook in the low sunlight like they were in the middle of a spin cycle. Ten years ago I'd have laughed at what I'd have seen as this bourgeois complacency; now, frankly, I couldn't give a toss. I felt that I paid my dues during the day. I felt that I did my bit, I didn't have to answer to anyone on that score. I had to move towards a lack of complication. I had to feel like I did now *all the time*. I had to feel vaguely pissed every minute of every day, I thought in a vaguely pissed way: that would see me right. Right? Drink clarified and redefined. I wondered if this was how people who believed in religion felt, they were supposed to be more content and live longer. (Longer? Eternally!) I needed a religion of alcohol. Alcohol and sex. Oh, and music too. The real holy trinity. Then I would feel happier day in, day out; and, as a divine bonus, think I was going to make it to heaven when I died. Life sorted. Death too. If only I could feel like this more often, I was sure it would prevent me getting entangled in situations I shouldn't have had anything to do with. As I pondered this some more, a hot air balloon came into view like a giant exclamation mark, the sort girls produced, rounded and coloured in. Christ, I thought, bloody school again. It was inescapable.

"Remember the first time we met?" Sarah said, reaching over for one of my cigars and the lighter.

"What? The actual first time? Not the other first time later on?"

"The first first time," Sarah said. "You were drunk, totally out of it."

"So were you -"

"It was the punch. Peter's punch. Everyone knew about Peter's punch."

"Looked like blood," I remembered. "But tasted good. He always made it the same way. His secret recipe. Who knows what he put in it. Something highly illegal."

"You were more drunk than me."

"No I wasn't."

"Were -" Sarah puffed out smoke at me.

"Wasn't," blowing it back at her.

"Were."

"Wasn't. Okay, I was. It was really romantic, our eyes

160

almost focused on each other across a crowded kitchen. I thought you had a squint."

"I thought you were short-sighted. Then we went out in the garden and went for a walk. I remember walking next to you. You put your arm around me. We carried on walking. It was a warm night. We didn't say much, did we? It felt good, your arm around me. I think I knew immediately we'd get married. I just knew." We'd spoken about this before, of course, but I liked it when Sarah recalled the story.

"We were holding each other up," I said.

"I was holding you up."

"That could be the truth."

"You know something, Harry Monk, I love you," Sarah said, leaning across towards me, an unsteady glass of wine in her hand, as though the glass was too heavy for her, particularly on its left-hand side.

"You know something, Sarah Monk, I love you too."

"That's good." Sarah giggled, putting the glass down.

"More wine? To celebrate?"

Sarah shook her head, "I'm drunk."

"Are you?"

"Can't you tell?"

"Well done," I told her. "It's about bloody time. You haven't been drunk in ages."

"I'm not supposed to. The tablets."

"Ah well."

"There's an enormous ladybird in the sky." Sarah pointed with her cigar.

"Yes, love." I poured more wine into Sarah's glass. "Blimey, you have got through it."

"No, there is. In the sky."

I looked up from pouring Sarah's drink, and she was right: a new red hot-air balloon with six black spots on its back had joined the first, a more conventionally coloured one of red, white and blue stripes like a misshapen stick of rock. "Fuck me," I laughed, "that's the biggest ladybird I've ever seen."

"Was that a request?"

"It could've been."

"I need the loo," Sarah said, "all this wine, but then." She put her cigar into the ash-tray, "Cigars, yeeugh!"

"You're funny, Mrs Monk."

She went into the house while I picked up my wine glass. A small fly had landed in what remained of the liquid at the bottom. I watched it flounder for a few seconds, before, in my contented state, flicking it out onto the table. I hoped that helped. I was sure that it would, though the fly would have a hell of a hangover in the morning. Did flies make it to a second morning? I wasn't sure. Oh well, not a bad way to go. Out of your tiny fly-like brain. I poured myself another half a glass, drank it down and went to find Eve.

33. Lewis

fuck that and fuck that and fuck that and fuck that and fuck that
fuck that and fuck that and fuck that and fuck that and fuck that
fuck that and fuck that and fuck that and fuck that and fuck that
fuck that and fuck that and fuck that and fuck that and fuck that
fuck that and fuck that and fuck that and fuck that and fuck that
fuck that and fuck that and fuck that and fuck that and fuck that
fuck that and fuck that and fuck that and fuck that and fuck that
fuck that and fuck that and fuck that and fuck that and fuck that
fuck that and fuck that and fuck that and fuck that and fuck that
fuck that and fuck that and fuck that and fuck that and fuck that
fuck that and fuck that and fuck that and fuck that and fuck that
fuck that and fuck that and fuck that and fuck that and fuck that
fuck that and fuck that and fuck that and fuck that and fuck that
fuck that and fuck that and fuck that and fuck that and fuck that
fuck that and fuck that and fuck that and fuck that and fuck that
fuck that and fuck that and fuck that and fuck that and fuck that
fuck that and fuck that and fuck that and fuck that and fuck that
fuck that and fuck that and fuck that and fuck that and fuck that
fuck that and fuck that and fuck that and fuck that and fuck that
fuck that and fuck that and fuck that and fuck that and fuck that
fuck that and fuck that and fuck that and fuck that and fuck that
fuck that and fuck that and fuck that and fuck that and fuck that
fuck that and fuck that and fuck that and fuck that and fuck that
fuck that and fuck that and fuck that and fuck that and fuck that
fuck that and fuck that and fuck that and fuck that and fuck that
fuck that and fuck that and fuck that and fuck that and fuck that
fuck that and fuck that and fuck that and fuck that and fuck that
fuck that and fuck that and fuck that and fuck that and fuck that
fuck that and fuck that and fuck that and fuck that and fuck that
fuck that and fuck that and fuck that and fuck that and fuck that
fuck that and fuck that and fuck that and fuck that and fuck that
fuck that and fuck that and fuck that and fuck that and fuck that

34. Harry

At the beginning of the English exam, I settled the Year 11s and reminded them what they needed to concentrate on. Once they were underway I didn't stop for the whole two hours, walking around, offering quiet words of advice and encouragement. The Year 11s were my kids and I was desperate for them to succeed. This was to help them get wherever they needed to get to, so I was going to do what I could. If they needed some mild guidance, then so be it. Ethics didn't enter into the process: the whole situation was far too distorted - the government's sanctimonious belief in endless progression, its fatuous targets, the constant painting of stones that went on - for anything like that kind of thought. Besides, it wasn't about any of that: it was about Kieran and Filipe and Sagheer and Grant; and all our little lives.

"What's happened?" I asked Alice when we went to the pub later on in the week. We'd hardly spoken since the phone-call about Lewis. She sat opposite me, keeping her hands on her lap. "I hardly seem to have seen you."

"Nothing's happened. You've been away a lot." Her eyes were vulnerable with tiredness, its bruising beneath them.

"True. It's been a pain in the arse. You look shattered."

"I am tired. But you are too. We both are."

"Have a couple of days off. Go away somewhere."

"I can't do that."

"No, I know you can't, you're too good, but you should. Alice, we'd such a nice time, and then -"

"We did."

"It's okay, I mean it doesn't matter. There's no pressure here. That's not what this is about. This is the last thing that this is about. I'm not making any sort of point. But you

164

seem a little distant at the moment. Look at you now. You don't have to be here if you don't want to be."

Alice's mouth flickered slightly at one corner. "Sorry, lots to think about."

"Work?" I said, not wanting it to be anything else. I could really do without it being anything else.

"Work," Alice replied.

"Another four-letter word."

"Mmm."

"It's the pressure of high office, being important."

"Must be." She almost smiled at me, before looking at her vodka, "The glass isn't clean." There was a smudge close to a section of the rim which faced her.

"I'll take it back."

"No, it's okay. Stay here. It's not too bad. I'll drink from it on the other side. I'm not sure I want it anyway." She turned the glass round, then sipped at the vodka as though it was very hot.

"Look," I said "don't you want to do this anymore? We can leave it for a while if you want. We can leave it for good, if you want that." Even *I* could pick these signals up.

"What d'you think?"

"Alice, whatever makes you happy. I don't want you to be unhappy. You're too important, properly important, for that."

"You can be very sweet."

"When I make a special effort," I said, winking.

"Either that - or full of shit."

"Definitely sweet," I said. I had meant it.

"Possibly it would be for the best."

"To give it a rest? Or finish it completely?"

"No. Temporarily."

"Okay," I said. "If that's what you want. If that's the best way forward." There was a silence between us then I said, "I've not upset you, have I? I've not done anything to upset you."

"No," Alice replied, "not at all. How could you upset me?" There was obviously no chance of that.

"Good. I really wouldn't want to, that's all." I rested my arms on the table. They faced Alice like an arrow-point.

Alice placed her hands over mine. "Things are a bit complicated at the moment. For both of us. Your mum. Then for me: school, that's one thing. There's too much to do. Every day chasing around, then I'm working till ten, eleven at night. It's bloody stupid, but it seems endless at the moment. Paperwork. And so, no I don't know if I've got the energy for - all this. I worry about it. I worry about how I'm going to meet you and what we're going to do, and will everything be okay when we're together. And I don't want to be worried about it. That seems to make a nonsense of the whole thing. Like you said. What d'you think? Would you mind? I'd appreciate the space. Sorry, I sound like some crass magazine, but you know what I mean. We've had a good time though, haven't we?"

"Don't make it sound like it's completely terminal."

"No, I don't mean to. But for the moment -"

I nodded, "Probably for the best." I bent forward and kissed the backs of both her hands.

"I'm saying it, and now I'm not sure."

Alice was very seldom indecisive, so I saw it merely as politeness, a warped decorum. "Alice, it's fine. You're right. Let's leave it awhile."

"Okay. If you agree."

"I agree," I said, stroking my chin. I felt calm, but I was glad that Alice was taking the lead.

"Okay."

"Agreed?" I said.

"I think so," Alice murmured. "I need to sort things out in my own mind. Get them clear. Like the bloody school. It's really getting to me at the moment. It never has done before particularly, and I don't like the way it is now. It's about getting my focus back, I think; yes, that's it: focus."

"When you've managed it, can you tell me how you did it? Let me know your secret. I'll do anything you want for your secret. Well, anything you'll let me do. You're in charge."

"That's a start," I said. We weren't usually so careless in a public place, but we kissed, and we held each other, and even though no-one else noticed, at that moment it wouldn't have mattered to me if they had.

Later when we'd returned to school to watch the summer concert we kept apart and paid no attention to each other. The concert was one of my favourite nights of the year. There were always unexpected children who got up on the stage; there were always a few performances that again reminded me why I did what I did. Tonight there was a very quiet girl from Year 10 who sang beautifully over a backing-track, there was a nicely choreographed dance from a lively bunch in Year 8 and there were two rappers from Year 9. The choir performed a great version of 'Stand By Me'. I was proud to teach at their school. I smiled at Alice once towards the end of the evening and she smiled back, a proper, unadulterated Alice smile, one that I realised I hadn't seen since soon after our hotel stay. If she thought she had to salvage some focus, then, I decided, I did too. Alice usually knew best. Funny, but it occurred to me that I was often quite happy to be told what to do by her. So - I had to focus on one thing at a time: I had to keep all of the things, such as they were, separate. Together, they might overwhelm me. Separately, I could cope. There was work, which was okay; there was the money situation, which was not; there was Sarah, who was both okay and not; and then there was mum.

I was seeing her the most regularly I'd done since leaving home. Dad also. And yet, of course, both were not themselves; dad to a lesser degree, but there was a sort of vacuum around him, as though he inhabited a world that was at one remove from the rest of us: everything about him was out of sync. And mum? Each visit was now unpredictable, unbalancing. For the time being, we'd decided to stop taking Eve because of the things her grandma might say in her presence.

She was sitting by the window when I arrived the following weekend, ladled into her adapted chair, head and

167

feet over-spilling either end. Turn her on her front, and she might be a tortoise. For some reason horse-racing was on the tv. I'd never known mum to be even remotely bothered by the sport - any sport really, but certainly not racing - not even the Grand National or the Derby, the extent of mine and dad's annual interest. "So, you're here," mum said as I came through the door, her face gripped by an antique mischievousness, alongside an almost boyish appearance, enhanced by the short hospital haircut.

"Yes, mum."

"I haven't seen you." Her voice was stronger now, but still rose and fell unexpectedly, so that I lost odd words here and there, and her sentences were even more disconnected. "You haven't bothered to visit me."

"Yes, I have. I was here last Saturday." I pulled a chair up next to hers. She was still wearing her hospital smock, even with the nighties I'd brought previously. Her legs were covered in a grey blanket. "I'm always here."

"I've been here for months now and I haven't seen you."

"Mum, you've been here five weeks and I've visited every weekend bar one. I was here last Saturday."

Mum seemed to soften, "Oh yes, I remember."

I smiled at her, "No you don't."

"Oh yes I do, I remember. Don't tell me I don't remember when I do."

"What did we talk about?"

Childlike, with no hint of irony, mum said, "We talked, yes."

"Yes, mum, we did. God, it's hot in here. Can I open the window?"

"Yes, open the window. It's the sun."

"It is hot, mum."

"It is hot, Harry, you're right. It is very hot. It's the sun. It's a hot sun. Look at it in the sky. It's a bloody hot sun. It's always shining. Every bloody day. It comes in through the window."

"You're not wrong."

"I know. I'm not. I'm never wrong, me."

"Are you not?"

"No. Never. Ask me anything, and you'll see. Go on. Try it."

"Anything?"

"Anything at all. Go on."

"Who's going to win?" I asked of the race on the tv.

"A horse," mum replied.

"Probably, mum - yes, that's true."

"You see, what did I tell you? Never wrong. Ask me another."

"I didn't know you liked racing."

"I do. Yes, I do. Yes. I. Do," she said staring up at the television. Then, after a pause, looking back at me, "No, I don't, you're right. I don't like racing. I don't know why it's on. Stupid bloody horses. Why do they bother? Somebody should tell them not to bother." I turned the tv onto a black-and-white movie, Jimmy Cagney was in it. At least, I was fairly sure it was Jimmy Cagney. It was either him or Edward G. Robinson. It was all big suits and machine-guns.

"That's better," mum said. "Better than bloody horses. They're a waste of time, horses. Get me a drink."

"The water?" I pointed at a plastic jug on the table next to her.

"Yes, the water. What else is there? What d'you think they give me? Champagne? They don't. Chablis? They don't. They give me water. They don't give me anything else." Desperation vied with anger in her voice, though her face remained impassive.

"Yes they do, mum. Look, there's orange squash over here. D'you want some orange squash?"

"No."

I poured the water into a plastic beaker, then lifted it to her.

"Hold it for me."

I held the cup and the straw to her mouth. She slurped it, stopped a while, then slurped it again, her face relaxing. "That enough?" She nodded. I put the cup down. "Is that better?"

"More," she said mechanically. I put the cup back to her mouth. I had become quickly sanguine. I felt a creeping fatalism about what was going on around me, I thought it was like being on a roller-coaster at the start, making that slow ascent to the top of the ride. I kept wondering if I'd made it to the summit yet, before realising that, because I was asking myself the question, I probably hadn't.

I was trying to describe this to Jon while we were on break-duty, how this could happen, how nothing could be counted on, when Jon asked me who a brown-haired boy with a bulbous head who ran past us was. "Sean White," I said, disappointed that Jon didn't want to hear more of what I had to say.

"White, that's it. He attempted some d-disruptive activity in my lesson yesterday. The rest of the class advised him against it."

"Another permanent exclusion. They're sending them all here now."

"Yes, it's been n-noted. The staffroom is in ferment." Both he and I leant against a window-ledge in the heat. I held my hand over my eyes to shield them from the sun. Jon had dark glasses on. He looked panda-like. Well, like a panda with no eyes.

"Anyway," I said, watching a game of basketball in front of us, "here's one for you - who's Sean's sister?"

"Surprise me."

"Tammy."

"Tammy Bolton?" Jon said, turning marginally towards me.

"Yup."

"No b-bloody wonder," Jon turned back again, as though the first movement had involved too much effort and the springs inside of him were more happily at rest straight on.

I watched the helicopter trudge across the cool blue limit of the sky. It made a sound like my own teeth being brushed. "And their dad is Simeon Ellis's brother."

"No. Too much."

"Yeah."

There was a pause, then Jon said, "But I thought Simeon and Tammy used to go out together?"

"I think he must be Tammy's step-dad. But they're all related to the Fairhursts in any case, it's as bad as the aristocracy, I think they're their cousins or something, and of course the Fairhursts are all intermingled with the Masons, it's the same granddad, y' know the odd one -"

"The one in the vest -"

"The one in the vest."

"T-tooth," Jon announced, "is stranger than friction."

Antwone, one of my favourite Year 11 students, came over to see me. It was nearly his last GCSE exam, and he came to tell me some news about a college place he'd recently been offered. Jon said hello to Antwone then went in to get himself a coffee. Antwone wasn't too keen on Jon. He'd once confided in me that he thought that Jon was a *batty bwoy*. I'd told Antwone that Jon wasn't, and anyway it didn't matter etc. etc. Antwone had begged to differ. I hadn't seen the point in pursuing the discussion. There were some debates with some people which occasionally weren't worth the hassle.

"You see, Mr M," Antwone said when he came over, "I been workin hard, innit. This month, man, work, work, work, I'm tellin you."

"That's good, Antwone."

"I realised, it did suddenly come to me. In a flash, man, in a gigantic, big, flashin explosion, I'm tellin you. I was thinkin, I need to get my ass to college."

"Good lad."

"So no ladies for the Antwone, Mr M. Not at the present moment, y' get me? Not at the present time. No ladies for the whole of the exam period. Period."

"No *ladies*, Antwone, no *ladies*?" I said. "That must be a shock to the system."

"You know what I'm saying, Mr M, you are understanding of my dilemma. None. For the whole period of these examinations. A bit of weed, innit, sir, but my studies have been taking precedence. They have been *precedential*. Man, you ask me anyfing, you test me on anyfing. Like History. Like historical stud-ease. In which I have been tested this very morning. Like Hitler. I was tested on Mr Ay-dolf Hit-ler. Hitler, he'd have a heart-attack if he was here now. Man, niggers in cars wid music on. Niggers wid gold. Ay-dolf, man, he'd have a heart-attack. That is analysis. That is fact. So, you see, dumb Antwone is transformed!"

"I never thought you were dumb, Antwone."

"No, Mr M, that is the truth, but some of dem other teachers," Antwone shook his head and looked to the sky, then looked back at me and then down to the ground. This was Antwone: theatrical bluster and then boyish humility. "You know what I'm saying, innit, sir?"

"I do, but I know you'll prove them wrong."

"Yeah, yeah, safe, sir, safe."

"Nice seeing you, Antwone."

"In a bitch, Mr M."

Did he really say that? "In a bit."

Kimberly appeared at my shoulder suddenly; reminding me of the shopkeeper in *Mr Benn*.

"Hi, Kim," I said.

"Was that Antwone?"

"Yes, it was."

"He asked me for a blow-job once, but I said no."

"Thanks for that, Kim."

"What?"

35. Lewis

luck mum sed the teachers are part of the government, thats what you gotta rember. there all part of the same thing, there there to keep us down, if we do anything they doant like they want to keep us down, they can be ok, doant get me rong there are sum ok teachers, that depute hibbert shes ok at your school but wen you luck arownd there all part of the same thing.

dad sed but it doant mater Lewis, mum mite be rite but that doant really change nothin, its what you want, its what you gonna do, nowon else is going to do it for you, wen people say that its true, i no im a useless bastad now, i no im no example to you now son but in the past i made sure i did what i had to, there is stuff that needs doing, its dog eat dog Lewis, you gotta be the dog doing the eating, you doant wanna be dog food.

you can do it, mum sed.

do what.

whatever you want.

i doant no what?

its time to work it out, a year your leafin school, a year you need a job, you gotta do sum planin, the future is on you reely quick before you no it, it gets quicker and quicker the older you get, you ask your dad that's rite isn't it, i mite be able to get you sumthing at co-op if you like. there in it together we gotta be in it together

do you agree miss.

36. Harry

Lying in bed that night, I thought how things seemed to be speeding up. I was reminded of one of those sixties reel-to-reel tapes unspooling itself quickly at the end. I never seemed to have time to think, never to have a second to myself, there was always somebody around, this conversation or that little chat: all talk, talk, talk, a public haze; or it was one event and then another event - and then, after that, yet another. It was like I was a rat with a series of obstacles to overcome, and now some vivisectionist was really beginning to take the mick.

"Go back on the tablets."

"I don't want to go back on the tablets."

"But only last month you said they were helping."

"The tablets screw me up, they turn me into a Stepford wife," Sarah replied. "But I forget, that's what you want, isn't it? That's how you like me best, little Miss Perfect, little Miss Perfect robot, that's how you want me to be, isn't it?"

"Don't be so stupid." I got up and closed the french windows. The air inside the room was immediately denser. The evening slid away into a deep blue distance.

"Don't call me stupid," Sarah said.

"*You're* not stupid, what you're saying is."

"Cut the teacher crap, Harry, I'm not thirteen. I'm not taken in by that bullshit."

"I don't want a Stepford wife," I said, sitting down again at the dining-table. "If I'd wanted a bloody Stepford wife, I'd have married one. There's plenty of them out there, they're not hard to find. Stepford bloody husbands to match. I don't want one of them, I want you. I want you back, *you*, the real you, like you were. My girl."

"This is me, Harry. This is me now. Everyone changes."

"Do they?" My hands rested on the table in front of me. Curiously they hardly seemed to be mine. I had to move them to make sure.

"You have."

"Have I?"

"Course you have," Sarah said. "You mean you don't think you've changed since you were twenty, twenty-one? How old were you when I met you, twenty-four? You mean you don't think you've changed since then? You're the same person now as you were then?"

"I don't know; maybe, maybe not."

"That's pathetic."

"I'm obviously older, and you change, I suppose, in the way you see things, but I think I'm essentially the same person now as I was then, yes. I haven't changed like you have. You're definitely not the person I met. And so what? Why should that make any difference? What right have I to pass any judgement? But this isn't you. That's the problem. Don't say that this is *you*."

"I'm ill. This is an illness. What, d'you think I can *learn* happiness again? Learn from the master. D'you think I can be educated into it? D'you think you can teach me how to be happy? You think it's as easy as that? You think you can sit down and you can lecture me on it. Draw a few diagrams on the wall. Ask a few obvious questions. How to get from here to there. You think I wouldn't do that if it was so easy?"

"I don't know."

"What d'you mean?"

"I don't know if you want to get better." There are times when you pull out the pin on a sentence when you know you shouldn't have, and you wait for it to go off. And this was one of those times.

"Bastard. How could you say such a thing?"

"No, you're right. Sorry." I stood up. I knew this was different. I thought I needed to be ready, though for what exactly I wasn't sure.

"How could you say it?"

175

"I've said I'm sorry. You're right, I shouldn't have said it. I was wrong." I accepted this, but it wasn't altering the course of what was going on.

"How could you even think it?"

"Okay, Sarah, you've made your point."

"IT'S AN ILLNESS!" She came at me, fist first at my chest, and then kicking too. I grabbed hold of her wrists and pushed her away from me, though still holding on. "LET GO OF ME!" Sarah kicked at me again, this time overbalancing and flying backwards, taking me part of the way with her; though, because I continued to hold her, allowing me partially to break her fall.

"Jesus, Sarah, are you okay?"

"No."

"Are you hurt?"

"No. Are you?"

"No. You caught me a couple of good blows though." I hauled her up.

"Screw you."

"No. Screw you."

"Na-na-na-na-na." I was sure Sarah almost smiled through this playground put-down.

"Na-na the na-na yourself," I said, the tension suddenly waning; but both of us fighting back the urge to admit it - just a sweet-and-sour silence till I said: "Let's not do this again."

"What? Let's not do what?"

"This -"

"What's *this*?" Sarah said apprehensively.

"What just happened -"

"Christ, Harry, I thought you meant -"

"What?"

"This - I thought you were talking about -"

"What?"

"I thought you meant me and you, I thought you meant -"

"Sarah -" I leaned towards her standing next to me and touched her cheek with the back of my fingers.

"Us. I thought you meant us. This." There were tears in

176

her eyes. I hated to see her cry.

"No, Sarah. How could you? How could you think that? Don't think that. How could you even begin to think that? You mustn't, mustn't. Not ever." We held hands facing each other. They were my hands. I held Sarah's hands in them.

"I could understand it. Look at me, I'm a wreck. Can't work. Can hardly bear to go out on my own. I'm a bloody useless wreck. I'd understand it if you wanted to leave me."

"I don't want to leave you."

"You can if you want," she said. "I mean, do if you want."

"Things will get better." Things can only get better.

"Will they?"

"Course they will," I said. "This is a blip. In a few years time we'll have forgotten all about it. These things come and go. One day it'll be gone. I'm sure that's what'll happen," I said, though I wasn't certain I believed it quite as stridently as I'd claimed. But then I wasn't certain I believed anything much of what I said. I wasn't certain that I knew where the pretence began and where it ended. So many stupid conversations. I had to make what I said *mean* something. What I wanted to do was to talk to someone without always marshalling and corralling every sentence. Just to say something straightforward that might be responded to straightforwardly. There must be conversations I could have like that, and maybe they would be a way back. A way back to what? A way back to how I wanted to be. Something about treating people right - properly, with kindness. The simple things, the human level. Doing the simple things right. It ought not to be hard.

"What would I do without you?" Sarah said, a faint smile painting her face, her large eyes glistening.

"I'm sure you'd be fine."

"I don't think so."

"I'm sure you would."

"Are you trying to get rid of me?"

"No," I said, "I was thinking more of the life-insurance,

177

you know if I did die. That'd sort things out. You wouldn't have to work for years. You could get yourself totally sorted."

"Harry," Sarah said, "don't say things like that, even as a joke."

"No," I told her, thinking it through once again.

"Not funny."

"No," I said, "I suppose not."

It was around this time when Roseanna taught me how to text. I'd thought that I had to identify every letter in a word until she showed me how, instead, the words might emerge of their own accord, mysteriously. We sat in the smokers' room and she guided me through the process. I could smell her perfume, her hair, and I made mistakes so that she carried on guiding me and I could continue to take her in. In one hand she held her cigarette, in the other she showed me how to text. She had long, bony fingers, and her wrist bone was prominent too: she was all juts and elongation - unfinished somehow - and I liked that about her. I insisted on writing words properly. "You really are a dweeb, aren't you?" Roseanna said, to which I replied in the affirmative. "I'm not going to start debasing the English language at my age," I said in my best *Spitting Image* John Major fashion. It occurred to me too late that Roseanna wouldn't get the joke. Likewise, there was a radio show that Roseanna had recommended I listen to - "there's lots of older music on there too," she said - and from time to time I'd caught bits of it. It was the show Roseanna liked to listen to when she woke up late on a Sunday morning, and one Sunday when I was driving to the tip I had the show on, and there was a song from the mid-eighties - a really overwrought, overproduced love song that I remembered from around the period I'd been seeing Abby - and it made me laugh to think that Roseanna, lying in her bed, would have had no idea about it - I hadn't heard it on the radio in years - and that she'd been what? six? seven? when it first came out.

We began to text each other now and then, sometimes at

178

work, more often than not outside of work. But while I thought it amusing - and I began to like having contact with Roseanna even if it was only a couple of slowly tapped-out sentences - I couldn't see the point of it. Why didn't we talk? Why didn't we speak to each other on the phone? Roseanna explained what the point was, but I remained unconvinced. I felt much the same way about email, which Roseanna was always using on her laptop contacting friends around the country, abroad. On the plus side, I did think, however, that if I could get hold of Colin's mobile number and his email address - not that I knew how, but.... - I might be able to utilise those as well as the ordinary landline number I had possession of, just to keep reminding him I was still around, still expecting news.

During our four times alone together, Roseanna and I had twice sat in my car and twice met in a pub, occasionally huddling with the thinnest of distances between us before either one or both of us would sit back in our seats. Whenever we were together we always seemed to be sitting, and there always seemed to be this careful choreography going on. This particular evening it was open mic in The Queen's Head. We were sitting even closer than normal to make ourselves heard.

"My first memory," I told Roseanna, "is of snow. I was two years old, and I think I thought the sky was breaking up. I thought it was coming down in little pieces. I kept expecting it to hurt. The cold, too, I remember the cold on my face, my forehead, my nose. Mum was really excited about it. She's always liked snow, mum. Her and dad went skiing a few times. She was holding me and pointing at it. Snow," I said, "that's my first memory, in answer to yours. Not as historic, I'm afraid, no great event. You have a really nice smile," I said quietly, almost as if I didn't want her to hear; and, in fact, as I spoke, I did begin to regret it. It felt like something I shouldn't have done. She was tying a knot in a black straw that had been in her drink. "Am I allowed to say that?"

"Maybe." She smiled at me again. She had a smile that

didn't quite believe in itself, only the start of her teeth and her chin jutting forward slightly. But she was still close to me. I could smell her last cigarette on her breath. I liked that. I picked up the straw and untied the knot in it. "Sweet talker. I bet you were a real womaniser in your day, you're so charming."

"In my day?"

"Well, you know -"

"I was always very picky, but now I'm past it -"

"I didn't mean - actually, yes, I did," Roseanna raised her glass to me, "old man."

"Thanks," I raised mine back.

"Don't mention it."

"Anyway, what d'you mean that you're not picky?" She crossed her arms with mock resentment.

"Still picky."

"I should think so too. Not that we're -"

"No, of course not." On the small stage over at the far end of the bar, the latest performer was playing keyboards energetically and singing in a punk-croon about the end of civilisation. He'd had a revelation about the nation, apparently, and this had caused him some privation. The keyboards were in danger of being destroyed as he reached his crescendo.

Later, after too many drinks, Roseanna explained why she and her boyfriend had split up. "We stopped having sex, Jason and me. We hadn't had it in months. Sex isn't everything, but I missed having it. I felt as though that was going to be it, no more sex ever, till I died, some shrivelled-up hag, and that wasn't an option. So we talked, like you're supposed to, like all the advice says you're supposed to; we talked about it, and we said, we're tired, we're busy - and we both were tired, and we both were busy - and then we talked some more about it. Didn't change much though. Still shagless. I say that: apart from five seconds late one Friday night."

"So Jason had to go. You young women are merciless."

"No, not exactly, I still loved him, it was difficult, but

we were turning into brother and sister - actually, I bet most brothers and sisters have a more passionate life than we did - and I like sex, I really like sex, and I couldn't do to be without it, then - no. No, I'm not going to tell you."

"Okay," I said.

"You won't tell anyone else?" She was, I noticed, manipulating the straw again, and it was as if a wax seal had suddenly appeared in the middle of it.

"Not if you don't want me to."

"No," Roseanna said; a little superfluously, I thought.

"No then."

"I'll tell you another time."

"Don't tell me at all if you don't want. That's fine."

"We're friends, aren't we?" Roseanna said, running a hand through her hair. Every now and again when she finished speaking her tongue darted to the corner of her mouth like there was something she had to get rid of.

"Course we're friends."

"I can trust you?"

"I hope so, I hope you do. I mean, you know you should."

"It's so ridiculous," Roseanna said, "you won't be able to believe it, but I'll tell you anyway. I think I should. It's funny, if nothing else. Okay - Jason had gone out drinking with his mates, Thursday night, his usual night out, and I'd gone to bed. I woke up about two. I can't believe I'm telling you this -"

"Don't -" Either do or don't, I thought, but we'll talk about something else if not: I realised I wasn't as interested as I was supposed to be.

"I woke up and wanted a drink of water so I went downstairs, and there was Jason -"

"Uh huh -"

"There he was in the lounge," Roseanna said, "wearing my clothes."

"Right." My straw. "Nice." Now this was more entertaining.

"A dress. One of my favourites, as it happened. A little

181

black thing I'd picked up for next to nothing in a charity shop. A bargain."

"Is he a similar size to you?"

"No, he's quite a big guy, the clothes were tight. I don't think he'd done it up at the back."

"What did you say?"

"I laughed, I didn't know what to say, so I laughed. Does that make sense?"

"It does," I replied. "It makes as much sense as anything else. More. I mean, what exactly were you supposed to say?"

"So I stood there, I was like, Uh? I was in shock, I was crushed. I think for a minute I thought I was still asleep, I thought I was dreaming, then obviously I wasn't because it was cold and my boyfriend was standing in front of me in one of my dresses. I laughed. Jason was standing there and he started laughing too. We were both standing in the lounge, laughing. I wanted to carry on laughing because I didn't know what else to do. Eventually Jason spoke. Standing in the bloody dress. My bloody dress. A real favourite of mine. Ruined, was what I guessed. I couldn't have worn it again anyway, not after this, whether it was damaged or not. Wearing my boyfriend's dress? No thanks. He said he hadn't done it before, that he was drunk and that he was only messing around, but I knew he was lying. It was obvious he was lying. Jason is a very poor liar. He gets his words muddled-up. Which I suppose is a good thing. Having to tell the truth because you can't manage not to. It ought to make life a whole lot easier, except when you really need to lie. So I knew. Suddenly things made sense - my clothes that I'd put in one place then found in another. Missing lipsticks -"

"Was he wearing -?"

"Lipstick? Yes," Roseanna said. "And make-up. The full works, it was rather a giveaway, it was so expertly applied. Better than I do my own. He'd obviously had a reasonable amount of practice."

Roseanna and I looked at each other and began

laughing. Then we drank our drinks and looked at each other again, and began laughing again. Some people nearer the stage turned round to look at us. There was bugger-all remotely funny about the bloke with the guitar and cowboy hat currently performing.

37. Lewis

anger mangement wos relaxation, this is were we lie on the floor and feel relaxd, we feel how it feels to be relaxd so its like how carm, your hart beat, your breathin, how gud it feels to feel like that, so this is how you want too be like carm and happy, it dus feel gud theres no dineyein it, it dus feel how you wud like to be a lot of the time tho it can get abit borin to

anger is gud, its hellthy its normal

gud self isteam meens we have less need of anger.

did you no that Roseanna?

i have to open my hands, i hold them tite wen im angry, i have to open my hands and let go of my anger, it is 1 thing to do anyway

there wos a jar at the frunt of the room, we had to rite down what had made us angry over the last week and put the words in the jar then miss blake tuk all the words out of the jar and rippd them up, there gon she sed, all that is gon she sed

you doant have to feel angry abowt those things no more

i think it workd, it was kinda funny anyway

im kinda thinkin those things are not there theyve gon

38. Harry

The next day, another hot one, Billy Edwards came to school with a knife. The first I knew about it was when Jack Dodsley, a boy in Year 9, charged down the English corridor shouting at me, "Mr Ward told me to get you. He's with Billy now, sir."

"What kind of knife?"

"A very sharp one."

"Yeah, very good, Jack."

"No, seriously, sir. It's, like, for real."

"For real, for real?"

"For real, for real."

"Okay."

"Don't believe me if you don't want."

Jon with Billy. Billy with a knife. Not good news. "I believe you, I'm sorry. Where?"

"At the end of the bottom corridor, down near history, along there. Mr Ward is trying to talk to him."

"Talk to him?" Jon talking to Billy. Even worse than I first thought.

"He said come and fetch you."

"Thanks, Jack. Do me a favour, will you? Go and find Mr Balshaw," I said, "find Mrs Hibbert as well, will you? And Mr Whitehurst, if he's around." Which I doubt, I wanted to add; but I had to play the game: the head would be able to sort it all out, or else what was the point of him?

"The lesser spotted Whitehurst?" Jack said.

"What's that?"

"Well - we never see him," Jack replied.

When I arrived at the scene there was a small clump of kids some distance away from Jon and Billy, being held back by a few members of staff. A number of the kids were shouting at Billy to stop being such a prick, but he wasn't paying them much heed. He was positioned in the cul-de-sac of the corridor holding a silver blade about five inches long. It was a odd-looking thing, not a kitchen knife, more ceremonial if anything: it wasn't a type of knife I'd ever seen before. Billy was pointing it at Jon who was standing placidly with his back against a display about nineteenth century slavery, his hands in his pockets, his moon-face in an ironic scowl.

"Alright, Mr Ward?" I said as dispassionately as possible, my heart blistering out a fiercer beat as I got past the kids and staff.

"Fine and dandy, Mr Monk," Jon replied, raising one hand lazily at me, as though he was relishing the attention. I wondered if Jon was party to knowledge the rest of us didn't have, like maybe the knife wasn't steel, that it was one of those whose blade would retreat into its handle when pushed against flesh or clothes. I had one as a boy, I remembered. But no, this knife wasn't plastic. It wouldn't retreat anywhere, would cut and slice. Still - Jon did seem fantastically assured. He might be posing for a photograph on holiday. Even his stutter had disappeared: "We're sorting a misapprehension out, aren't we, Billy?" Billy said nothing. "Aren't we, eh? Billy - seriously, young man, give me the knife and then we can all go and sit down and talk about it."

That was enough for Billy, "I'm not talking to you. I haven't brought this to *talk* to you, you fat fuck."

"You don't have to talk to me. That's perfectly reasonable. You can converse with whomever you want. Even Mr Monk. Isn't that right, Mr Monk?"

"Even me."

"Fuckin' talk," Billy said. "You're all fuckin' talk. The whole lot on y'. Yap, yap, yap. Don't come any closer," he warned me, "cos I will do it, I'll stick the fat fuck." I stopped a short distance away, weighing up what I could do. Billy was positioned in such a manner that while Jon had no chance of escape, anyone approaching the two of them was also in danger. I didn't think Billy would actually do what he was threatening - it seemed above and beyond what he was capable of - but I wasn't totally certain; and I didn't want to find out I was wrong by annoying him.

"Billy was on his way to find Asif," Jon explained. "He didn't like it when I suggested that that wasn't his brightest idea. We brought our conversation down here, out of the way."

"He pushed me."

"I *guided* you."

"You gripped me up."

"It wasn't like that, Billy."

"No, I think you were right there, Mr Ward," I replied, "best thing you could've done. C'mon, Billy. You don't need this. Put the knife down, and then we can all just crack on. Forget this happened." I edged a few feet nearer, my hands up, palms open, in front of my chest. Billy was jittery, his body stuck with the knife, as though he'd woken up that morning with it growing from his hand. It was like the seconds themselves were shaking, and Billy was trapped inside them. I was now quite close, about the length of my body away.

"Stay the fuck back. That Paki thinks he's the big man. Needs a fuckin puff to protect him."

"Whatever you're angry about, I'm sure we can sort it out," I said quietly. The air seemed thinner in this little cave of space; as though there wasn't enough to go around.

"We are sorting it out, aren't we, Billy?" Jon said. Unnecessarily, I thought; just shut up, Jon, you don't have to prove anything here. Let him work it out for himself, give him some time. Sometimes, people didn't know when to stay stumm. "Aren't we? Sorting it out. Getting it sorted."

"No, we're not."

"We are, Mr Monk." Jon raised half an eyebrow at me.

"No, we're not."

"Oh yes we are." More pantomime.

"No, we're fucking not," Billy said, and he swung his right hand into Jon's thigh, like a punch, I thought, nothing

187

more than that. Jon grabbed at the side of his leg and looked at Billy, gone out, "You st-stupid twat, you've st-stabbed me."

"Yeah," Billy was saying, as if happy to agree it was a nice day. It seemed to me that there were maybe a couple of seconds when nothing much happened, there was something like a collective gasp of realisation, before, all of a sudden, noise, screaming. Other members of staff who had arrived were shouting at kids to move away; there was tussling at the edge of my vision.

"Fucking hell, Harry, l-look."

"Jesus, Billy."

"Yeah," Billy said again as he made to stab Jon a second time. Jon turned and crumpled in on himself, then slowly collapsed to the floor. Billy twisted towards me. Everything was happening in slow motion: it was a frame, a frame, a frame at a time - as I saw the blade, this weird-looking thing. Then time quickened up again, double-speed, triple-speed and I threw myself at Billy, back on the rugby pitch, flattening the fly-half. I felt the knife slide across my shoulder as I thudded into his midriff, knocking him to the floor. He seemed to be shouting out and I was on top of him reaching for his hands, and I felt a finger or two break as I grabbed hold of the knife from out of them; and then I was scrambling it away to Arun, who was low-down next to me. "Stupid fucker," he said; but, for once, that might not have been aimed in my direction.

There was chaos: people everywhere; clamour, movement. Staff surrounded Billy and me. I thought I could pick out Jon's voice, "The twat's stabbed me. L-look. There's blood." Billy was bucking beneath me, then he spat in my eyes, so I put my hand over his face and held his head down against the floor. I really wanted to hit him, the spit dripping down my cheek into my mouth, but I just managed to restrain myself. Other hands were pulling him away: two or three people had taken hold, and I raised myself onto my knees, happy to let him go. I wiped the spit from my eyes and mouth then dried the backs of my hands on my trousers.

I finished this job off with some tissue from my pocket. From being on my knees I stood up and steadied myself against a wall. I felt blood trickling down my arm and back so I touched at the place with my fingers and found where it was coming from. I dabbed some more at it, looked at my fingers, then dabbed at it again. The pain I expected was, curiously, not there. Feeling a little dizzy, I focused on the wall - to drag myself away from the danger of keeling over, then saw Jon sitting on the floor, looking dazed, but still conscious, holding onto the side of his thigh. Balshaw was shouting "Call an ambulance! And the police. And get those blasted kids back in their classrooms!" I peered around me, everything almost subaqueous, saw children being shepherded in various directions, some standing their ground and arguing; Billy being hauled up, sitting and weakly trying to lash out at those who had hold of him; Alice on her mobile-phone; and Roseanna coming towards me. I made my way over to Jon and half-stumbled, half-sat down next to him, "Are you alright?"

"Yes," Jon replied, "n-never better."

"All the fun," I said, though my voice seemed a long way off, and all I could feel was the cold wall behind me. I thought of Goose Fair, and taking Eve with me the previous year. All the fun. Roseanna crouched in front of me and Jon. She wiped at my shoulder. "Hello," I said to her, "sort Jon out, Roe, will you? I'm fine."

"Are you sure?"

"Sure. A scratch, a scratch."

"You don't think I'll d-die, do you?" Jon said immediately to Roseanna, still starring, and with his girl. "You don't think this'll kill me, do you? I can't die like this, in this shit-hole."

I glanced down at where Roseanna was looking, at Jon's hand, holding onto the side of his thigh. Blood was slowly seeping through his fingers. "Jon, listen," she said, "I don't think it's too bad, I really don't. I think you'll be okay. Hold onto it. Keep pressing it tight. The ambulance'll be here in a minute."

Through the windows, above the children, the adults, I could see the helicopter swooping over the building. Blood was dripping down my arm. I crossed my left hand onto my right shoulder and closed my eyes.

39. Lewis

billy lost it big time today, he wos luckin for asif today, i no becos he told me asif wos ded, sumthin hed sed to billy, billy went of, i had your leson i went to your leson

next thing i new its kickin off, word is there billy is there, billy had 1 of dads knifes, 1 of dads!?! i wos well shockd, wen did billy get that knife i dunno? wen did he, i want there, he robbd it, dad will batter me if he finds out, dad will batter billy to, i cudnt beleaf it, i was like guttd

i wos shouting at billy but he wos not lissening sum twat teacher wudnt let me threw, go speak to him, i wud have spoke to him if i cud, i wud of got the knife of him im sure hed just lost it cos of asif and his disrespek

wen he stabd word i cud not beleaf it, i wos like o no for f**k, billy you dick, i thort word was ded, that big man monkey got billy, i sore you there, wat did you think.

billy beter not grass abowt the knife, it will be so f**kd up if he dus, if dad notises it will be f**kd up, ill be in so much s**t and sinkin fast, i gotta wotch out hear

40. Harry

"Daddy," Eve asked after I was discharged from hospital the following afternoon, "how have you hurt your arm?" I was sitting in the armchair in the front room, cricket on the tv. She was standing in front of me.

"Oh, I bashed it. It'll be okay."

"You weren't here."

"No, I wasn't."

"Where did you go?"

"To a hotel."

"You're always going to hotels."

"I'm lucky, aren't I?"

"Are you?"

"I am."

"You are. Do you know why?" Eve asked.

"No."

"Because you've got me."

"Well, that's true."

"It's very, very true."

"It is."

"It's got lots of bandages, daddy, can I kiss it better?"

"Very gently, darling."

"I will be gentle, daddy."

"I'm pleased." Eve sat on my knee and kissed my shoulder. "It feels better already."

Eve kissed me again. "There," she said. "I might be a doctor when I grow up."

"What a good idea," I said. "Mending people with kisses."

"Can you mend people with kisses?"

"I'm sure you can."

Dad rang and told me how proud he was, "I mean what I say, son. I don't say it lightly." Here was something, at least. I had to admit: I liked his praise, even now. "Your Uncle Ted too, he sends his best wishes. Mary and Bill as well. I've had a lot of people come up to me and ask how you are, genuinely concerned. Everyone thinks you did a brave thing. And you did. I haven't told your mum about it though. And I did ask the nurses not to mention it either. I thought it might worry her or confuse her. I didn't think it would be fair."

"I'm sure you're right."

"How are you?"

"I'm fine. Bit of a scratch across my shoulder, a few stitches, but apart from that. I was very lucky. I don't think it dawned on me at the time, it happened so fast. But, y'know, today, sitting around, thought it through a bit more. But there we are. All okay." My mind felt a little mossy, but basically I was telling the truth.

"I hope they throw away the key."

"They won't. He's just a crazy, mixed-up kid. There's lots of them out there. And they're not all children."

"And they don't go around stabbing people."

"True."

"And how's the other feller?"

"Jon's going to be fine. They'll let him out in a few days I think. He was only grazed really. Well, that's a bit unfair, bit more than a graze. But again, very lucky. His thigh and, well, his bum."

"Where had the little bugger got the knife?"

"Stolen it from his older brother's not so secret hiding-place."

"Why did he have it?"

"Protection. Dunno. Drugs, another possibility." Drugs were easily available on the estate, as they were pretty much everywhere. I remembered one class of fifteen year old boys I'd taught a few years earlier, who, contrary to accepted wisdom, were far easier to manage in the afternoon than in the morning. This was because they enjoyed Skittles and Maltesers washed down with Pepsi for breakfast, but a sandwich and spliff for lunch. With that

193

class, there was always a hazy post-prandial inertia. I often wondered whether some suspect aromatherapy might be employed more widely within schools to similar effect. Calm. Get the beta brainwaves in the ascendancy. Better for learning with. "Listen, I thought I'd wait a bit till I next come up and see mum, maybe the weekend after next, dad. I don't want her to see me with my shoulder like it is. And driving's a bit difficult at the moment."

"Very sensible. She can't expect to see you every weekend anyway. The drive. The petrol. She talked more again today though."

"Did she? That's good."

"Didn't all make sense, her memories are all mixed up for one, but she was talking. It's interesting to watch her, she's excited, I think, when another word or phrase returns to her. We spoke for a good ten minutes."

I was getting tired of hospitals, but I visited Jon a couple of times. "Mentally, though, I-I don't know about you, Harry, but I'm not sure of the cost. Bound to haunt me for some c-considerable time to come, I'd have thought. Extended summer holiday will prove invaluable though. All the way through to Christmas, with a f-following wind. A two-hemisphere summer. Recovery cannot be r-rushed, don't want to be set back, that's what the consultant said. Might give me time to nurse the sitcom to fruition as well. Nurse, I can't help myself! Take my mind off other things. Th-therapy. Got an episode in my head where a devilishly h-h-handsome teacher gets stabbed in the stomach, but saves the day all the same. Talking of which, good likeness of me in the p-press, I thought. Janet chose well. She ransacked mother's house as I understand it. Yours, on the other hand, Harry - thought you looked under the w-w-weather, if you don't mind me saying. Still, bit of an ordeal and all that. Particularly at your advanced age."

I returned to school a few days after the incident to a standing ovation from the staff, though a large number of them didn't understand why I'd come back so rapidly and thought I should have taken Jon's route. I just wanted to be there, I don't know what I'd have done with myself otherwise. Daytime tv would've finished me off. I was constantly asked how I felt, and the truth was I felt fine: what had happened had happened and I wasn't going to dwell on it. Anyway, some of the kids had collected enough money to buy me a huge bar of milk chocolate. There was only one place I could be.

However, it seemed as though the stabbing had been a catalyst for a further downturn in behaviour, rather than affording, as I'd hoped while I was at home, some chance for Alice and Balshaw to assert their authority again. It didn't help that counsellors had been assigned to the school to deal with any symptoms of post-traumatic stress disorder caused by the stabbing. Children were allowed to visit these people if they were feeling at all worried by their experience, however tangential their relationship to it. Concerns had a tendency to emerge during double maths.

It was towards the end of June, not overlong before the summer holidays. Now, however, the Peter Wallingford pupils went to a school where a teacher had been stabbed. I could see that a growing minority of them were taking a certain kind of off-kilter pride in this. There was more cockiness, more surliness evident in even the most mundane of daily occurrences. Children as young as twelve or thirteen were questioning everything they were asked to do, from waiting properly in the lunch-queue to completing work. Most would then eventually conform; though not before an abrasively negotiated disobedience had been slithered through. A majority of the staff were just about holding their nerve, but even those as experienced as me were becoming frayed with it: that pettifogging wore everyone down in the end. Many of the staff were fast becoming as restless as the pupils. I couldn't believe how quickly these things slipped. It didn't take much, a few bad days strung together. A few more bad days soon after that. Before long, you could see how people thought Peter Wallingford had always been like this, and always would be. There was a sense of collective failure.

I found myself having to sort problems out both in my own department and also in the school generally. My teaching was being constantly interrupted as I had to visit other classrooms to remove troublemakers or quell whatever else was taking place in there. I knew though that any success I achieved in these situations was solely dependent upon me, and nothing to do with the school or a general craving for order to reign. It was respite based on personality - not strategies or structures or any innate desire for harmony - and while that massaged the ego from time to time, it didn't bode well for the stability of the institution.

Even I could do little about the massed fight that took place on the Yard one lunchtime between what seemed to be most of the Year 9 and Year 10 boys. Younger children were flapping around, trying to get out of the way. Teachers on duty tried to prevent what they could, but it was difficult when there were around eighty fourteen and fifteen year olds scrapping all over the place. Balshaw excluded a few ringleaders; however, it was unclear who'd been involved, even after examining the footage from the cameras: everyone had worn a cap or a hoodie or both, and there wasn't a great deal of difference in those.

There were kids openly smoking in the yard, and the numbers on the corridors during lessons were rising day by day. Whitehurst seemed to have disappeared completely. He was often out of school at meetings or conferences: conferences entitled 'How to Make Excuses and Run'. Alice was doing her best, but mostly in terms of crisis management rather than anything that might redirect the school. I often saw her calming children down, calming parents down, calming staff down. She was human prozac. More and more staff were taking more and more time off, which meant the school was increasingly full of supply teachers, most of whom could barely keep kids in their classrooms; or who, alternatively, came once and didn't return. The record from arrival to departure was half a lesson, a supply teacher arriving then walking out after thirty minutes with Balshaw chasing her into the car park, telling her she'd never work in the City again, and her telling him to piss off, and did he think she cared?

This was also the term when the City had recruited a group of South Africans to work as the core of supply. It was, I supposed, on a par with the fifties and getting people in from the Commonwealth to do all the menial jobs the home population didn't want. Now the menial job was teaching. Mostly these South Africans were decent people who were singularly unprepared to teach in inner-city England. Being a teacher in South Africa automatically conferred some respect; it was a shock for them that precisely the opposite was true in the country they'd come to work in. As a consequence they tended to locate a corner of their classroom and then watch the ensuing mayhem, like a witness to an alternative cabaret. The City had hired the South Africans on a collective one-term contract, however, so they had to work. And, in point of fact, no-one else wanted to come to The Peter Wallingford School anyway. So maybe a purse-lipped bemused-looking South African at the front of the class was marginally better than no-one. But only marginally.

Among the black South Africans there was a white guy as well, Boeta - a huge bloke with a vast late-nineteenth century beard. He looked like an archetypal Boer, I thought, like his covered wagon should be waiting outside. I got talking to him. Boeta had been at a loose end, when, aged seventeen, he'd signed up for the South African army. He'd fought in Angola for two years and then he'd been brought back to help quell the township violence of the late eighties. His eyes tightened when he talked about this, though he didn't reveal much. Now he and his wife were travelling and teaching. They didn't intend to stay in England long. This struck me as sensible especially as their next contract was in Bermuda. It did begin to get me thinking, though, about a more radical move and I spoke to Sarah to see what she felt about possibly relocating abroad. Once you're better, I said to her.

Boeta was present with me when Nick Richardson, a lad

in Year 10, deliberately put his hand through a pane of glass and then tried to put his head through the one next to it (Vyvyan in *The Young Ones* came to mind.). Boeta and I prevented Nick completing his mission, which meant he decided he wanted to head-butt me instead. Pane of glass: my face. It was, I thought, an interesting comparison. Boeta and I eventually quietened Nick down and prevented further blood decorating my suit and shirt.

As June turned into July there was increasing quantities of the red stuff: kids in fights, kids in accidents (Staff First Aider: "Oh yeah, he has broken his arm." Other member of staff: "How d'you know?" Staff First Aider: "His arm's got two elbows."), a little craze of kids throwing things at each other indiscriminately: chocolate chip cookies, bottles, cans, coins, stones, some lead piping someone found lying around. It was getting too hot as well. The classrooms were too hot, the corridors were too hot, the Yard was too hot, and, partly perhaps as a result of this - "the mad blood stirring", all that - the slightest disagreements were escalating rapidly, and even the kids were at a loss to explain: "I dunno, I were feeling pissed-off, I 'ad to 'it *someone.*" It was the predictable unpredictability of it all. Every day something else happened that I least expected - or something happened involving children that I least expected. It was like an epidemic, and the most unlikely students were victims of it, usually placid kids losing it as well as unstable ones. We were sitting in our own sweat before we even moved to get up.

41. Lewis

school is like mad there is allsorts going of, there needs to
be security

i stopd cummin for abit, i fount a mint bike beter than my
old one and 1 day i rode of into the countryside. it wos
reelly hot, i wos sweating cobs, i wos sokd to the skin, i
rode to the river, i wos thinking i mite have a swim, there
were lotsa people there old people and small kids, they dint
like me being there they were suspishus, the sun was
shinnin it was bakeing, i got abit pissd of with this little kid
i shudnt have dun but i did, his granma gave me sum jip

i rode away and wos on my own, i fount a nice place and i
lay in the sun, i closed my eyes and i wos dreaming, i woant
tell you what i wos dreaming, it wos gud it was a gud day
peacefull i lissend to sum sheep they wos purrin like cats,
like cats that wos cool, everything wos real quite, sleepy
yawn, the cows purrin the river insecks the sun wos like it
wos strokin my face, sownds funny i no but it wos gud

but wen i came back to school WAM

its like evryone is loonytoons

its like a gud time, theres always sumthing to see, the
teachers doant like it there always mardy, at least you try
and be friendly, ive been gud in your lessons doant you
think, i sit quitely doant i, you are being nice to me which is
gud?

42. Harry

It was Ray's fiftieth birthday meal. I nearly decided not to go, thought I might ring and say that either Sarah or Eve or I was ill. In the end, though, I knew I better had: it was Ray, after all, and I also hadn't seen Ray's wife, Maureen, for a while. I liked being with them both. They plainly adored each other and I enjoyed that sort of longstanding soppiness. The meal was in a French restaurant in the centre of the city. In an area where bars and restaurants had proliferated over the previous few years, this was one of the most durable venues in town. It had used to face the old *Evening Post* building, but that had been demolished to make way for a cinema/restaurant complex, and so now Punchinello's was in direct competition with chain cafes and bars. Except that Punchinello's was the only place where you could eat properly. It was intimate and quirky; I'd eaten with Sarah there in the past.

When I arrived the rest of the guests, including a faintly spaced-out Jon ("M-medication."), were already seated and looking at their menus. They'd met half an hour earlier in a nearby pub and were therefore relaxed and happy to see me. I'd been saved a seat at the end of the table. Roseanna was sitting next to me on my left. Opposite Roseanna, to my right, was Martin, a French teacher and one of the best teachers, per se, I'd ever worked with. Martin was in his early fifties, an old friend of Ray's and one of those charismatic entertainers whose stage is a classroom; the type of teacher even the toughest of kids respond to and work for. The guy was, in my opinion, a pedagogical genius. He was also a supplier of strong concoctions from his hipflask which he always brought out on evenings like this. Tonight's liquor was something he'd got hold of while holidaying in the Philippines the previous summer: Martin had a slug, then passed the hipflask to me and then to Roseanna and Jon. It was good stuff, its glow spreading quickly as we all listened to Gareth Murray tell the story of his ex-wife's breast enhancement, "She'd been going on for years about how her tits were too small. They *were* pretty small, but I liked them. Big tits have never done that much for me, to be perfectly honest; legs are more my thing, I guess - sorry, Jane, but it's true. Anyway, I like the petit lady. As my ex-wife was, and she was a lovely-looking woman. But she didn't like her tits. Used to stuff her bra with all sorts of crap: socks, specially bought things - chicken fillets, that's it - , I don't know what. So she's badgering me and badgering me about this, this is when the kids are young and she's at home and not working.

"It gets worse, I'm not even allowed to see them any more, and so, after a period of renewed pressure, I give in and write her the cheque. Four grand. Four thousand smackers. Two thousand quid a tit. Not that you'd ever only ask for one, I suppose. Having said that - in some circumstances… But that's not the point. What is the point, Jane? I'm getting to that, I'm getting to that now.

"The point is she has her tits done, my ex-wife, enlarged from an A cup to a C cup, I think. I've never understood that. What does that mean? A cup? C cup? I don't know. But they're much bigger, let's put it that way. And even though they're swollen after the surgery, they're going to stay bigger, that much is obvious. And then, a week after the operation, before I'd even properly seen those tits, let alone touched them, done whatever it is you do with a pair of larger tits that you don't do with a pair of smaller ones - alright, Steve, thanks for that information; before all that, she's buggered off with this other bloke. This dick called, ironically, Richard. Dick. The ironies are endless. Met him in am-dram. It'd all been done for him. He liked large breasts by all accounts, there'd been a history of them. Four bloody grand they cost me. Four thousand pounds. All for him. For his pleasure. Should've given him the money - he could've stuffed it down her bloody bra, that would've done the job.

"So it was all rather bleak. But, y'know, the upshot of this, was that eventually I met my new wife. And she, let me tell you, is a wonderful woman. And she has rather a large pair of breasts. And they're all her own. She was born with them. Well, not exactly born with them, but potentially, y'know, they were there or thereabouts."

By the time we ate our puddings, the atmosphere around the table was extremely convivial. The fact that Roseanna had begun moving her foot along the back of my leg as we began our main course meant that the evening was improving all the more. Roseanna continued this, then moved her foot along the front of my leg, before, miraculously - because Roseanna maintained her seated posture perfectly, as far as I could see - she'd reached my crotch; it must be her long toes, I thought, or she was double-jointed, perhaps both; and I began laughing, which thankfully chimed in with the end of one of Martin's stories about shooting squirrels.

It was soon after this that Jon followed me into the Gents. "How's your new chum, Harry?" We were standing a urinal apart, me looking at the wall, Jon staring downwards.

"Chum, Jon?"

"Your chum, Harry. Tongues are wagging."

"Alice?" I peed easily, aware that Jon was struggling to begin.

"No, n-not Alice."

"I was going to say -"

"Old h-hat?"

"Not the nicest way of describing her."

"You're incorrigible, Mr Monk."

"I have absolutely no idea what you're talking about." I zipped myself up as Jon started to pee.

"Harry -"

"What?"

"Our young c-colleague." There was something surprisingly stony in Jon's voice.

"Oh."

"Well?"

"Because I'm friends with Roseanna."

"Friends." There it was again.

"Chums, Jon."

"That's not what's being said, old man. I'm merely keeping you up to date with the jungle-telegraph, the gang have been talking, it's of n-no interest to me one way or the other."

"Thank you for your advice."

"I wouldn't like to see it be the progenitor of anything problematic. Tears before bedtime."

"I'm sure you wouldn't," I said. "Not that there's anything that could, you understand."

"Splendid."

"It is."

"It's all to do with the size of your b-b-balls apparently," Jon said as I made to leave.

"What? What are you talking about?"

"Apes, chimpanzees and promiscuity. It's to do with the relative size of their b-bollocks. The apes that have comparatively large balls are more promiscuous than those who d-don't. Human males are somewhere in between."

"Worth remembering," I said, looking in the mirror, wondering how big my balls were, comparatively. "I can't believe I'm in a bog with you discussing the size of bollocks."

"Be c-careful, Harry."

"That's what I'm thinking, Jon."

"You know what I mean."

"Christ, Jon, what exactly would you know about it?"

"Absolutely bugger all, obviously."

"Sorry, I didn't mean that to come out as it sounded."

"Don't worry about me, old man, I'm spectacularly heartless, I'm a c-cold, clinical, calculating machine, you can't upset me. I'm invincible. Look, I've got a scar to prove it."

Towards the end of the evening, Roseanna and I escaped

from the rest and went to a club. It was a dark, dingy place concertinaed over a number of floors. It seemed as though the rooms got smaller the higher up we went, so that by the time we'd reached the top there wasn't much more space than that occupied by a tiny bar and half-a-dozen seats. We'd bought drinks in the first bar prior to carrying them upstairs. I held Roseanna's hand to guide her through the crowds in the corridors, on the stairs. I held her hand and I liked the feeling of that, of gently pulling her along. When we reached the top we found a dark corner to sit in. We sat up close. I liked the physical feeling of her next to me: her leg, her hip, her arm, alongside mine, just fabric away. We picked up our drinks almost together, laughed at this absolutely together, watched each other as we drank deliberately together, till I tried to catch Roseanna out, and she followed a split-second behind. Slamming our glasses down, we half-turned towards each other and smiled. I suppose we could have kissed but we didn't. Roseanna was very drunk, for one, and I…. well, I wasn't really sure if I should. Instead we hugged and held each other.

Okay, we might have kissed a little.

After a while, Roseanna said, "Can we get out of here? Can we go and get some air? I'm wankered."

"Are you? Hadn't noticed."

"Yes you had."

"Maybe I had."

It was warm out on the street and lighter than it had been in the club. We walked a short distance; I felt elated in the fresh air.

"Oh Harry," Roseanna said, "I can't even walk straight."

"You're a complete drunkard, Roseanna Stiles."

"I think I might be."

"No *might* about it, missus."

"Will you go off me, Harry, because I'm a slave to the bottle?"

"No. As if. It's quite fetching really."

"Are you sure?"

"Absolutely. We need to find you a taxi."

"Harry -"

"C'mon, drunkard. You'll catch cold."

"Hey, sir!" I looked around and it was Kim - dressed in jeans and a crop-top and looking at least eighteen - with an older lad, whom I quickly recognised to be Shane, her brother: he'd always had a sloping, skiddy, almost skiing, walk, and that's what I noticed first. Secondly, the bruising around his eyes like he was wearing a Lone Ranger mask. "It's Mr Monk," Kim said to Shane, "and Miss -"

"Miss Stiles."

"Miss is new," Kim told her brother.

"Alright, Mr Monk, how's it going?"

"It's going fine, Shane," I said. Shane's smile suggested he thought it was too. "How about you?"

"Yeah, yeah, can't complain."

"Where've you two been?"

"Picked her up from work," Shane replied.

"We've been on a staff night out," I said. "Mr Chiltern's birthday. You just missed everybody else."

"I might come and see you," Shane said. "Thinking of going to college in September."

"Good idea."

"I'll call in and see you."

"You do that."

"Bye, Mr Monk," Kim said, and then to Roseanna: "and, you know - you too."

"D'you think," Roseanna said tipsily as we watched Kim and Shane wander off, "d'you think anyone knows who I am?"

"I do."

"Yes," she replied, "but you don't count."

43. Lewis

today wos another gud day, lotsa gud days, yeah, yeah, yeah, and ill tell you about it

dad wos in a gud mood, doant ask me why? i doant no, but he sed lets go out for a ride

a ride.

yeah

how?

you can pull me along on your bike

ok sound

i got sum rope out of the shed, we tied it round under the seat of my bike, dad held onto each end, we rode down the street, me pullin him along, it was nackrin to start with, i wos chuggin along

cum on slowcoach dad sed

allright allright

you cudnt lift ysen over a can of coke

funny

i no

huh

once i got going it wos real gud, dad wos laffing gud lad, i wos peggin it. dad wos like yeah i wos like yeah, we wos bommin down the street laffin and laffin, it was like top, it was like hahahaha and burstin inside

44. Harry

There were other things to think about. Sarah and I were fast running out of money, any money - loans, space on credit cards, anything. I kept trying to work out how long we had left before trying hard to ignore the answer; and of course Sarah still didn't know the extent of our problems. I became tetchy one evening after I'd opened a credit card bill and got to see how much extra Sarah had spent, alongside some I knew about.

"Listen, Sarah," I said, "I've told you. We keep talking about this, and these bills keep coming in. We can't carry on spending at this rate."

"Alright," Sarah replied, "Okay, you're right, I'm sorry. I try to go into town on my own and I think it'll cheer me up, and I don't know why I bother because I hate it as soon as there's more than three people in a shop with me, but then it does cheer me up sometimes, for a short while -"

"I know, darling, and I don't mean to be uptight about this, but we can't go on in the same way, we simply can't."

"Is it that bad?"

"It's getting that way."

"I'm sorry."

"We'll manage," I lied, "but we've got to stop spending so much."

"I know."

"It's crap, isn't it? You should have married a banker. That's *banker*. 'B' for -"

"That's what I thought you said." When she smiled I felt peppier again.

"Yeah."

"Harry, couldn't we dip into our savings? Why don't we use some of that to clear some of this?"

"I don't want to use the money for that. We have to

imagine it isn't there."

"I know I'm the one who's been spending, but if it'd put us right -"

"We'll think about it. But better we pack in the over-spending."

"I suppose," Sarah said.

"And that money is supposed to be for something big - or just to have - for the next few years."

"Couldn't we use some of it? There's no point being worried when we don't need to. There's enough worries without piling unnecessary ones up as well."

"Let's give it some more thought." My words came out hard and hollow, shells of themselves.

When, the next day, the bank statement arrived, it was even worse than I'd previously believed, and I knew I'd have to come up with something better. I wouldn't be eligible for a loan so soon after the last one, credit card companies were having nothing more to do with me and the house was already re-mortgaged. What, I wondered, actually happened when you no longer had any money left to pay anything to anyone? How long would it take? *No money:* how would that play out exactly? Like having no air. Would they send the heavies round? I wondered if I could be heavier than them. Probably not. But part of me wanted to know, to find out. An odd, desperate, obscure part of me - which I needed to ignore.

I had to get hold of Colin. Even if it meant borrowing the money back off him. Christ, Colin was made of the bloody stuff, wasn't he? His DNA was almost certainly a combination of pound signs and numbers with plenty of zeros on the end. I would go down to London and meet him. That was one thing I could do, at the beginning of the summer holidays. I needed to do something, and that was one thing; and maybe, I thought, there was, in fact, something else. The large end-of-year school trips were coming up soon. I needed money and I knew where a reasonable sum would be. I could borrow it, maybe. Before anyone knew. Short-term. To see me through.

I was thinking about this in the early hours after I'd woken with a start again. At night, I would wake suddenly, sometimes gasping for air or feeling that I had to get up and walk around the room, my heart jump-started and my legs jolting. I usually had no recollection of the bad dreams that had engendered this agitation, but there was too much on my mind - it was kaleidoscopic, patterns of worry shaking in and out of focus, not in my control - and it might have been any of it. It was like the bad dream had left a patch of glue in my brain. On one occasion, I dreamt that Billy Edwards was waving a knife in my face, and then it wasn't Billy, it was Colin; but that was only one night. I couldn't manage what happened in my sleep. I felt a bit like Ray Liotta in that sequence towards the end of *Goodfellas* where he's racing around from one thing to the next in a coke-fuelled haze. It might have helped, I thought, if, like Ray Liotta, I'd been similarly stoked.

I would, for example, have enjoyed it more when I was taking Eve round the supermarket and we bumped into Ryan and Claire. I might have told Ryan what I really thought. I might have worked out what I really thought. It was after the riots in Oldham and Burnley, and Ryan was keen to expound. "It's what we were talking about," he said. "Round at yours."

"You were more switched-on than me," I said. (In fact, the one overtly politicised Moslem student in school - Naveed - had said to me after Burnley, "You Western imperialists are getting what's coming to you. This society is so decadent, man. It needs sorting out. Properly, man. I mean, starting again." I didn't know if Naveed was joking or not, so I smiled with a grimly fixed lower-lip.)

"It'll get worse," Ryan said.

"It's the weather," I replied, "nice summer evenings. They're bored. They want something to do. Nothing on the telly. The telly is particularly rubbish at the moment. I mean, *Big Brother*."

"They have to be taught how to be British," Ryan said, "it's as simple as that. We - I mean the likes of me and you

- we don't do things like that."

"Maybe," I found it hard to be bothered combating Ryan's views, however easy it would have been.

"You lot in schools."

I snorted. School at the moment was just making it from one end of the day to the other without finally losing it. Counting the lessons down. Eve tugged at my hand mutinously, "C'mon, Daddy."

"How's Sarah?" Claire asked.

"She's fine."

"Tell her I'll give her a call."

"Yeah."

"Oh, well done, by the way," Ryan laughed. "Have-a-go hero. And I always thought you were a wimp."

"Right again," I said.

Cocaine might have helped when visiting mum as well, though the conversations would probably have been no less distorted. It was looking unlikely that she would regain the use of her left-hand side, certainly in the immediate future, and that she would have to use a wheelchair, possibly for the rest of her life. She hadn't taken too kindly to that news. As a result, she and I were having plenty of discussions about the pointlessness of it all, which, one afternoon took a whimsical turn: "I've lived too long."

"Mum, you're sixty-eight -"

"I'm done."

"No you're not. You're just feeling sorry for yourself."

"Suppose. But look at me. Maybe someone's trying to tell me something."

"Who?"

"I don't know. God."

"God?"

"Yes. Maybe God is trying to give me a hint. That I'm nearing the end."

"Listen, if God thought he wanted you to be near the end, surely he could do more than send you a hint."

"Suppose."

"Anyway," I said, "you don't believe in God."

"I might be having a rethink."

"Mum -"

"What's wrong with that?"

"Nothing. Except you know as well as I do that he doesn't exist."

"*You* might know that."

"Have you seen an angel?"

"You think I've gone potty -"

"I'm not saying that."

"I've had a bit of time to think. God has given me the time."

"Well done, God."

"He loves us all."

"He doesn't love me."

"He does."

"I think you'll find he doesn't, because I don't believe in him. I think that'll annoy him enough to mean that his love isn't forthcoming."

"Oh, Harry. Still, one day -"

"No, mum."

"You can save it right to the end you know."

"I'll bear that in mind."

"Frankly, you might as well get in touch then. You've nothing to lose."

"Mum, I love you very much. More than God does, actually."

"I don't think that's possible."

"I think it is."

And now I really was plunging earthwards, really plunging, at pace, everything hurtling towards me - somebody must have told Alice something, because she came to find me one morning in the English Office and asked me to accompany her; and once we were in her office another conversation soon got completely out of hand: "What's your point, Harry?"

"What exactly is yours, Alice?"

"That you embarked on this relationship with me -" She stood above me, while I chose to remain seated.

"I didn't *embark* on anything."

"Okay, overdramatic word - given," Alice said. "That we got to know each other, that we enjoyed each other's company, that we got to know each other well, or so I thought, that we made love, that we slept in the same bed together, that we've been close, Harry, that we've had that trust, and now you believe you can do what you like, just like that? You think that because you've had enough, I've had enough as well? You think you can dispose of me, just like that?"

"Dispose?" I replied. I leant back in my chair and put my hands on the top of my head like a prisoner-of-war. "Dispose?"

"Okay, pedant, again the wrong word in your cold, logical universe - but this is how I feel - *embarked* is how I felt; *dispose* is how I feel. These words mean something, this matters, Harry, however much we were fooling around - listen to me, fooling around - I'm not a bloody teenager - fooling around? But I'll tell you what: *you* don't decide when you finish with me, Harry. Finish! That's what comes with working with kids! You don't decide. I decide *with* you. We decide. Together. We come to an agreement about this. Together. This is as intimate as it gets. This is adult. This is adult life. If you want it to finish, you want it to finish, but not like -"

"Hang on, Alice," I said, now leaning forward, elbows on my knees, my hands at prayer, my chin resting on my two thumbs, "you said we needed a break from each other. And you were right. It was you who suggested it. It was you who wanted it."

"Not so you could start seeing someone else."

"I'm not."

"I don't think even you know when you're telling the truth. You lie all the time. Every time you open your mouth. I think you've forgotten what the truth is. It's not that hard, the truth, Harry, it's all very straightforward. It's what actually is happening, what's actually happened. It's all clear. The point is: there's a right way and a wrong way to

213

do this. And you're doing it the wrong way. As usual. Wake up to yourself."

"Who am I supposed to be seeing?"

"Harry -" Alice said as though she really couldn't credit she was having to. She turned away from me, towards her desk, shaking her head.

"No - tell me."

Quietly: "No, I won't. No wonder you can cheat on your wife."

"With you, you mean?" I sat back again, putting my right arm behind my neck and rubbing my left shoulder.

"Alright, so I'm no better, but at least I'm aware of it."

"And I'm not?"

"I don't know - are you? Or am I *inconvenient* now? Like poor Sarah. Am I in the way?"

"Sarah doesn't need your sympathy."

"Sarah needs everyone's sympathy."

"Alice, I didn't mean for the any of this to be hurtful."

"Mean? No, you don't *mean* anything," Alice said. "Actually, you don't: you don't mean anything."

"Mean? I don't even know the meaning of the word, that kind of thing?"

"Piss off. Arrogant arsehole. You think you're so bloody clever. What's clever got to do with anything? You think your cleverness matters?"

"Look, I'm sorry. But I've been upset about this too. It's not just you, y'know. Everything's too complicated. I want to simplify it all."

"You've said."

"It's true. I can't deal with all this - it's what you said. I need to sort things out too. We both need to."

"If I see you with that *girl* -" Alice said.

"What girl?"

"If I see you with that girl -"

"What's *that girl* got to do with anything?"

"I don't know. What are you, her knight in shining armour? *Save me, Harry, save me.* You tell me."

"Yeah, I'll tell you: nothing, Alice. Nothing. This is

about me and you, solely me and you, nobody else. This isn't about anybody else but me and you. For god's sake. What interest d'you think she's got in me? You think she's interested in me?"

"Now you put it like that."

"Exactly."

"You're a sad-sack bastard and she's at least got time on her side, she's got years on you. But I'm telling you, if I see you with her, if I see you sniffing around her -"

"It's nice to know what you really think," I said. "Let it out, love."

"Likewise, you fuck," Alice replied.

45. Lewis

My wordsurch abowt wot makes me happy

S	S	I	I	A	R	U	M	A	S
P	T	W	F	U	M	T	N	J	E
J	T	Q	O	P	I	Z	Z	A	L
A	M	U	M	R	P	I	Z	Z	I
M	A	K	V	X	D	O	N	U	T
S	H	A	P	P	Y	Z	B	W	V
P	E	W	M	Q	D	A	D	E	S
U	R	K	Y	U	D	E	T	X	S
N	P	V	I	N	M	W	K	Y	I
J	X	A	P	B	L	E	N	O	M
Z	F	L	O	R	D	A	Y	B	C
C	O	M	P	U	T	E	R	R	J

DAD
FLORIDA
MUM
COMPUTER
COKE
PIZZA
SAMURAI
MISS STILES
JAM SPUNJ
MONEY
SWORD
BIKE

46. Harry

I had to return to thinking about the money situation. There were no more excuses not to. I'd decided that I was definitely going to travel down to London and meet up with Colin once the summer holidays started. Meanwhile my idea for a temporary reprieve had returned to me more clearly formulated as well. It came to me wholly one morning as I woke. It was like the idea had been taking shape overnight and was waiting for my consciousness to make itself known. It required that I had the guts to walk into an empty room with an empty briefcase and then walk out again with a fuller, heavier briefcase. The test would be momentary, the risk slight. The idea proved to me that too much of my recent life had been an exercise in limitation: limits which had been set by no-one but myself. The risks I'd taken - with Alice, I supposed, and latterly, though not to the same degree, with Roseanna - were commonplace. This financial solution would be different, might free me up. I would solve my money problems in the short term, then I would go and meet up with Colin and solve them in the long-term too. And fuck everything that was in my way. Fuck that; and fuck that; and fuck that too.

But I wasn't going to fuck Roseanna. I was going to have had to make do with a few hugs and kisses. This was further brought home to me on the evening the staff went out to celebrate the end of the school year. I'd picked Roseanna up in a taxi I'd ordered and then once in town we'd gone somewhere on our own for a while before meeting up with everyone else in a bar that was housed in a converted church in the Lace Market.

Midway through the evening, I went to buy a round and when I returned Roseanna was talking to someone whose name I missed, but who was, Roseanna said, a friend from university. I watched as this old friend of Roseanna's talked to her. He was the same age as her, fit-looking, muscular, confident. She seemed different with him. They were standing close together because of the music pounding the bar. Roseanna leant into her friend and touched his arm. I sat down with my drink and watched, and felt as though that was all I wanted to do; and then felt as though that actually was all I didn't want to do. The truth of the matter was coming to me, but I wouldn't allow it to surface. The truth of the matter was: well, yes, I knew - Roseanna was ten years younger than me and she had all those things ahead of her, the stuff I'd done. I'd had my turn. And though part of me wished I was ten years younger, that was self-indulgent nonsense. If I liked her so much, it was clear I had to get out of her way; get her out of my head. But, hell, in the meantime, if this was how it was going to be as a consequence, then I was paying, that was for sure, with a deadened, nauseous, lumpy feeling. I sat with my drink and talked with Ray for a while instead. I had to get myself back on track. As with everything else, talking to Ray made that seem possible.

After a few minutes, I returned to Roseanna and her friend and told her I had to leave, and did she want to share a taxi or was she staying? I had a headache coming on, I said. Roseanna said she'd come with me. I said, No, no, stay, enjoy yourself, you deserve it, end of your first year, all that. But Roseanna insisted. As we left the bar, I wasn't sure what I was playing at, and, as we reached the taxi-rank, I told her so.

"What d'you mean?"

"I mean I brought you out here because I was jealous of that bloke talking to you. I'm sorry. Let's go back."

"No, it's alright," she said. "Loser. Not really, I'm joking. I'm tired. I'm happy to go home. And anyway he's a bit of an arse."

We sat in silence in the taxi for a few minutes, then Roseanna spoke as if everything was okay. She was telling me a story about somebody she used to work for, but I wasn't listening properly. "Harry, are you alright?"

"I'm fine," I said. I marvelled at my own brittleness. I knew what I had to say. It wasn't a big deal. I'd got myself into this situation, and now I had to get myself out of it. "But I don't think you need me."

"No, I don't. That's right. I don't need anybody."

"No, I mean - you really don't. You really don't need to have anything to do with me."

"I know I really don't. But I'm not sure what that's got to do with anything. I don't think that makes any difference, does it? It's only - what is it we're doing exactly? You blow so hot and cold. I'm confused."

"I'm sorry."

"Okay," Roseanna narrowed her eyes like she was having trouble seeing, or maybe to make herself see more clearly, "fine. But why all the stringing me along? I mean, if you think it bothers me, if you get a kick out of this, well - it doesn't. But why all the other stuff? What was that all about? What a waste of time. You need to leave people alone."

After the taxi dropped Roseanna off, I noticed there were three missed calls from Sarah on my mobile, all spaced within a twenty minute spectrum. I thought it too late to ring her back, wondering what it might possibly be this time, but I would soon be home, so there was little point worrying.

I could tell from her breathing that Sarah was nearly asleep when I entered our bedroom. "Did you have a nice time?" she said dozily.

"It was okay, everyone was in a good mood," I replied. "But Friday nights in town aren't really my cup of tea."

"I can imagine," Sarah said.

"Busy," I said. "A cattle-market. You'd have hated it."

"Horrible."

"Did you ring me?"

"It was nothing," Sarah replied, her voice warm and sugary with tiredness. "I was lonely and I wanted to talk to you."

"Sweetheart," I said. "I thought something bad might have happened again."

"Sorry. Useless, aren't I?"

"Wonderful, more like. Sorry, I didn't hear the phone ring. The music in the bars. It's hard enough hearing people standing in front of you."

"I was going to text you, but I didn't think you'd be able to open it."

"True." Then, jokily: "Texting? What the hell's that?"

"It doesn't matter," Sarah mumbled, "you're here now."

"That's right, I am." I got into bed then I reached over and kissed her goodnight. I remained sitting up and drank a glass of water while Sarah went quickly to sleep. I watched her while I drank, my head back against the wall. I watched the rise and fall of her breathing. It was unhurried, deep, regular. She was happy while she slept; it was good to see her happy. I gently touched the top of her hair. What was that line? *I hope you're with someone who makes you feel safe in your sleep.* Did I do that for her? Did I? Probably. Should she feel safe with me around? Probably not. I put my glass down on the bedside cabinet, then leant over and kissed her again. I wondered what all my chasing around was about. Always, for as long as I could remember, these distractions. Why couldn't I settle to something? Really settle to it, so that there was nothing else - or that beyond whatever it was I could find, that the rest would become peripheral; rather than, at present, when I felt as though everything peripheral was somehow central to me and all the decisions I made. It was like distraction was at the heart of me, in my heart.

Monday or Tuesday, I'd sort the money out. Eventually mum would get better. Sarah, Eve and I would go on holiday, leave everything behind for a week or two. I'd make that happen. Course I would. Think I couldn't? Course I could. It was a weird time alright, but it would rectify itself. I smiled at the sudden realisation of my good fortune, put my head on my pillow and was soon asleep. I remained untroubled throughout the night.

Refreshed, the next day I drove to Lancaster. Dad was more and more deflated, though typically he didn't say much to me, and I wasn't about to launch into twenty questions. I moved some heavy flowerpots around the garden and sorted out a small leak under the sink. I made us some lunch - chicken sandwiches - and we finished the crossword.

I went to see mum. She was sitting in her chair by the window. I'd bought her some flowers, though she was reluctant to let me change the dying ones in the vase on the window-sill next to her. I said I'd have to bring her another vase; she agreed with me, saying I should've been more prepared. I was never prepared for anything, she said. She remembered when I was a boy, she said, and then she recounted a story about me as a seven year old that I'd no recollection of and couldn't be certain whether she was inventing or not. Next, unpredictably changing tack, she said, "Are you alright, Harry?"

"I am alright, mum."

"Are you sure?"

"Totally."

"You don't let me down, do you?"

Let you down. "I hope not."

"I was just checking."

"How would I let you down? I wouldn't want to, so you better tell me how that might happen."

"Oh, I don't know. If you're *not* letting me down then that's fine. Is Sarah any happier?"

"She's doing okay."

"Do you make her happy?"

"I try."

"Do you?"

"Yes." I caught sight of our reflection in the window-pane. It was a withered, lop-sided world in there.

"It's very easy to give up. Don't give up."

"No, mum."

"I'm not giving up."

"Good," I replied.

"I thought I was, but now I'm not. Too obvious."

"I'm glad. And you're right, you know me too well - I'm having a bit of a rethink, but I'm not giving up."

"Why haven't you put the flowers in the vase? They're wasted over there."

"You didn't want me to." I discreetly checked my watch. Not that I wanted to leave her particularly; more that I wanted to get home.

"Why wouldn't I want you to? These ones are dying."

"Easily sorted out," I said, taking the vase down from the window-sill. "Everything's easily sorted out," I said.

I raced from the hospital straight back home. The motorways were relatively empty and I put my foot down. I thought about what mum had said to me; she was right, of course, but that was the old me, the one who hadn't come to his senses etc. etc. Things were going to be different now. I'd convinced myself of this point. I needed to pay attention to what I had. I needed that clarity.

"Harry," Sarah said as soon as I came through the door, "I got a phone-call today."

"Yeah?" I said, shutting the door behind me and putting my keys and wallet down on the table next to it. My head was still clammy with the road. I was happy to see her. "Are you alright?"

She was facing me in the hallway, her arms wrapped around herself, "An anonymous one, it upset me."

"Why, love, what is it?"

"I want you to tell me if it's true or not."

"Sure - what? What is it, Sarah?" It was obvious that she thought I should know what she was referring to.

"Tell me if it's true, won't you? At least tell me if it's true." She looked as though she'd been crying, though that wasn't out of the ordinary, and it might have been about anything.

"Hey, girl, c'mon." I wasn't sure where to start. I moved over to hug her, but Sarah put her hands up to prevent this. "What's the matter?"

"There was a woman on the phone, there was a woman,

she said you were having an affair -"

"What?" I said. "Who with?"

"What? How many are you having?"

"I don't mean that - I mean, what, with her?"

"She didn't say - not with her, she didn't say it was with her, I don't think - I don't know -"

"Are you sure it was a woman? What was her voice like? Could it have been a girl? Come in here with me," I said, leading Sarah into the living-room and sitting down next to her on the sofa. I touched her nearest arm. She flinched, but I wasn't going to be defeated. This was not going to end badly.

"I don't know - a woman, a girl, I don't know, I don't care - tell me: is it true?" Sitting there in her white tee-shirt and skirt, she was narrowness, tendons, bones.

"Oh, for God's sake, Sarah, some malicious cow, probably that bloody girl I've told you about -"

"What girl?"

Shaking my head: "That bloody girl in Year 10, Kimberly -"

"I don't know about any girl -"

"I've told you about her, she's always following me around, I told you about her before - she's got some sort of crush on me, she's called here before, I have told you." In fact, I had. "It'll be her, I'm telling you, little bitch, for fuck's sake, this really pisses me off -" In fact, it did, and I felt stronger because of it.

I thought I was free, but Sarah wasn't going to let go. "Are you having an affair?"

"Love -"

"Don't -"

"Well -"

"I need to know -"

"Of course I'm bloody not! Sarah -"

"Tell me the truth - I've been so worried - I need the truth."

"Sarah - Sarah - angel," I took her in my arms, "of course I'm not." I was, strictly, not lying to her; and I

223

believed myself. I believed what I said. I just had to get through this. "How could I? Course I'm not. Little cow, wait till I see her on Monday. Love, how could you think such a thing?"

"I didn't know what to think - I didn't know -" She was crying again, tears tracing her face.

"You don't believe it, do you? I couldn't do that to you, Sarah. I couldn't. I love you, I love *you*. How could I do that?" I had to get through this. I would get through this. The last few months were shrinking into the crisis of these seconds, minutes.

"I know," Sarah replied. "I knew. I know it, I know it. It's only, I'm at home, I stay at home all day, I'm scared of going out, and I think, What does he see in me? I'm just a little nobody. I can't even get a job. I don't like going out on my own. I don't like talking to people on the phone. What d'you see in me?"

"Sarah -"

"I don't know, I need to get myself sorted out, I need to get back to work, I need to be a proper human being again. I shouldn't have let this get to me, it was silly, I know, but I've got too much time to think about it. I'm on my own far too much. I know you wouldn't do that, of course I know you wouldn't. Why would somebody ring?"

"I've told you, this Kimberly, she's got a crush on me, can't think why, silly girl. I've told you, worse than a crush, actually, bigger, it's pathetic. She's always around. It's been getting on my nerves but I thought it would all blow over eventually. I thought that by September it'd be over and that I'd leave it for now, y'know, that in the summer holidays she'd find herself a boyfriend or something. I'll speak to her on Monday, I'll sort it out then. There," I said, putting my hand to her cheek. "Sarah, I love you -"

"I don't know why, I'm such a mess."

"Shall I tell you why?"

"Yes."

"Shall I?"

Sniffing: "Yes."

"Well, you're beautiful, for a start. I know that's superficial - but there you go, that's how I think, I'm superficial - you're fucking gorgeous, and when I say fucking, that's what I'm getting at. And we've known each other now for how long? It's a long time, it's ten years or whatever, but you still turn me on, and I know that's not everything; in fact it's hardly anything at all, but, still, it can't be bad, can it?"

"No."

"And I love how funny you are -"

"I'm not funny -"

"Oh you are. You make me laugh, you're always making me laugh, we're always laughing. You're an intelligent, beautiful, funny woman. Did I mention you were intelligent? Because that's important too, so I'm not totally lightweight, you see. I have a deep side to me, y'know, a real deep side. I even read books now and again. Books without pictures. Did you know that? Did you? We talk to each other about all sorts of stuff and you make me think differently about things I obviously hadn't thought about properly before. Because that is all terribly, terribly important. But then there is also your arse," I said, putting my hands inside the back of Sarah's knickers, "and there is your neck - did I tell you that I love your neck? Did I tell you that I love you? Did I mention that to you at all?"

"Harry, I was scared."

"Hey -" I held her on both sides of her face as though I was going to kiss her on the mouth.

"You won't leave me, will you?" Sarah said.

"Don't be silly -"

"You won't ever leave me, will you?"

"You silly thing -" I brought her close to me and held her.

"I'm sorry -"

"You've nothing to be sorry about. I'm the one who's sorry. I'm sorry -"

"I shouldn't be so paranoid - I need to sort myself out -" Sarah said. "I'm going to sort myself out. I can't go on like this. I'm going to get myself right. You watch. And today, another thing, I saw that woman with her son, remember the one I told you about ages ago, who used to bring her son to playgroup. Remember? There was something wrong with him. You know, autistic or something. This was last year, eighteen months ago. We bumped into them a year ago, well the mum mainly, I forget where. The son caused a few problems. And anyway, she stopped bringing him. There were some words, I think. I stayed out of the way, didn't say anything when I should have. But I saw her today, and her son. She's Kate. The boy's called Tom. He's big for his age. And I just thought - I invited them round. I don't know if she'll come, she seemed a bit suspicious, which I understand. And then this, Harry - a weird day."

47. Lewis

dad sed well clean the swords

i sed yeah ill do the knifes

dad sed well do the knifes another day, you can do a sword and ill do a sword, ill show you how

i no how

do you

ive wachd you enuff

allright but well do it together, its 1 thing waching

so we got the swords off the wall, we wos sat out the back.

we both wore gloves becos the oils in your skin can mash up the blades, you wudnt think that wud you.

we used rise paper and sword oil, we did it slowly, we did it carefully. we wos presise.

i did a mint job with my sword dad sed, we had a smoke to selebrate

the swords are on the wall agen all shinnin

48. Harry

I was on a mission. I could only think that it was Alice who had phoned. Roseanna didn't have my home number, only my mobile, and anyway, it didn't seem like her. But then if it had been Alice surely she would have explained who she was to Sarah and what had happened. She wouldn't have given me the luxury of an escape route. Maybe it *was* Kimberly. Maybe it was somebody else, as yet unidentified. I decided I needed to work on both Alice and Kim. Subtly. Pretend Sarah hadn't even mentioned the call to me. Lead up gently to an overwhelming question.

"Kim, have you ever phoned a teacher at home?" Perhaps not quite as I'd intended. Sometimes I opened my mouth and the sounds that came out were a surprise, even to me.... At the bottom corner of the Yard four crows were rolling around together like a small dog tussling with itself. Firstly I'd thought them a dog, then realised my mistake when it flew apart, and kept on flying.

"No, sir, why would I?" Kimberly replied. "I have enough of you lot here, let alone out of school."

"Are you sure, Kim?" I tried to sound as uninterested as possible.

"I've never phoned a teacher at home. That's gross!"

"Somebody phoned me on Saturday, I thought it might be you. It doesn't matter, I just wondered." I watched the crows regroup and battle it out, canine again.

"Why would I want to phone you? No offence, sir, but what would I want to say to you? I think you might have gone a bit nuts, sir. Too much sunshine. Too many late nights. You ought to take it steady. Didn't you ring 1471?"

Maybe the heat *had* got to me: "The number was withheld."

"Oh."

"Yeah." The crows took off once more, this time over the building. Strange though. I wondered what they'd been doing. I supposed that I looked as odd to them as the other way round. Still, fair play, they'd managed a high quality dog impersonation. Judged in terms of being a dog, those crows deserved proper praise.

"What does that mean?"

"There's a block on it. I'm sure you know. You can't find out who phoned you."

"Why would you want to do that?"

"If, I suppose, Kim, you didn't want to let the people taking your call know who you were."

"That's clever, isn't it?" Kimberly said.

"I suppose it is, yeah -"

"Have you ever used it, sir? So someone didn't know who *you* were."

"No, Kim, I haven't. I don't do things like that. I'm happy for people to know who I am."

Smiling, she said: "I might try it in the future."

"Kim, don't push your luck -"

"I don't know what you mean, sir." On this occasion, for once, her fluttering coyness perfectly done.

At the end of school, I went to visit Alice in her office to find out what she knew. To my surprise, she was pleased to see me and said she had something to tell me almost as soon as I sat down.

"What's that then?"

"It's good news really."

"Yes?"

"I've started to see Simon again." She gave me a big smile, though there was a faint flicker around her eyes.

"See him?" I said, understanding only as I said it. *See him? Simon?* Jesus. I felt my lower back stiffen and I shifted in my seat.

"Yes, you know. We've - this sounds odd, saying it like this, but I'll say it anyway - we've been out together. The cinema. A restaurant. Out, like that. Dates. Dating. It sounds silly, doesn't it? He's back, I suppose. Not back

229

exactly, but -"

"That's good. That's nice. I'm pleased." I was sure I nearly meant it. But *Simon*! Back with *Simon*! After all she'd said about him. Hadn't she been telling the truth? "Are you pleased?"

"Yes."

"Good. Then I am too. For you. If it's what you want -"

"Yes, it is," Alice replied.

"For you - not the boys." Not that it was any of my business.

"For me. I found I couldn't throw all the time we'd had together away. You can't assume it'll vanish. And, you know something, I've missed him."

Missed him! "I'm pleased then. I'm pleased you're happy."

"Thank you," Alice said. "D'you want a tea or coffee?"

"No, no thanks," I said. "We ought to have something more celebratory. Anyway, I need to be going soon." A thought suddenly came to me. "One thing: does Simon know about -"

"Us?" Alice said, switching the kettle on.

"Yeah." I remembered fucking her on the office floor. It was like I was talking to a hologram of the Alice I'd fucked. The fucking was still taking place, and I was talking to someone who wasn't really there.

"Yes, he does."

"How is he about that?" I asked.

"He was the one who left me -"

"True."

"So he hasn't got any rights in the matter, has he?"

"No, I don't suppose he has." I leant forward, looking at the floor, and brushed my right hand through my hair. My hair felt as though it needed a wash, my hand clammy as well. Another hot day, but I wanted to shiver.

"We're taking it very slowly, one step at a time," Alice said. "Listen to me!"

"How long's this been going on for?"

Putting the tea-bag in her mug: "A while. A few weeks."

"But I thought you said - I mean, it wasn't long ago you hated me."

"I wanted to make you sweat, Harry." She looked down at me. "No, actually I did hate you."

"Thanks." I sat back, smiled and shook my head. I really didn't have a clue what was going on around me. I was in the middle of a game of blind man's buff. Things got funnier and funnier. I started to laugh.

"What are you laughing at?"

"Nothing. Everything."

"I'm a right old cow, aren't I?"

"No, not really. What do Nick and Tim think? I suppose it must be good for them, their mum and dad back together."

"They don't know yet. We're not going to tell them until we're really sure what we want to do," Alice said. The kettle boiled. Alice poured the hot water into her mug, and stirred the water round the tea-bag. "I hope you don't mind, I've been telling them I've been meeting up with you when I've been seeing Simon. They thought that had been going on anyway, so I didn't think there was any harm done. Was that alright?"

"You might have mentioned it, but I suppose you weren't talking to me, and it's too late now," I replied. Then: "Do they know my telephone number? How old's Tim's girlfriend?"

"Why?"

"Oh, nothing," I said. "Doesn't matter." It was like an Agatha Christie. Who did that make me? Hercule Poirot? Miss Marple?

"Are you alright?" Alice asked, sitting down opposite me. The initial fretfulness had eased and she now appeared relaxed, in charge.

"I'm fine."

"You look pale. Are you sure you're alright? Another thing, I wanted to say thank you."

"What for?"

"For what happened. Between us. You helped me out.

231

You were a friend. It meant a lot to me."

"I do my best," I said. "Service with a smile, that's me. I should wear a badge. Little smiley-face logo. But we had a good time."

"We did." Alice smiled. "Anyhow, that's what I had to tell you - that's it."

"I'm chuffed for you. D'you know what? I'm really, really chuffed for you. Sorry, if that sounds false, but I'm telling the truth, believe it or not. This is the actual truth, from me, for once - I'm pleased you're sorted."

"Thank you," Alice replied. "And I believe what you said. For once. It's not often I do, obviously. I don't want it going to your head."

"You wouldn't let me."

"No. Big enough already."

"Well," I said, "I'll see you tomorrow then."

"I'll be here," Alice said. "I might *still* be here. I might set up a bed."

"A hammock in your office."

"Yes."

"You're right," I replied, "I might not be in."

"Okay, I'll see you when you come back. Tomorrow. Results day. It's up to you. I'll be here. Take care," Alice said. "Look after yourself."

"Yeah. And you. Well, I need to get home."

"Good idea."

"Yes, it is."

Before that, there was something else to do, however. I took my briefcase into the school office. The office was empty, as I'd known it would be; all the admin staff had gone home: their chairs were under their desks, their computers were switched off. Only their manager was left, and she was meeting with Whitehurst in his office. I clicked shut the door behind me so that I would hear anybody returning. The trip money was in bags in the safe which was located in a small room off to the left of the main one. I went into the room but left the door to it open. I knew the combination of the safe, so, after slipping on a pair of

232

plastic gloves I'd taken from the school nurse's room and then checking behind me through the open doorway, I turned the wheel accordingly. It felt a little bit like I was starring in my own film. Everything enlarged, in saturated colour. The safe-door opened: inside, on a shelf, were the cotton bags. There were four of them, two red and two yellow, one for each of the remaining Year groups in school. I checked behind myself one last time and even scooted quickly back into the office to make sure it was still deserted, before returning and putting the four bags into a Sainsbury's carrier: one, two, three, four. I wrapped the handles and the top half of the carrier around the rest of itself, then put it into my briefcase which I clicked shut. Next I closed the safe and locked it, then peeled off the gloves. I felt much more distanced from what I was doing than I'd expected: this was what I had to do, and I was doing it; but it wasn't me. I picked up the briefcase and walked back into the office. The main office door was still shut. I opened it. There was no-one in the corridor. Hang on, there was: Lewis Tuckwood. "What are you still doing here?"

"Nothing."

"Bit late, isn't it?"

"'Ad a detention."

"Right. I should get home now then."

"Yeah."

"Have a nice holiday."

"Yes, sir, and you."

Sir. Blimey. What had got into him?

I knew there was no camera to avoid as long as I now walked up the stairs opposite the office to the staff-room and then back into there. Next I could exit the staff-room from its furthest end and return to the English office before leaving for home as I normally would. I thought about the money I had in my briefcase. About five hundred children were going on the trip, each paying ten quid a time. Some would have brought cheques, but most would have paid by cash; or, at least, that's how it usually was. I thought I could reckon on three thousand. That ought to see me and Sarah and Eve right for the summer holidays. That ought to pay some of the bills, and also allow us to have a decent time during the break. I'd worry about the rest in the autumn after I'd seen Colin, and had had more time to think. Christ, I was tired. I walked up the stairs, the warm air like quicksand closing over my head. Nearly at the top, though, I tripped and the briefcase slipped from my grasp. It bounced down the stairs and sprung open at the bottom next to Lewis' feet. The Sainsbury's carrier had unwrapped, some of the money and cheques flung across the floor.

"You alright, Mr Monk?" Lewis said.

"Yeah," I said, less concerned about my throbbing knee than the escaped contents of my briefcase. If Whitehurst or anyone came along now.....

"D'you want any help pickin this up?"

"Yeah, please, Lewis," I replied, hobbling back down towards him, trying desperately to stay calm.

"I think I'll 'ave some of this."

"Yeah."

"There's loads, int the'?"

"You're right. I knew I had something else to do, thanks, Lewis, dropping my briefcase has reminded me," I said as we collected up the money bag's contents. "Look on the bright-side I suppose, even though my leg's killing me. This all needs to be in the safe. I'd completely forgotten about it."

"Don't know 'ow you could forget about this lot, must be all the money you're on."

"Must be."

"Anyhow, y' right, it does need to be in the safe. Don't want it goin missin now, do you? You'd get the blame."

"True."

Having returned the bags to their rightful place, I quickly left school. I waved to Lewis as I drove past him. I drove down to the river, close to Trent Bridge, across from the back of County Hall, its peppermint green roof like some incongruous marzipan. People were enjoying the July sunshine, some walking along by the river, others on bikes. There was an ice-cream van further up the road: I wondered about going to buy one as it was hot in the car with the air con off. I opened all the windows, but there was only the faintest of breezes. The sky was scuffed with thin cloud. On the river some oarsman were practising. I looked at the river, the geese waddling along the bank, pigeons too. All this bloody wildlife. Two men jogged past the car. Perhaps I'd get fit again. Properly fit. Go to the gym. Run a marathon. Well, a half one. With Ryan. In fancy-dress. For charity.

I needed air. I was sweating heavily and it would do me good after being cooped-up. I got out of my car, locked it, then stood still, uncertain where to go. My body felt as though its joints were jammed-up and waxy. I felt as though we were on the verge of seizing up. A walk would sort me out. I went over to the ice-cream van and bought myself a cone with chocolate sauce on. There was heat outside my head - I could feel it particularly on my left temple, my left cheek - and there was still heat inside my head too, but that was fading. Things seemed clearer. I turned around. Facing me was the war memorial, a vast grey-bricked monument with one large central archway and two smaller ones. I crossed over the road and walked into the memorial gardens, past the fountains and people sitting on benches or lying on the grass. I started to relax, started to breathe properly. So much to see and do, think about. All good. One moment and then the next, and then the next, after that. Happiness prevailed. I walked up onto the road again and looked across at the skyline, the dome of the Town Hall, the castle on the left-hand side, the cranes among the taller buildings to the right. The wink and gleam of them.

Closer to me, I noticed there was a game of football taking place on the recreation grounds. I finished my ice-cream, wondering why anyone would be playing football in the height of summer, but I supposed it was August soon, and even the professional game was due to kick off within a week or two. I walked towards the match to see what it was all about. It was patently more than a kick-about: the nets were up, there was a referee, there were fifteen or twenty people on the touchline. It was greens against yellows. I watched from a distance. The standard of the football seemed reasonably useful, though I wasn't totally sure. A few minutes into the game, there was a scramble in the goal-mouth and the red keeper booted the ball away. Unfortunately the ball hit the back of the referee's head as he was running out of the penalty-area towards the halfway line, knocking him over, and then slowly ballooning over all the outfield players and also the keeper himself who watched it float into the corner of the goal. I continued to have no idea what the purpose of the game was, but at that point everyone started laughing, the twenty-two players, the people on the touchline, me. The referee picked himself up and fought hard to keep a straight face while signalling a goal, but then his face cracked too. Players from both sides were congratulating him. He acknowledged them by getting down on one knee and raising his fist to the sky. Then he stood up, blew his whistle and the game began again. I watched, and soon a seriousness had descended once more, but it was an altered, more relaxed seriousness, one changed by what had happened. A better seriousness, if anything, I thought.

I walked back towards the river, taking the mobile-phone from out of my pocket, wondering why I needed it. I didn't need it. Not in my new simple life. How many times was it that you had to make a call, that somebody desperately had to call you? Maybe once. A month? A year? A lifetime? It wasn't as though I was never far from a thousand phones if a call really and truly had to be made. Christ, what exactly would that call be? What good would it do anybody?

I held the phone in front of me like it was a dripping ice lolly that might stain my clothes, and returned over the road to the river. I walked past the geese, a few of which hissed at me. That's right, I thought, villainous, boo! There were steps to the waterside which I went down, still holding the mobile as if it was contaminated. I made sure no-one was looking. The rowers were upstream. There was a little girl slightly older than Eve close by, but she was walking in the opposite direction. I lobbed the phone into the water. It hardly made a sound.

49. Lewis

my dad sez you can allways tell when the police and that are hidding sumthing becos they are politer not like normal, monkey was politer tonite. he was kinda nice hard to beleaf but trew, he had loadsa money in his briefcase, it went everywhere we pickd it up

i came back to school to give you this exersise book but i cudnt find you, then i didn't no if i wud give you it, i doant no if its a good idear or not, i mite rip sum off the pages out

but this is all abowt me like you askd for a long time ago and i wantd to show you that i did it

Nigel Pickard was born in West Germany in 1966.
His first novel, *One*, was published by Bookcase in 2005.
He lives and works in Nottingham.

Acknowledgements

Special thanks to Martin Stannard, Rosie Garner, Stephan
Collishaw, Dave Holloway, Jenny Holloway, Martyn
Turner, Ally Turner, Rob Bray, Beryl Miles, Jim Buckle,
Ian Collinson, Phil Davies, Leah Wain-Reid, George
Norton and, most of all, Jane Bonnell.